Castaway

Castaway

Advocate and Fanatic

Writers Club Press
San Jose New York Lincoln Shanghai

Castaway

Writers Club Press
an imprint of iUniverse.com, Inc.

For information address:
iUniverse.com, Inc.
5220 S 16th, Ste. 200
Lincoln, NE 68512
www.iuniverse.com

ISBN: 0-595-15719-X

Printed in the United States of America

This book is dedicated to the love of my life and my best friend. I'm well aware of just how lucky I am. I love you.

Advocate

This book is dedicated to the people who taught me how to laugh—my parents and my brother. No one could ever have a better family than the one I am blessed with. I love you.

Fanatic

CONTENTS

Acknowledgements

Several people were instrumental in the preparation of this book. We are very pleased to have this opportunity to acknowledge them.

Jen Badman, Barbara Davies, Liz Harrison, and Maggie Sheridan: The book is better because of you and your technical skills. Thank you.

Mya L. Smith: Your tireless efforts to create and maintain a webpage for us is/was appreciated more than you will ever know. From the bottom of our hearts, thank you. We highly recommend her company, Twin Creations (http://www.twincreations.com).

Medora MacD and Maggie Sheridan: Your ideas for the book jacket were awesome. Nobody does a summary like you guys.

Barbara Davies, Judith Kuwatch, Medora MacD, Stephanie Solomon, and Jan Trumbo all lent us their talent with their wonderful guest panelist articles. You get the credit for several good belly laughs. Thank you.

This is also my big chance to say how much I enjoyed working with Fanatic. It was truly an experience!

Fanatic would like to say the same but she is tied up right now. Literally. By Advocate. Send help, please.

INTRODUCTION

'Castaway' is intended to be read as though it is a weekly, real life, episodic television series. It may remind you a lot of the summertime game show that was a ratings blockbuster, and dominated water cooler discussions for weeks on end. That's okay. It should. 'Castaway' is a parody of not only that show, but the entire television industry. It's a spoof and all meant in fun.

We are not going to be politically correct in this series. If you like PC humor, don't read this. If you still read this and don't like it, don't write us about it. We plan on bashing stereotypes (hey, they exist for a reason, folks) and exaggerating about as many people and places as possible. It's all in the name of humor. If it ain't your cup of tea, swim on, matey, this here is our island.

This work of fiction is intended for mature audiences only. There are adult themes and language, nudity, sensuality, sexuality, alternative lifestyles (including depictions of homosexuality), and the like. We believe that most parents would consider these elements to be too strong for viewing by persons less than 18 years of age. If we were a film, we would have an "R" or an "NC-17" rating.

The biographical information contained within is meant to enhance your reading pleasure and clue you in on the characters' histories and backgrounds. It's *crucial reading* if you want to get the most of the show and understand the personalities involved. And, since 'Castaway' starts off with sixteen contestants and several additional characters, comprising the production crew and network employees, you'll consult it often. We did, and we wrote the darn thing.

Also, the Bender Television Broadcasting Channel (BTBC) has invited a series of expert panelists to comment on their new hit show, 'Castaway'. These four experts—a novelist, a psychologist, an anthropologist and a sociologist—will discuss the import of the series on our daily lives. Their articles appear at the end of certain chapters and are disbursed throughout the book. There is also the lone postal worker presenting her side of things.

Now, sit back and relax. Grab some snacks and a beverage and turn on your television. A press conference explaining the show's premise is about to begin....

*   *   *

"Is this thing on?"

"Okay...I'm Joan Fogarty, the executive producer and host of what's going to be the hottest new show of the summer season 'Castaway'. One of the castaways is going to win a million dollars."

<Joan grins toothily>

"Let me give a brief rundown on the show's premise. We've taken 16 American strangers and stranded them on an uninhabited island in the middle of the South China Sea. They have to survive with no modern conveniences."

<A round of grumbles goes 'round the room>

<Joan chuckles>

"It's perfectly safe. The castaways are provided with all the fresh water and rice they want. We also have a first-aid hut set up across the island and staffed with a full-time medical staff."

<A reporter raises his hand and asks, "What does it take to win the million dollars? What are the rules?">

"I was just getting to that. Okay...the castaways will be broken down into two teams, the Alphas and the Betas. The teams will compete with each other in a series of challenges."

<Joan smiles as though she knows a secret she's not quite willing to share>

"That part is going to be really fun. The team that loses the challenge has to vote one of its members off the island. So the number of castaways is always shrinking. The winning team is granted immunity from losing a member, and gets a luxury item as a prize."

<Several hands shoot up but Joan ignores them>

"I already know what you're going to ask. The luxury items range from tools or materials to make the castaways' daily survival easier...to more frivolous, fun items. It's different with every challenge. But for more specifics about the rules you should visit our website. All your questions will be answered there."

<Joan looks offstage, noticing that another producer is waiting in the wings, ready to announce his new show. She decides there is always time for one more plug>

"The season premiere is this Friday. Don't miss it!"

<Fade out>

Castaway Biographies

THE ALPHA TEAM

Name: Jason
Age: 21
Marital Status: Engaged
Occupation: Recent Yale Graduate
Hometown: New Bedford, Rhode Island
Castaway Quote: "To quote from one of my personal heroes, Andrew Carnegie, 'And while the law of competition may be sometimes hard for the individual, it is best for the race, because it ensures the survival of the fittest in every department.'"
Luxury Item: Razor
Vital Statistics: I am just over six foot tall, in great shape, and rather a young Robert Redford look-alike
Biography: Jason graduated in May summa cum laude from Yale University, double-majoring in Political Science and Economics. Accepted into Harvard Law School for the fall, Jason is engaged to marry Victoria, daughter of Senator Penent (D-MA), over the Christmas break. His future career plans include expanding his dot.com venture (www.mybiz.com) and pursuing legislative office because he knows what is best for the country.

*   *   *

Name: Marty
Age: 38
Marital Status: Divorced
Occupation: Army Corps of Engineers
Hometown: Seattle, Washington
Castaway Quote: "I don't know how those girls are gonna make it on the island. I mean, they get mad if they break a nail. How are they going to survive? They'll be lucky there are some men there to protect them."
Luxury Item: His lucky lure
Vital Statistics: Six foot four inches of opportunity, solid muscle with brown hair and eyes
Biography: Martin is a construction foreman in the Army Corps of Engineers. One of his current projects is rebuilding some of the stores harmed in the recent World Trade Organization riots in downtown Seattle. "It was a real lucky break for us those labor-breaking, scum-sucking financial guys came here. We have plenty of work to keep us busy through the summer and into the fall." When he's not on the job, Marty is at the lake fishing.

         *   *   *

Name: Marva
Age: 26
Marital Status: Married with two children
Occupation: Housewife
Hometown: Stone Mountain, Georgia
Castaway Quote: "I've always wanted a little adventure, like Scarlet found when she met Rhett."
Luxury Item: Picture of her kids

Vital Statistics: I'm average height and weight, have brown hair, but I do have clear, blue eyes

Biography: Marva is a stay-at-home mom, raising her two children, Edwina (three) and Hubert (one), while her husband drives a truck. Prior to joining the Castaways, Marva had never traveled more than one hundred miles from home. Her biggest adventure to date has been to go to the annual Snellville, GA charity tractor pull. She is looking forward to seeing the ocean for the first time, but knows she will miss her two sugarplums terribly.

       *   *   *

Name: Molly
Age: 44
Marital Status: No marital status given
Occupation: New Age Guru
Hometown: Palo Alto, California
Castaway Quote: "It's only when you release your fears, your inhibitions, your negative energy, that you can embrace what it truly means to be human, to be alive. I look forward to escaping the trappings of modern day society and contemplating my place in this world."
Luxury Item: Her crystals
Vital Statistics: I'm tall and willowy, like a young sapling; my hair has a touch of gray, denoting wisdom, and I have brown eyes.
Biography: After recovering slowly from a traumatic bee sting as a child, Molly has devoted herself to alternative medicine and allowing her mind to develop to its full potential. Recognizing the sham traditional medicine has become, she earned her degree from the Wee-Wong-Woo Institute of Healing, Meditation and Nutrition. Molly is

macrobiotic and a yoga master. She looks forward to doing her morning routine on the sand.

*　　　　*　　　　*

Name: Russell
Age: 52
Marital Status: Divorced
Occupation: Professor
Hometown: Dallas, Texas
Castaway Quote: "I have long wanted to participate in a study like this. I think it's great to see Natural Man and Natural Woman emerge."
Luxury Item: Viagra
Vital Statistics: Height: 72 inches, Weight: 211 lbs, Hair: brown, Eyes: blue
Biography: The dark-haired and distinguished Russell has been voted Most Popular Professor and Best Kisser for the last five years at the University of Texas, Dallas. A scientist (bio-chem) with a sense of humor and a great car, he is an advisor to many of the young, blonde first year students. "It's my solemn duty to help them find their way in this world." He is regularly seen at the campus gym working out with weights.

*　　　　*　　—　*

Name: Ryan
Age: 28
Marital Status: Single
Occupation: Survivalist
Hometown: (Undisclosed), Kentucky
Castaway Quote: "I will win."

Luxury Item: Swiss Army Knife
Vital Statistics: Six foot tall, athletic build, black hair, blue eyes...not that it's any of your business.
Biography: Ryan is a survivalist from Kentucky. Forced at a young age to assume responsibility for her brothers—after her parents were killed in a mysterious government-caused* car crash—she has worked in a number of industries. Skilled as an EMT, a mechanic, a volunteer fireman, a munitions expert, a nationally ranked marksman and a short order cook, Ryan is an invaluable asset to her community, somewhere in the Kentucky hills.

The BTBC takes no responsibility for content of the supplied Castaway bios. The BTBC is confident that if the government says it was an accident, it was an accident.

*　　　　　*　　　　　*

Name: Tony
Age: 19
Marital Status: Single
Occupation: Counter Clerk at 7-11
Hometown: Miami, Florida
Castaway Quote: "I'm young, I'm fit and I'm already tan."
Luxury Item: The Patch
Vital Statistics: 74 inches, 143 lbs, blond hair, green eyes
Biography: Tony is a recent graduate from Central Miami High School. Currently employed at 7-11, his plans are to attend the DeVris Institute of Technology and become a photocopier repairman. "I really dig reproduction, man." One of his favorite hobbies is rolling his own cigarettes. His only concern regarding his island adventure is the

apparent lack of tobacco plants on the island. He is hoping to discover other indigenous plants one can smoke. He plans to inhale.

*   *   *

Name: Yun-kyung
Age: 31
Marital Status: Single
Occupation: Veterinarian
Hometown: Boston, Massachusetts
Castaway Quote: "If there are any ill or injured animals on the island, I will be happy to take care of them. For free."
Luxury Item: Rubbing Alcohol
Vital Statistics: I'm petite, with glossy black hair and brown eyes.
Biography: From a typical underachieving Korean family (father is a scientist for the CDC, mother is a published novelist, both brothers are cardiologists), Yun-kyung devotes her professional and personal life to saving animals. A board member of PETA, ASPCA and PAWS, she is also active with Greenpeace, Earth Day and Save The Whales, Inc. She shares her home with ten feral cats, four dogs, two bunnies and a turtle.

THE BETA TEAM

Name: Arturo
Age: 32
Marital Status: Single
Occupation: Stylist
Hometown: San Francisco, California
Castaway Quote: "Only in America would I get such an opportunity. I love this place! I love this place! Girlfriend, did I mention I love this place?!"
Luxury Item: Scissors

Vital Statistics: I am a dark and beautiful Latino man. What else do you wanna know? Oh, and I never touch refried beans. They go right to my hips, girlfriend! I gotta stay lookin' good.

Biography: Arturo, born in Rio de Janeiro, Brazil, became a U.S. citizen in 1995. He is the head stylist at an exclusive San Francisco salon and plans to use his winnings to open his own business. Arturo lives alone except for his Persian cats Fluffy and Mugums. He is looking for new inspiration for the styles of Summer 2001 because retro is dead.

*   *   *

Name: Bill
Age: 28
Marital Status: Single
Occupation: Software Designer
Hometown: St. Louis, Missouri
Castaway Quote: "I'm going to tackle the island with brain power, not brawn. Survival, like anything else, can be easily predicted when mapped out mathematically using the appropriate computer model."
Luxury Item: Dental Floss
Vital Statistics: Height: 73 inches. Weight: 192. Eyes: Brown. Hair: Brown. Shoe size: 11
Biography: Bill has a Masters Degree from M.I.T. in computer engineering. He lives in the lower level of his parents' home, sharing space with his ant farm and parakeet. Bill works for a software company designing video games. After a hard day at work, Bill likes to relax by dabbling in C++programming, building matchstick suspension bridges and calculating the exact number of years, months, days, weeks, hours, minutes, and seconds before the sun finally burns out.

*   *   *

Name: David
Age: 65
Marital Status: Widowed
Occupation: Minister
Hometown: Tucson, Arizona
Castaway Quote: "The time of reckoning is upon us."
Luxury Item: Bible (King James Version)
Vital Statistics: 68 inches, 247 lbs, gray hair, hazel eyes
Biography: David has been a minister of the gospel for over 40 years. He is the father of three grown children and grandfather to thirteen. He is an active school board member, who believes in emphasizing the classics in the curriculum. David intends using his winnings to open Arizona's first drive-thru ministry, Give God the Gas. In his spare time, David enjoys playing with model trains.

*   *   *

Name: Dawn
Age: 21
Marital Status: Single
Occupation: Farm Worker
Hometown: Rain Tree, Iowa
Castaway Quote: "At first, I didn't think Mama and Daddy would even let me fill out the application. But after I explained that we would be filmed the entire time and that nothing inappropriate could possibly happen, they agreed. I'd like to take this opportunity to say hello to my Aunt Margaret who works at Rickie's Diner in Rain Tree. That's Rickie's Diner—home of the 'belly buster' steak combo and the 'all you can eat' corn bar. 555-CORNS. Open 7 days a week. No credit cards or personal checks, please."
Luxury Item: Shampoo

Vital Statistics: Well, I'm taller than my mama and younger sister, but shorter than my older sisters and all of my brothers, of course. I'm a size 8, except in those fancy designer brands. Then I usually just go into the dressing room and try on two or three different sizes. My hair is light brown, except in the summer when I work outside. Then it's more of an ash color.

Biography: Dawn lives on her parents' corn farm with her 4 brothers and 3 sisters. She is a clarinetist whose hobbies include cooking, cross-stitching, and canning. Someday, Dawn would like 4 children (2 boys named Ethan and George and 2 girls named Cindy and Agnes) and her very own John Deere tractor. With a radio.

         *   *   *

Name: Desiree
Age: (age withheld)
Marital Status: Single
Occupation: Fashion Model / Cosmetics Spokeswoman
Hometown: Manhattan, New York
Castaway Quote: "Everyone thinks models have an easy job. That all we do is stand around and look pretty. Well, I'm here to bash that tired myth to pieces. Sometimes we have to sit in one pose for a really long time without moving, and then the wind comes along and musses our hair! We earn every penny!
Luxury Item: A mirror
Vital Statistics: I'm 5 foot 9. And way, way skinnier than all those other cows who dare to claim the title: Super Model. I have baby-blue eyes, auburn hair—this week, and a peaches and cream complexion to die for. But best of all, my hips are perfectly proportioned to my waist. I'm famous for that.

Biography: Desiree began her modeling career at the tender age of (withheld) in 19(withheld). She is a graduate of the acclaimed FiFi LeFranc School of Professional Modeling, where she received honors for her achievement in 'posture' and 'navigating dimly lit catwalks'.

*   *   *

Name: Joe
Age: 35
Marital Status: Divorced
Occupation: Bartender
Hometown: Hackensack, New Jersey
Castaway Quote: "I'm here to see if I can do it—meet the challenge and be stronger for it."
Luxury Item: A frisbee
Vital Statistics: 6 ft. 2 inches tall, 190 lbs, brown eyes and hair
Biography: Joe is a bartender by night, stay-at-home dad to his 8-year-old son by day. In high school, Joe was an all-state quarterback and wrestling champion. He is an accomplished piano player who enjoys traveling, camping and playing ball with his son. If Joe wins the million dollars, he intends to resume his malpractice claim against his divorce attorney.

*   *   *

Name: Shannon
Age: 25
Marital Status: Single
Occupation: Administrative Assistant
Hometown: Los Angeles, California

Castaway Quote: "I hope to learn as much as I possibly can from this unique experience."
Luxury Item: Her journal
Vital Statistics: I'm 5 feet 3 inches tall and around 122 lbs with blonde hair and green eyes.
Biography: Shannon originally hails from Denver, Colorado. She is a budding novelist with a B.A. in Communications from UCLA. Shannon is an only child, and is eagerly looking forward to the communal living experience the island will provide. Her hobbies include reading, kick-boxing and cycling.

*   *   *

Name: Tanesha
Age: 28
Marital Status: Single
Occupation: Athletic Recruiter
Hometown: Detroit, Michigan
Castaway Quote: "I'm gonna win me that million dollars because I'm the best...hands down. I am gonna be stronger, tougher, and smarter. My focus will not waiver. And no droopy-assed honky is gonna stand in my way!"
Luxury Item: A toothbrush
Vital Statistics: Black. Guess the rest, fool!
Biography: Tanesha was an alternate to the women's 400-meter relay team in the 1990 Olympics. Today, she is an athletic recruiter for the University of Michigan's Women's Track Team. Tanesha believes in sharing of herself and twice a week counsels troubled African-American youths in the area of race relations at her local community center.

PROLOGUE

Sold My Soul to the Devil

Gulls cried overhead, swooping playfully back and forth in front of two women slowly making their way down a secluded sandy beach. They strolled arm-in-arm at the edge of the salty surf. The taller woman's long dark hair blew gently in the afternoon breeze, her face the very picture of contentment. Her younger, fair-haired companion laughed heartily at something the taller woman said, giving her a little shove and causing a long finger to waggle affectionately at the smaller woman's antics.

Their faded blue jeans were rolled up to their knees, the occasional spray of seawater dotting the denim. They splashed along happily, sharing wholesome looks of devotion and basking in mutual admiration.

A few more steps and the younger, shorter woman stopped her companion with a gentle tug of her arm.

"Can I ask you something?" she questioned earnestly, looking up into sparkling eyes, her heart on her sleeve for all the world to see.

"Always," the other woman replied seriously, squeezing the younger woman's shoulder with reassuring tenderness, instilling confidence with a look in her eyes that screamed, 'You can always ask me anything!'

"Do you ever get that 'not so fresh' feeling?"

"SWEET JESUS! GODDAMMIT!!!" Clint Bender roared, slapping his open palm down hard on the long oval table. The room's occupants flinched, snatching up their coffee cups so as not to lose a precious drop of the aromatic elixir.

The tape stopped mid-frame, the brunette's mouth frozen open, her answer unheard, the sound of the sea birds replaced by the boom of Bender's hand, which still echoed off the wood-paneled walls. The big man straightened indignantly, tugging up his large, silver belt buckle with thick fingers.

Six sets of eyes immediately trained themselves on the polished wooden table, as their owners mentally braced for the pending explosion that was sure to make Hiroshima look tame. Someone would pay for this horrendous oversight, and each of them mentally thanked their deity of choice that it wouldn't be them. Not today. At least, not for this.

"I thought I told you to cut out or at least fast forward over that feminine shit!" Bender complained bitterly, his voice filled with equal parts anger and genuine disgust. He pointed in horror to the large flat screen mounted on the boardroom wall, as though he had been forced to sit through John Tesh in concert. Twice. "You know I hate that crap! Goddammit! Now I've gone and lost my appetite!" he whined, his words taking on a slightly piteous edge.

"I...I...I'm so sorry, Mr. Bender," the projectionist sputtered, his suddenly sweaty finger nearly slipping off the 'pause' button on the remote control. "We just got the season finale tape a few minutes ago. I didn't have time to edit…"

"Shut up, boy! I don't want excuses," the network owner reprimanded, his dark eyes filling with righteous indignation as he pushed off from the table and stepped closer to his perspiring employee. "If God had meant for me to know about those nasty female problems, he wouldn't have blessed me with a pecker, now, would he?" He cocked his grizzled head. And waited.

The projectionist, who also happened to be the Vice President of Programming for the fledgling network BTBC (Bender Television Broadcasting Channel), glanced helplessly at his colleagues, hoping one of them would jump in and save him from trying to answer what he had assumed was a rhetorical question. The other executives refused to meet his needy stare, instead concentrating on their doodle-filled legal pads, or warm coffee cups, or bright enamel nail polish, anything but him. In this business it was sink or swim, and not a single soul in that room was willing to let go of their own life preserver to lend him a hand. Especially not when the biggest shark of them all was nipping at their heels.

Bender glared at his employee for several seconds before it became clear that the flustered young man wasn't going to respond to his question. "Get your ass outta here 'fore I decide to fire ya right here and now! And take that Goddamn worthless tape with you!"

The programming VP nodded vigorously on his way out of the room, careful to press 'eject' before disengaging his cramped finger from the 'pause' button. He walked away on slightly shaky legs, thankful to be going to *his* office instead of the Unemployment Office. It was more than he had expected going into this meeting.

Four years after its inception, and a year after its purchase by Bender, the network was still floundering in last place in every major market and time slot. In response, Clint Bender had decided to take a very *personal* interest in his investment.

"Oh, and just so you know," Bender suddenly continued, his deep voice halting the rapidly fleeing man just as he was about to open the door, "I'll be stoppin' by your office later."

There was a moment of stunned silence before the Director of Marketing coughed "Flotsam," under his breath, his curled fist only barely muffling the word. A round of sniggers went round the room.

The Programming VP's face paled and his loud gulp heralded his final descent to the bottom.

*   *   *

Shannon Muldoon stood impatiently in the private waiting room next to the boardroom. Leaning her shoulder against the wall, she smoothed her russet-colored linen skirt with a restless hand, wishing she had bothered to eat breakfast that morning. Her stomach growled furiously. Who knew the meeting would take this long? Her boss was already more than 45 minutes late. *When is Rita not late, Shannon? You certainly know every time her little visitor is late, because you're the one who gets sent to the drugstore to buy another box of Clear Blue Easy. 'Easy' was one of many four letter words that described Rita.*

A large window, coffee-colored vertical blinds partially open, divided the private waiting room and the boardroom, allowing the young woman a view of the posh interior. Its plush red carpet, black walnut furnishings, and expensive, if slightly gaudy artwork, were all meant to impress potential advertisers. Green eyes with more than a hint of blue rolled at the stuffy atmosphere and its equally unimaginative occupants.

Shannon snorted loudly. *Look at the drones. If one of the reps from Nike or Pepsi asked any one of them for a kidney, that fucker Bender would sharpen the scalpel himself, then offer a lung to boot.* She winced internally. *God, I'm almost one of them.* She figured she'd earned that charitable 'almost' because she knew she was pathetic but still remained hopeful for a better life.

Glancing at her watch, Shannon gave her boss another 5 minutes before she had to leave for her appointment with a publisher. Today she was taking her first step toward that 'better life'. Nothing was worth this.

Though her job title was Administrative Assistant to the President of Programming, she was more than that and everyone knew it. She was Rita's right hand, a junior executive of sorts. But without the big office. Or fancy car. Or money for nothin' and chicks for free. Oh yeah. She especially missed that part.

She was tired of the endless bullshit, late hours and missed appointments. She couldn't remember how many times she'd been paged during class or a date. Her beeper had gone off, sending her scurrying like the slave that she was, during her college graduation ceremony and her Uncle Patrick's wake. She'd been called away in the middle of a root canal, and even while she was being happily seduced by her roommate's sister.

And, unbelievably, her boss's timing had on several recent occasions been even worse. *Every single time I get close…* Shannon closed her eyes and shook her head in dismay, biting her lower lip as the wicked, prophetic words rang out in her head…taunting her with their cruelty. *"I don't give a flying fuck if you're in the middle of the biggest 'rock my world', 'the eagle has landed' orgasm in the history of mankind. Strap-On-Sally can just go slinking back home, 'cause when I page you, I expect you to drop everything and come running!"* Shannon's mind mimicked the words perfectly, causing a shiver to chase its way down her spine. *How could anyone relax under those circumstances?!*

"Oh my God," Shannon moaned, her mouth dropping open in a moment of clarity. "That bitch has made me impotent!"

The boardroom was soundproofed but she could tell something unpleasant was happening by the look on everyone's faces. Which, she contemplated, was pretty amazing considering she had never seen a more stressed-out bunch of people to begin with. Shitting bricks didn't begin to cover it. These people were the Chihuahuas of the human race. A harsh scolding from the big boss and they just might piddle on the rug.

*   *   *

"Goddamn, people!" Bender boomed, shaking his head back and forth. He watched the credits roll for what was supposed to be their answer to the current game show craze and that 'Real Life' primetime show. "No wonder we're dead ass last! What's this show supposed to be about again, Rita? And who is that ugly woman?"

Rita, the President of Programming, clicked her long red nails together nervously. Jesus! Was Bender going to make them justify each of the characters on their new series? "Ahem," she cleared her throat nervously. "It's called 'Castaway'. They aren't actors; they're real people we're going to maroon on an island. We start out with 16 castaways, broken down into two teams, and they have to 'survive' with no modern conveniences. Every few days they vote to lose a member. The last person left wins a million dollars. They leave on Monday for Paradise Island."

Bender's eyes widened perceptibly when he heard the amount.

"The castaways go through a series of challenges and compete with each other. And we film it all."

The big man scratched his jaw. If presented correctly, *this* could have potential. "So it's a 'Lord of the Flies' eat-or-be-eaten show?"

"Not exactly."

"They hunt each other with tranquilizer darts or taser guns to thin the weak from the herd?"

"Umm…No." Rita's eyes lit up. *But that's not a bad idea.*

Bender blew out a disgusted breath. *So much for potential.* "And people want to see this because…?"

They don't, asshole. That's why we're in last place! Rita stilled her nervous fingers, wishing she had a cigarette. "We expect conflict and excitement." She glanced down at her note pad, knowing there was nothing written on it that would help her. "Our market research told us the ugly girl would appeal to overweight teenagers with acne, insecure single women ages 18-28, and nearsighted male computer geeks ages 30-40." She drew her eyes up to meet Bender's and felt her pulse begin to increase. *Oh no! He's going to say he'll see me in my office later, too!*

Bender took a calming breath and was about to speak when the Director of Network Research stepped in to defend his work. "Mr. Bender, our test groups were meticulously..."

"Boy, you couldn't find your own buttocks with both hands. Shut up and sit down!"

Properly spanked, the Director of Research gladly took his seat. "Yes, Mr. Bender," he mumbled.

Bender turned and pinned Rita with an intense stare. "*I'm* going to tell you how we can fix this damn show. I want a whole new group of people on that island."

Rita nearly fainted. It had been hell picking these sixteen out as it was. "Mr. Bender, with all due respect, it will set us back at least three months with all the background checks and psych profiles...And we have the crew on the island already. We're ready to go."

The stare she received from Bender reminded her of the dead-eyed fish on ice at the local Chinese market. "There's no Goddamn way we're *not* shooting this, starting Monday. Do you have any idea what it would cost to delay the rollout? My God, Rita! I expect you to recast it over the weekend and get them on the plane to be there by Monday. And the first person I want you to find is a lesbian. Some men find that...appealing."

Rita resisted the nearly staggering impulse to roll her eyes. "No. Really?"

"Don't play dumb." Bender straightened his tie, proud of his hipness, despite his age. "I know what's hot, dammit! And I want you to find me a big old 'I'm going straight to hell but I'm gonna have me some tits along the way' lesbian. And I want her to be good-looking, too." He started gesturing wildly. He was on a roll. "I don't give a shit how much zit cream advertising we'll lose. I want her to appeal to red-blooded American men." With that proclamation he puffed his chest out so that it extended just a hair beyond his belly.

"But our audience is primarily f…"

"Who the hell is that?" Bender suddenly pointed toward Shannon, who was doing her best to hide behind the partially closed blinds. Caught, Shannon began squirming under the weight of their stares, ruffling her bangs with a nervous hand.

Rita rolled her eyes. Shannon was always getting into some sort of trouble! "That's my assistant, Shannon Muldoon. She's probably looking for me. We were…"

Bender scratched his jaw speculatively and motioned toward Shannon with his chin. "Have her come out from behind those blinds so I can see her better."

As fast as her three-inch heels would allow, and anxious to save her own ass, Rita ran over to the window and tapped on the glass. She motioned wildly for Shannon to stop hiding, and silently mouthed 'be nice and smile' to her scowling employee.

Bender moved a step closer and cocked his head, carefully studying Shannon who, though she felt very much like a chimp at the zoo, managed to plaster on an insincere smile. "Hmm…She's a pretty little thing." His eyes swept over Rita's assistant. "All fit, and sweet looking." His face creased into a broad smile. "She's like the perfect kid sister— that everyone still wants to fuck," he said with a grin. "Goddamn, she might even be a natural blonde!"

Rita's hands unconsciously moved to her platinum hair.

"I want her."

"She's yours."

"For the show, Rita!"

"Oh." Rita began clicking her nails again. "I knew that. Whatever. She's available."

"You'll have to get her to agree, but still fire her. It wouldn't look right for one of our employees to be one of the 'castaways.'"

"She's fired." Rita winced internally. Shannon was going to be hard to replace.

"How old is she?"

Rita bit the inside of her cheek, careful not to smudge her blood-red lipstick. "How old do you want her to be?" she asked carefully.

"Over 21."

The President of Programming breathed a huge sigh of relief, glad she wouldn't have to get a fake birth certificate drawn up. Things like that were so time consuming. "She's twenty-four or twenty-five, something like that."

"And you're sure she'll say yes?"

Rita snorted. "Oh, I'm sure. We *own* her."

Bender knew the type. Young. Ambitious. Unable to say no even when their boss was sucking out their last drop of life blood. "Well now," he chuckled, plopping back down in his high-back leather chair. "That's a bird of a different feather."

The network owner glanced over his shoulder at his intern. "Go tell Ms. Muldoon to wait in Rita's office. This meeting is nearly over." Dark eyes danced with merriment as a simple idea formed in Clint Bender's brain. He focused on Rita. "With Shannon's help, we might just have a show after all. See, this casting shit is easy."

*   *   *

"I'm fired?!" Shannon screeched, still not believing her piss poor luck. Not only had she missed her appointment with the publisher, but now she was out of a job too!

"It's the opportunity of a lifetime," Rita corrected with forced cheerfulness.

Shannon narrowed her eyes. "Oh, excuse me if I don't jump up and down for joy, Rita. I've *seen* the concept paper on the show. It sucks, by the way. And I don't have any survival skills. They'll vote me off first thing." But even as Shannon protested, her own idea began brewing.

The publisher whose appointment she had just missed was, at best, marginally interested in her novel. Hell, if she hadn't flirted with the poor man mercilessly she probably wouldn't have got an appointment at all. Maybe she just needed something more interesting to write about…like life as a castaway?

"I'll hire you back when you get the boot." There was no way this girl would last long enough to win any real money. "And you get severance pay for your unexpected termination. It's more than your original salary would have been," Rita pressed, certain her own job was on the line.

"And if I say no, do I still get the severance pay?"

A spray of diet Dr. Pepper hit Shannon squarely in the eye as Rita choked and sputtered. "What the hell do you think, darling?"

"Don't call me that. And I hate you," Shannon ground out forcefully. God! She didn't have a choice. Her student loan payments alone would cripple several South American nations.

Okay, Shannon girl. Time to salvage what you can out of the shit heap currently known as 'your life' and make the best of things. "Maybe you're right, Rita." Shannon took a deep breath and let it out slowly. *Just say it! It's not like you really have to believe it!* "It could be the opportunity of a lifetime."

<Fade out>

EPISODE ONE

Just Sit Right Back and You'll Hear a Tale...

It was hot. Okay, not just hot. It was excruciatingly, brain meltingly, you've just left a sweaty ass print on every surface, 'God, my bra itches', hot and humid. Shannon scratched the item in question and seriously considered going au naturel for however many days she lasted on the island. She was just starting to warm to the idea when several cameramen moved closer.

The TV crew constantly scanned the castaways, hoping for something...anything that would make good film. Bender had offered a $2000 bonus to the first cameraman to capture a fight, another $1000 if it was between two women, and $1000 more if anyone lost their clothing. Somehow Shannon doubted that he meant the cameramen.

But the castaways weren't fighting...they weren't even talking. They were pretty much keeping to themselves, nervously looking out across the ocean or leafing through the 'Meet Your Fellow Castaways' brochure that the production crew had passed out when they departed Borneo.

Shannon lifted her ponytail off the back of her neck, allowing the salty breeze to dry some of the perspiration that had gathered around her T-shirt collar. *I might as well check out the bios and see who I'm stuck here with.* She had taken a few moments to glance around at the other people on the deck. But they were still a bunch of nameless faces.

"Lazy bastards!" she hissed loudly, her eyes darting across the glossy brochure. The camera crew rushed over, hoping to film something interesting, only to have Shannon turn her back to them and face out toward the rapidly approaching island, as she continued to read.

"Cut!" a heavyset man snapped loudly, lowering his camera and shooing away the second shooter. "Look…" The man tugged his own brochure out of his back pocket and found Shannon's face among the other castaways. "Ah…okay, Ms. Muldoon, here's the deal: You signed a contract saying you would let us film you. You can't keep turning your back every time we come around. So, give us a break here, all right?"

The young woman didn't move.

"It's really not a good idea to get on the camera crew's bad side," he added impatiently, his voice taking on a slightly menacing tone. "You don't wanna know how big I can make your ass look, sweetheart."

Shannon turned around very slowly and smiled her sweetest smile.

The cameraman smirked over his victory. Screw that seminar on 'Conflict in the Workplace' the Bender Television Broadcasting Channel had made everyone take. He knew how to handle a blonde. "All right, Ms. Muldoon. What had you so upset a moment ago?" He crouched down in front of Shannon, adjusting his camera. A second more and then a red light next to the lens began to blink.

The blonde held up her 'Meet Your Fellow Castaways' brochure for the camera, her fake smile still plastered across her face. "Well, I was looking at my biography. You know, the one based on the information that *I* so helpfully provided." She opened the book and pointed to the page with her photo and bio. "My degree is from USC *not* UCLA, and it's in English Lit., *not* Communications."

"Oh great. Another bitch," the cameraman groaned, knowing they'd simply edit it out later, but in case they didn't, he adjusted the lens and doubled her chin for the hell of it.

"And I was especially wondering how my brother and sister were going to feel about finding out I'm an only child! This..." Shannon shook the brochure, "...is nothing but a crock of..."

The blinking red light clicked off.

"Over here, Pete!" another voice called from across the boat. "That annoying space cadet is seasick and puking her guts out. C'mon!"

As quickly as he'd come, Pete, the cameraman, disappeared.

Shannon shook her head in disgust and watched several drops of sweat blotch her picture. That lazy bitch Rita hadn't even looked at the gazillion page form Shannon had filled out. "Why am I even surprised?" she asked herself wearily. This was television, after all, where bullshit was passed around as readily as a whore at the Democratic National Convention. *God only knows what I'll find on the island. I'll be lucky if they're not selling me off to slave traders!*

The boat slowed, then stopped and several crewmembers scrambled to drop anchor.

Curious eyes studied the island still about 300 yards in the distance.

Black Death Island.

Shannon snorted quietly. BTBC had billed it 'Paradise Island' until some industrious intern from a competing network found out that even though the island was 'officially' unnamed, inhabitants from the neighboring islands had been calling it 'Black Death Island' for several hundred years. Shannon's lips curled into a smile as she remembered her boss' reaction to the news that the island had been a refuge for plague bearers and lepers. It was excellent, although Shannon was still holding out hope for a full-blown stroke.

Joan Fogarty, the show's host and executive producer, jumped up onto an empty crate to get everyone's attention. Shannon had heard Joan was a nice woman, despite the fact that she was known for being peppy to the point of psychotic. "Okay, Beta Team..."

All eyes turned to her and several castaways stepped closer.

Pale brows creased as Shannon glanced at the people scattered across the deck. *We're the Beta Team, huh?* Out of the corner of her eye she could see another small group clustered at the opposite end of the boat.

"This is as far as we go." Joan smiled and Shannon thought she caught a hint of sympathy in her voice. "You have to make it the rest of the way to the island on your own."

Joan leaned against what appeared to be a stack of crates under a dark cloth. "There are two bamboo rafts near the stern."

Only one person looked in the right direction.

"Beta Team gets one of them. It should hold three people." This started a few murmurs. "The rest of you will get your first taste of these lovely waters. And don't worry," she grinned again, showing off two rows of perfectly capped teeth, "the water snakes aren't poisonous." That was a little white lie. Damn! She loved her job.

A tall, well-built black woman standing behind Shannon began chanting, "Oh, sweet Jesus, oh, sweet Jesus," under her breath.

A camera moved in for a close up.

"Now for the fun part," Joan continued, causing Shannon's stomach to clench. "Under this tarp…" she kicked the black, slick cloth with the toe of her boot, "…are some things that will make your island stay a lot easier. You've got two minutes to take what items you can and be in the water. Anyone who's left on the boat after two minutes is up will cause their entire team to forfeit the items you selected from under the tarp."

The Beta Team was clustered together now; hanging on Joan's every word. "And just to make it a little more interesting…you'll have to compete with the Alpha Team for what's under the cloth."

A new group of people suddenly joined the Beta Team. Shannon had seen a few of them but assumed they were more TV people.

"GO!!!" Joan shouted.

And all hell broke loose.

*   *   *

Ryan Stryker sat near the diving platform of the boat, as far away from the other people as possible. She couldn't decide whether to turn her back to the ocean and risk a Navy SEAL coming up out of the water and attacking her, or to turn her back on the mangy-looking boat crew. So she kept spinning around in the seat, never staying in one position long enough for someone to get a clear shot. She was smarter than those government bastards.

"What's up with her?" a young man asked his companion. Both looked exactly alike—tall, gangly, hair in the latest floppy style favored by the younger set, tips dyed blond for no apparent reason.

"Must have been a bad hit," the floppier of the two replied. He reached up and scratched his arm where The Patch was securely fastened. Had it only been fifteen minutes since his last cigarette? Well, his second last cigarette. He had had his first last cigarette two hours ago when they left port. He figured he wouldn't be able to bum another one off the crew at this point, so he reached into his backpack and pulled out another patch, affixing it to his other arm. Maybe that would help.

The engines died. Taking a deep breath and drawing out her Swiss Army knife, Ryan leaned over the edge of the boat, plunging her head into the warm tropical waters. She scanned the underbelly of the boat for the SEALs who she was sure had to have cut the gas line.

All she saw was a school of bright orange fish swimming past the nearby coral reef. She speared the nearest one with her knife.

Returning to the surface, Ryan shook the water from her hair, nailing an Asian woman, whom she immediately recognized as Yun-kyung from the 'Castaway' brochure, sitting six feet away. The woman looked up and saw the fish impaled on Ryan's knife. "OHMIGOD!" she shrieked.

Ryan twirled around once. Twice. Nothing. "What? Where are they?" she asked breathlessly.

"You. Killed. A. Fish."

Ryan squinted and eyed the ten-inch beauty. "Yeah. Haven't you heard of sushi?" She brought it to her mouth and took a bite, spitting out the small bones as she chewed.

Yun-kyung leaned over the side of the boat and hurled.

"That's good, Cap'n," Joan called from the other side of the boat.

Huh. Whatever the network had in store for them was starting.

One of the camera crew came and stood in the middle of them, flapping his arms like a rabid turkey to gather the group. "Everyone! Huddle up! Huddle up!"

The eight contestants who had been sent to that end of the boat followed directions a bit warily. Without a megaphone or clipboard, he clearly lacked the authority necessary to convince them of anything.

Ryan smiled as she looked at her teammates. This game was as good as in the bag. She could already imagine her new government surplus tank parked next to her command center. Let those government bastards try to come get her then! Her team consisted of the two floppy boys, two old men, and three women of no consequence. Like stealing money from a federally insured bank, baybee.

"We just put down anchor here," the crewman said. "It's up to you to get to the island when Joan gives the signal. In a moment, you and the Beta Team will compete to take the supplies from this boat to the island."

"I think we can work out an equitable distribution among ourselves," interjected one of the women. She was, kindly put, middle-aged. Her eyes were a bit too tight and her lips a bit too plump, clearly showing heavy reconstruction had taken place in the not too distant past. There are reasons work like that doesn't have a money back guarantee. Molly was a walking, talking reason.

"You will have two minutes," was the final instruction from the crewman.

All the team members cursed except the youngest female. She just looked terrified.

"Everyone put on your lifejackets and then we'll start."

After carefully inspecting hers, Ryan slipped it on and secured it about her chest. She watched the youngest woman struggle for a moment before stepping over. "Relax." Ryan worked quickly and soon had the woman encased in a lifejacket as well. "Can you swim?"

Baleful blue eyes met her own. "Not well. I've never been around the ocean before. I'm Marva, by the way." The woman held out a timid hand.

Ryan grasped the offered hand firmly. "I know, I'm…" she hesitated, almost giving one of her many aliases before settling on the truth, "I'm Ryan."

"We just had a little crick out back behind our house growing up…it wasn't quite so deep," Marva continued nervously.

"And it didn't have sea snakes," a cameraman sniggered.

Marva wavered, and almost fainted, clutching the rail to keep upright. The look Ryan fixed on the man caused him to find other more interesting subjects to shoot.

Ryan focused on Marva. "You stay with me; understand?"

A nod and a pathetic smile of relief.

Ryan nodded. *Oh well, all great leaders need a loyal lackey. This one looks harmless enough.* They were herded over to the other team. Joan stood in the middle of them, her whistle hanging around her neck and bandana tucked in her back pocket, her clipboard and megaphone in the ready position. She looked like an ad for the sequel to 'Jurassic Park'. Everyone knew how well that turned out. Their own damn fault for hiring that 'Fly' guy.

"Go!!!"

*   *   *

In two long strides Ryan was at the supplies, tossing aside the tarp. "You, twitchy blond boy, into the water!" she barked from her crouched position as she scanned the packages, tools, and bundles. "When the supplies start coming overboard, you load them into the raft." Ryan sniffed the air and licked her finger, holding it up to the breeze in order to calculate the wind speed, direction, and the exact trajectory necessary to put the raft in the proper spot. Then she marched over to the raft and simply dumped it overboard.

Twitchy blonde boy, otherwise known by his mother as Tony (strangely, his father called him twitchy blonde boy, too), scratched at his nicotine patches. Could these get wet? "But…"

Ryan shot up, grabbing Tony by the front of his T-shirt, pulling him close enough to smell his smoky exhales. "MOVE. MOVE. MOVE!!!"

Without thought, Tony dove overboard. Several other castaways joined him, automatically responding to Ryan's order. One was even from her own Team.

Ryan turned to a wide-eyed Marva. "Go with Tony and stay with the raft. You'll be fine. I'll join you in another minute and a half."

A geeky looking man from the Beta Team almost corrected Ryan. She was, after all, nearly 4 seconds off in her calculation. But his mouth clicked shut when he got a good look at what was in Ryan's hands.

Ryan flipped open her six-inch, custom-made Swiss Army knife and began cutting away some loose bindings that held the supplies together. "Here," she dug out a standard issue military entrenching tool and handed it, along with the tarp, to Yun-kyung, who took them, then simply stared at them in confusion. "JUMP, JUMP, JUMP!" Ryan roared causing Yun-kyung to scream in terror, her shoes making a mysterious, wet swishing noise by the time she reached the railing.

Two more Beta Team members suddenly decided that the water snakes looked a lot friendlier than the tall, crazy bitch wearing camouflage shorts and carrying a huge knife. Stealing their team's raft, they dove into the water. Screw the supplies.

It was the Beta Team's first demonstration of teamwork.

With amazing speed and efficiency, Ryan began sorting through the supplies, disregarding some, tossing others directly into the ocean, and passing the things that wouldn't float to her waiting teammates before they disappeared over the boat's edge.

Shannon looked on in horror as the best of the supplies disappeared faster than virgins on prom night. The members of her team who hadn't jumped overboard at Ryan's command were simply standing there, too shocked to move. Who *was* this person? Every time a Beta Team member even got close to the supplies, the tall brunette would growl at them like a rabid dog. Okay, a rabid dog with perfect breasts. Shannon unconsciously licked her lips.

Ryan suddenly looked up from her task, her eyes locking on Shannon's. For a split second, neither woman moved, each held captive by the other's gaze.

It was just enough time for two Beta Team members to scramble past Ryan's defenses, allowing them to snatch some of the booty. The larger of the two men accidentally bumped into Ryan, causing the woman to stumble a couple of steps forward but not fall.

"Sorry," he mumbled, before running to the end of the boat and jumping off.

Ryan quickly straightened, shooting an evil glare at Shannon, who was clearly a government spy, probably ATF, sent to distract her and keep her from winning the million dollars. How did the Feds find out she had a thing for short, green-eyed blondes? Damn that time she used a pay phone in '93!

"I got somethin'! I got somethin'!" A slender Hispanic man, with a heavy accent, wearing matching hot pink Polo shorts and a short-sleeved silk shirt began prancing around the deck, wildly shaking his prize. He had no idea what it was. But he didn't care. The boys from his flower arranging class would be so proud!

Ryan took a menacing step toward him. This had to be Arturo from the Beta Team.

"Don't even think about it, girlfriend," Arturo reprimanded, his tenacity stopping Ryan dead in her tracks. His limp wrist flicked twice as he snapped his fingers dramatically before holding his nose with one hand and plunging overboard.

"Fuck!" Ryan growled. She had let a Nancy boy hairdresser escape with something! The survivalist quickly shook it off. No matter. If it was something critical she could always go on a midnight reconnaissance mission and get it back later.

"Twenty seconds, castaways," Joan called out, directing two of the cameramen to focus on the people swimming to shore while one focused solely on Shannon and Ryan, the only castaways left on deck.

Shannon looked down at the remaining supplies then back up at Ryan, who had resumed her position guarding them. "You can't carry them all."

"Neither can you. And if you stay here your team will lose what they took."

"Fifteen seconds!"

"Ha! So what?" Shannon put her hands on her hips and cocked her head to the side. "Your team already has everything worth taking. The Alphas have much more to lose than the Betas."

Damn, she could be CIA! Since when did they start using logic?!

"Ten seconds!"

"Shit!' both women muttered simultaneously, each grabbing a bundle in her arms.

"You first!" Ryan ordered.

"No, you!"

"You!"

"Five seconds!"

Shannon gave in first, running for the edge of the boat, only to have Ryan dive past her and disappear into the salty water with barely a splash.

The blonde came up for air, sputtering and spitting, still clinging to a large plastic covered bundle. The words 'toilet paper' were staring her in the face. Cool!

No one from the boat called after her so she assumed they had made it off in time. Using the toilet paper as a floatation device, Shannon scanned the water for Ryan. Everyone else appeared to be more than half way to shore. After several long seconds, when Shannon was beginning to wonder if Ryan's supplies had caused her to sink, the tall woman popped out of the water about 20 yards ahead of her. Her big ass knife was clenched between her teeth, sparkling in the sunlight. And her supplies were neatly secured on her back.

"How in the hell did she do that?" Shannon marveled.

Something slimy slithered between Shannon's thighs. "Jesus!" she shuddered in revulsion. It reminded her of her high school boyfriend. "I hate you, Rita!" she screamed as she paddled to shore.

<Fade out>

EPISODE TWO

Paradise Lost

The camp was quiet. Very quiet. Eerily quiet. The quiet before a shit storm hits you full in the face and there-isn't-a-scrap-of-toilet-paper-in-sight kinda quiet.

The eight members of Alpha Team were scattered around their campsite. Compared to Beta Team's, it was luxurious. Marty and Ryan had constructed two bunkhouses that could withstand up to a Type II monsoon.

The tarp that had nearly drowned Yun-kyung during her swim to the raft was now stretched between two palm trees and one of the bunkhouses, providing a shady escape from the heat. All in all, it was a somewhat upscale version of a Girl Scout camp. Russell was particularly looking forward to the pillow fights at night.

Ryan sat by the campfire and was carefully feeling her scalp for the transmitter that had to be there. *How else did they know to put that luscious little thing on the other team?* It must have been put in the one time she had gone into the hospital. Her second-in-command had—gasp!—filled out forms giving her name and other personal information. Now, all of it was housed on big brother's computer, there for all the intelligence world to see. *So maybe it isn't an implant, but still, if it is...*

She'd have to be sure to deny her true feelings of instant attraction to Shannon. *No, don't even think her name, Ryan. It's bad enough you looked it up in the 'Castaway' brochure. If they know you want her, they'll torture you with not having her. You must be strong. Like John Wayne when he wanted Maureen O'Hara in 'The Quiet Man'. Strong.*

Tony came bounding over to the others, holding a bamboo tube in his hand. "The mail came!"

Fucking postal service is everywhere! Not even communications on the island are safe! Ryan immediately took the tube and inspected it for bombs.

"Give that to me, you loon." Marty snatched the tube out of her hand and pulled out the parchment. The others waited eagerly for him to read it aloud, though Yun-kyung was unsure whether he was capable of such an advanced skill. "It's a map," he announced, leaving the veterinarian to continue wondering.

"What should we do with it?" Marva asked. She was still a bit overwhelmed by everything going on. Since her swim to the island, she had tried to remain as close to Ryan as possible. The tall, dark-haired woman was a bit paranoid, but she was a whole lot safer than her other teammates. While Russell gave Marva the impression that if she wasn't a virgin, he wasn't interested, Marty had no such inhibitions.

"This is so fuckin' cool!" Tony said, pumping his arm. "Let's go! I bet this is our first challenge. We need to get to that 'x' first so the other team has to lose a person."

Ryan shrugged. "I dunno. Sometimes it's good to weed the garden."

Suddenly, crystals were swinging around, flashing rainbows in the air as Molly twirled her necklace and chanted.

"Peace...harmony...love...unity."

"Yeah, yeah, yeah, come on, Granola, let's get going." Marty pushed himself to his feet and dusted the sand off his shorts. He hated it when he got sand in the crack of his ass. Very annoying.

One by one, the team began following him into the jungle. Like lemmings taking that extra step, they followed his lead.

*   *   *

The map was not very helpful. It appeared to be drawn by a dyslexic sixth grader wearing a cast. Actually, that wasn't too far from the truth. But Joan's production crew didn't like to tell her that to her face.

They marched in single file. There wasn't any real need to do so, but all of them had watched jungle movies in the past and were going with tradition. Jason followed directly behind Martin, trying to glance over the older man's shoulder for a look at the map.

"So where do you think they're sending us?"

"I hope somewhere with a Burger King," Tony whined, licking The Patch he had just removed from his shoulder. He hoped against hope the nicotine would enter his bloodstream faster that way.

"We've only been here thirty hours," Jason observed, glancing at his watch.

"How can you eat at those horrific fast food restaurants? The amount of abuse the animals suffer prior to being brutally slaughtered and then consumed by arrogant Americans such as yourself is…"

Tony stopped and faced Yun-kyung. "Are you telling me you don't like BK?" He sounded personally offended, as if it were his fattened calf she had refused.

"Like? No, I *don't* like a corporation that helps destroy the rain forests in South America. Did you know that more than half the species in the world live in the rain forest? And you're killing them for your Big Macs?"

"Those are at MickeyD's. BK has the Whopper." Tony knew his fast food menu items. "And isn't it MickeyD's that's destroying the rain forest?"

Marva shivered. "I hate clowns."

Everyone turned to face the housewife. "Huh?" Jason managed on behalf of the group.

"Clowns. You know, ever since 'Poltergeist', they've scared the crap out of me. When my daughter, Edwina, was born someone gave me a stuffed clown for her. Well, first thing I did was stick that thing down the garbage disposal. I didn't want it coming to life in the middle of the night and strangling my little darling."

Ryan nodded solemnly. It wasn't entirely implausible.

"So, we don't go to McDonald's," Marva continued. "Ronald scares me."

"I've always wondered why he feels a need to disguise his true identity," Ryan confided. "If his burgers are such a good thing, why does he have to dress up like that? If not to fool us?"

Yun-kyung rolled her eyes and started hiking again. It wouldn't be worth the oxygen expenditure to try to reason with her teammates.

"Let's go, ladies," Marty called out, meaning the rest of his team. The two young boys were barely old enough to have hair on their balls and Marty considered Russell a bit of a pansy, being a schoolteacher and all.

An hour later, the group stopped. Marty carefully studied the map and glanced around trying to get his bearings.

Russell shook his head and sat down on a large boulder.

"Do you need help?" Marva asked sweetly. She was used to driving with her husband. That man could get lost even in little Stone Mountain, Georgia.

"No!"

"Sometimes it helps to get another opinion –"

"No!"

"We all need help finding our way," Molly said. "Without others to act as our compass, we are adrift."

"It's this way," the construction foreman insisted and stormed confidently into the bog in front of them. Despite his determination, his steps soon became very slow. It was when he was a good fifteen paces

away from the rest of the team that Marty realized where he was:
Quicksand.

"Oh shit," he whispered, not wanting any of the others to hear. He
was certainly manly enough to swear around them, but far too manly to
sound panicked.

Perhaps he could outrun it.

Moving as quickly as he could, he managed to sink to his hips.

Shit! Fuck!

He glared at the cameraman who was filming his descent into the
sludge. "You wanna give me a hand here?"

The cameraman shrugged. "I'm union, buddy." Saving dumb ass
contestants wasn't in his contract.

"Little help," Marty said in as casual a tone as he could manage.

                    *   *   *

By unanimous consent, Ryan now led the team. In possession of the
slightly soggy and gritty map, the survivalist set off at a rapid pace for
their destination. Also by unanimous consent, Marty had been sent to
the rear of the line. Quicksand stinks like shit on your shoes on a hot
summer day.

Ryan wondered if Shannon—*no! don't think her name!*—was already
at their destination. Was the jungle heat affecting her? Was her skin all
slick with sweat, little droplets gathering between her lush, ripe breasts?

The cute blonde reminded Ryan of her first love, the tragic Chloe.
They had been grade school sweethearts, though everyone thought they
were just playing Barbies together. Just like Barbie, they were going to
have it all. Including a non-functional male to serve their every whim.

Then, one day, Chloe got a retainer. At first, Ryan thought it was
kinda sexy, the way it made her mouth all sparkly. But then...

The voices came.

They were playing a hurt-comfort scene with Barbie and Skipper when Ryan first heard it. It was a weather forecast. Coming from Chloe's mouth.

Soon, stock market quotes came.

And—gasp!—top 40 hits.

Hearing Casey Kasem's voice and a cheesy dedication to someone's dead pet iguana coming from her beloved's mouth was too much to bear. Ryan made her own long distance dedication and broke up with Chloe.

That night, in her despair, Chloe forgot to take out her retainer. It choked her during her sleep.

Ryan never truly recovered.

*　　　　　*　　　　　*

Shannon leaned against a tree. The same tree that they had passed at least once an hour for the past four hours. And she knew damn well that it was the same tree, because David, the portly religious guy, felt the need to scratch tiny crosses on every conceivable surface to mark their trail. Shannon was standing as far away from him as possible. She didn't want to be saved! At least by him.

This was their first challenge—a competition between the Alpha and Beta Teams where the loser would have to select one of their team members to leave the island. And the winning team would receive a fishing rod. So here they were, hopelessly lost in the middle of the dense, uneven, jungle. Using a hand-drawn map provided by Joan, trying to find a secret location somewhere in the center of the island before the Alpha Team did.

The young blonde smacked another buzzing insect, surprised that, despite the fact she was hungry, tired, bug-bitten, and sunburned, she was in pretty good spirits. This was the first time in she didn't know how long that she wasn't at Rita's immediate beck and call. No organizer, no Palm V, no pager, no phone. She felt positively naked…Ohh…naked…that got her thinking about Ryan.

Closing her eyes and using the rough tree bark, Shannon decided to give herself a good old-fashioned back scratching. Eagerly, she allowed her thoughts to wander to a certain blue-eyed castaway. Ryan had her curiosity piqued. She would be the perfect protagonist in a story! A female anti-hero; all rough and psychotic on the exterior, but with a heart of gold. And even if she didn't have a heart of gold, she still had perfect breasts! A woman couldn't have everything, could she?

Shannon's frantic movements against the tree slowed and shifted into a languid swaying motion. God, but that bark felt good against her itchy bug bites! Ohh…scratching an itch…that got her thinking about Ryan again. Thick dark hair, tall, muscular but still feminine—assuming you overlooked that big ass knife, and forgot about the fact that she was dressed for combat, and didn't dwell on her ability to cause the loss of bladder control with a single stare. *Okay, so I like 'em butch! Sue me!* Oh yeah. Ryan could scratch her itch.

A soft moan escaped Shannon's lips.

"Oh, Channon! Chica, when is the wedding between you and that tree? And how come I wasn't invited?!" Arturo stamped his foot petulantly, resting his hands on slender hips in mock irritation.

Shannon's eyes popped open and she immediately flushed, realizing that her movements against the tree were bordering on pornographic. *Oh God, I can't be horny! It's too hot to be horny. I'll melt! No more thinking about Ryan.* But for some reason, that solution was immediately disregarded as unacceptable. *Okay, I can still think about her. But only when I'm alone. God, I'm weak!*

Shannon stepped away from the tree and tried to scrub the blush from her face with her hands. "My name is Shannon, not Channon." Could that Fernando Lamas accent be for real?

"That's what I said, girlfriend: Channon."

Shannon's gaze dropped to her feet. "I was just...um..."

"I know what you were doing, or at least imagining doing." Arturo giggled like a 12-year-old schoolgirl. "Too bad there are no cold chowers on this island. Oh my!" He slapped his cheeks with the palms of his hands. "That Desiree person is finally finished arguing with Tanesha. I absolutely *must* go talk to her about her hair. Tsk...Tsk...How can she not know Clairol #36 Auburn is out this season?"

Arturo pointed back to the tree behind Shannon. "I hope you two will be very happy together," he added before flittering over to Desiree.

When she felt like her face was no longer lobster red, Shannon took a step to rejoin the group. They had to find their way sometime! Shit! She just knew they had already lost this challenge, which meant their team would be minus one member by tonight. She only hoped it wouldn't be her.

"Ms. Muldoon?" a voice queried from behind Shannon.

The blonde nearly jumped out of her skin. She had already forgotten several cameramen were hovering around like vultures, capturing their every move. "Yes?"

The man dug a note out of his pocket. "I was asked to give this to you...Um...in private. But...well, um...the only time you're not near the group is when you're taking a lea..."

"You were watching?!"

"NO!" the cameraman denied vigorously.

"Pervert!" Shannon snatched the note out of his sweaty hands.

The man shifted from one foot to the other. How was he to know what she made that little side trip earlier for? He was only doing his job!

At the sound of raised voices, the shooter moved toward the group. Surely a clawfest between Arturo and Desiree would count as a catfight! Oh yeah. That bonus was in the bag! "Big screen TV, here I come," he chuckled as he moved into position.

Shannon held the note in her hands without opening it. Oh God. Someone had to be dead. Why else would she be receiving personal correspondence? Her pulse began to pound, and she slowly opened the creased paper. Her eyes immediately scanned to the bottom of the message.

FUCK! It was from Rita! Would the woman ever leave her alone? What did she want now? Her firstborn? A kidney? For Shannon to drop everything and run home so she could go to the nursing home and visit Rita's senile Grandpa, all the while pretending to be the executive? *Ha! She can just drop dead. I told her I wasn't going to do that…again. I have my pride!*

Irritated green eyes scanned the telegram that had, apparently, come via the neighboring island.

Shannon:

Keep your eyes off Ryan's boobs! (Too bad too, she does have nice tits). We had to cut out that whole bit on the boat where she looked up at you and froze. Bender just went ape (deleted by government censor).

This is coming directly from Bender, so pay attention:

"What in the (deleted by government censor) does that stupid blonde (deleted by government censor) think she's doing? She can't be the lesbian! She's the (deleted by government censor) girl next door!"

Can't you start making doe eyes at Joe instead? He's nice looking. A few days in the jungle, and Ryan will be just as hairy. Anyway, Bender is hoping for sparks between Ryan and Tanesha. Or, in the alternative, that Martin will be able to turn her. So hands and eyes off!

For clarity, I repeat, while on the island, YOU CAN-NOT BE GAY!

The person directly above you on the food chain,

Rita

"Who in the hell does she think she is?" Shannon said angrily, balling up the note, but stuffing it in her pocket instead of tossing it on the ground. Who knew how long that toilet paper would last?

"Give it back! Give it back!"

Shannon's eyes were drawn to her teammates, several of whom were hunched over the incredibly useless map, while the others appeared to be engaged in a game of 'keep away'.

"Give it back!" Bill, who was by far the quietest member of the Beta Team, was nearly in tears. Joe and Dawn were gleefully tossing something to each other over the software designer's head. And every time Bill got close to reclaiming whatever it was they were throwing, they'd launch it beyond his reach again.

"What's going on here?" Shannon stalked over to Joe, Dawn, and Bill. "Hmm?"

Joe and Dawn's gazes dropped sheepishly to the island floor. "We were just having some fun, Shannon," Joe admitted guiltily, digging the toe of his boot into the moist soil.

"Let me have it," Shannon demanded, holding out her hand and doing a very good imitation of someone's mother. "Am I the only adult on this entire team?"

No one answered.

"Thank you," Bill said to Shannon, as he plucked his pocket protector from her hand and slid it neatly into place.

Shannon shook her head sadly, wondering if a single day went by in grade school where someone didn't kick Bill's ass. "Bill, how did they let you on the island with that?" She motioned toward the bright white pocket protector. "That can't be what you selected for your luxury item."

"He wouldn't get on the boat without it," Dawn piped up. "He convinced Joan it was part of his clothing."

"It is," Bill shot back. "It's perfectly logical that something worn on your person, at all times, be considered clothing."

Shannon's pale brows creased. "But you don't have anything with you. What is the pocket protector supposed to protect against?"

"I don't know!" Bill cried. "It's always had something before!" The man fell to his knees and began to sob. "How am I supposed to function without my mechanical pencils?!" The sobbing intensified.

Shannon's eyes widened and she took a quick step backwards. This was clearly someone a few gigs short of a hard drive. *Oh, hard...I bet Ryan...Stop it, Shannon!*

Heedless of the piteous cries, David walked over to Bill and laid a comforting hand on the shaking man's shoulder. "It's all right, son," the preacher said in a soothing voice, giving him a reassuring squeeze.

Bill buried his face against David's ample stomach.

With a final pat on the back, David took a step away from Bill and directed his statement to the group. "I propose that if we keep walking in circles, never finding our way out of the center of the island, we eat Bill first."

"What?!" Bill screamed, rising to his feet.

Dark eyes trained themselves on Bill. "It's God's way, son. The weak shall perish from the earth. God proclaims..."

The entire group started to groan. "Enough. Shut the hell up with that God stuff. Why don't we just eat you, porky cracker?" came the varied replies.

"You are not logical! You are not logical!" Bill screeched to no one in particular, his eyes darting wildly from person to person. "I will not be eaten by you unevolved, under-educated cretins!"

"What do you mean 'unevolved'?" Desiree asked in a confused voice. "What do you care if I'm seeing anyone, geek?"

Bill cocked his head to one side, as if examining another, far lesser species.

When Bill didn't answer her quickly enough, Desiree turned to the group. "Will someone please tell me why Bill is crying and talking about croutons?" She was even more confused than before. "Will we be having salad later?"

Ignoring the idiot model, Shannon held up placating palms. "Look, Bill, I'm sure David was only joking." She glared at the minister who was sucking in his stomach, trying not to look like too much of an appetizing meal himself. "No one is going to...."

With a speed no one would have suspected the uncoordinated man possessed, Bill lunged for the map, tearing it out of Tanesha's hands before disappearing into the jungle.

The Betas stared at each other in shocked silence before it finally registered that Bill had completely snapped and made off with their map. A round of curses rang out as the entire team took off after their rogue member.

*   *   *

Three hours later, Bill crashed through the jungle into a clearing littered with several benches and a glowing fire pit. Sitting there, looking extremely bored, was the Alpha Team. Thirty seconds later, the scratched, panting, sweat-soaked Betas stumbled into the clearing, hot on Bill's trail.

Ryan did her best not to laugh. And she thought *her* team was a bunch of candy-asses! The Beta Team was beyond pathetic. Well, except for Shannon, of course. But even if Shannon turned out to be a candy-ass too, Ryan had a strange feeling she could live with it. Oh yeah. Shannon could melt in her mouth anytime. The survivalist had to bite her tongue to stop from moaning out loud. Spy or not, she needed to meet this woman. Hell, she just needed this woman, period.

Suddenly, as if sensing her thoughts, intense green eyes focused on her for the briefest of seconds before flickering back to Joan.

Joan shook her head ruefully, wondering why Bill had attached himself to her leg like a wayward puppy. This first challenge wasn't meant to be that difficult. "I'm sorry, Beta Team. The Alpha Team was here first."

"Duh!" Joe shouted out as he tried to walk off his charley horse. For someone who spent his days in front of a screen, Bill was surprisingly fast. It's amazing what the threat of cannibalism will do for a man's athletic ability.

"You may go back to your tribal village, Alpha Team," Joan announced for the cameras.

Like we're gonna go someplace else. Ryan wiped her hands on her shorts as she stood up to leave. *Why are my hands sweaty all of the sudden? It's because she's here. God, if she makes my palms wet like this, just imagine what she can do for other places.*

One by one, the victorious team trooped out of the clearing. Ryan made sure she was last to leave and just as she passed Shannon, pretended to stumble. It wasn't the best plan, but, damn, she had to find a way to get her hands on the pretty blonde and she was in a pinch. "Uff," Ryan grunted, clinging on to Shannon tighter than a T-shirt to Brittany Spears.

"Are you okay?"

The question was asked with such sincerity, it took Ryan's breath away for a moment. "Uh, yeah," was her articulate reply.

"Be careful; it's getting dark."

Regaining her balance, Ryan flashed a cocky grin. "All the best things happen in the dark. Don't you be getting yourself voted off here now." With that and a pat on the butt, Ryan hurried after her teammates.

"Moving on…" Joan tried to regain Beta Team's attention. "This location, at the very center of the island, its heart, is sacred. It is here, on hallowed ground, that the Tribal Council meetings take place."

"Bring on the vote!" Tanesha called impatiently.

Joan ground her teeth together. Did these people have no sense of the dramatic? "Tonight," she paused for effect, staring into one of the rapidly zooming cameras, "you'll lose one of your own."

Every member of the Beta Team fixed their eyes either on Bill or David.

Shannon pushed sweat-drenched bangs off her forehead with the back of her hand, doing her best to catch her breath. Other than Joe and Tanesha, she was the only member of her team who hadn't collapsed around the fire pit. "Somehow, Joan, I don't think that's going to be a problem."

<Fade out>

Castaway Farewell (David)

David looked up at the cameramen and waited for his cue to begin. When he received it, he nodded solemnly.

"For those of you who need to be reminded, I'm David. And I know with the certainty of a righteous man that it was the Lord's plan for me to remain on the island and win the million dollars." He shook his head sadly.

"Now that I have had time to reflect, it is clear to me exactly what happened. My fellow Castaways are under the influence of Satan!" David's face turned beet-red and he grabbed at his non-existent collar. "Why, when I woke up my team for what I hoped would be the first of many sunrise services, do you know what they told me I could go do? Do you? God surely never intended a big stick to go there!"

David's body began to quake. "Servants of the Lord, such as yourselves, cannot begin to understand the depravity and debauchery that I have been subjected to while on this island of sin! The longing looks! The lustful, lingering glances! And all between two…???" A loud, unidentifiable noise drew David's attention away from the camera. He sneered but nodded. Taking a deep breath, he wiped his sweaty brow.

"For the trials I have endured, in His name, it is the Lord's will that I receive at least one million dollars no later than 2 weeks from today. God's children," he spread his hands in entreaty, "only YOU can rectify the wrong committed here today."

The camera motioned for David to wrap it up.

The big man leaned forward, nearly pressing his face against the camera lens.

"Failing to heed my warning will lead to eternal damnation for you and your children! Doomsday is upon us!"

A Preparation H commercial broke into to David's words.

<Fade out>

Panelist's Article: Going Postal by Jude Courtlow, Postal Carrier #666

Due to the number of complaints the BTBC received due to its portrayal of the US Postal Service in recent episodes of Castaway, the BTBC has agreed to allow them equal time to air their grievances.

I simply had to say my piece about BTBC bashing postal workers. We have feelings too, you know. Okay, so maybe they are mostly feelings of rage and paranoia.

The main problem with the *being everywhere* theory is this…

There are just some neighborhoods and districts we won't go into. We may be prone to exterminating one another, but we are not going to be taken down by the outsiders.

Why, in the name of the postmaster general, would the government use us to spy?

It is not like we have time to thumb through the billions of brown paper-covered magazines that sift through our hands each day. Like we give a flying fig who is reading Militia Today or The Advocate (although I liked the cover with Melissa Etheridge on it). It is not possible for us to read every postcard coming from foreign countries. (I love their stamps though.)

The United States Postal Service is singularly responsible for the greatness of this country! We, the postal workers of America, are the most under-appreciated workers in the country.

Do you think we are respected for carrying a stupid letter across the country for 33¢ or making sure all the tampon samples get delivered?

I'll wager not one of the BTBC's creative (I use that word loosely) team took into account how frustrating it is to deliver welfare checks to undeserving lazy-assed loafers. No, all BTBC brain trust could come up with is: let's poke fun at the greatest organization in the US of A.

All right, that's it. I am mad as hell and I'm not going to take it anymore.

Furthermore, the postal service IS fucking everywhere. Every time you lick a stamp or an envelope you are spitting your DNA all over the world. We can get to you anytime we want. We have many skills. We literally know where you live. Think about it!

So, my advice to you is to lay off the USPS, because you never ever know when one of us will be lurking nearby.

PS—Could I get the phone number of that Shannon chick, please? I already know her address.

EPISODE THREE

Raindrops Keep Fallin' On My Head

It was cold, kinda like the Clintons' marriage bed, but at least the island had hopes of warming up in the future.

The castaways stood on the beach, shivering, waiting for the next challenge to begin. They were dressed in swimsuits and T-shirts, looking out at the murky blue ocean and the gray sky overhead.

"I've got a bad feeling about this," Bill whined. As if hearing him, lightning streaked across the sky. "Is this safe? I mean, statistically speaking? Shouldn't we wait until tomorrow for this?"

"Sissy boy," Marty muttered under his breath. He didn't understand why they even had to do challenges. The Beta Team was worthless. Couldn't they just vote all of them off at once and be done with it?

"All right!" Joan called out, jumping into the middle of the loose circle. "Is everyone ready for our second challenge?" Lackluster responses met her enthusiasm. She frowned. Perhaps they should attach cattle prods to the cameras to generate some excitement. A good zap or two might pick up the energy level. "Here are the rules: each team is to swim out to its flag. Once there, you need to dive down to the ocean floor and get the treasure chest. The first team to bring its treasure chest to the

29

shore wins the competition. The winners will get immunity and the contents of the chest. The other team will lose a member."

I like the contents of her chest, Ryan thought lecherously, studying Shannon intently. She hadn't seen the luscious little blonde for almost twenty-four hours—far too long for Ryan's peace of mind.

Shannon caught the look in Ryan's eyes and smiled shyly. Well, she thought it was a shy smile. Ryan thought it looked a little like gas. She decided she would find Shannon a natural remedy for it on the island.

"Go!" Joan shouted, ruining the moment.

The teams raced toward the water and then stopped.

"Damn!"

"It's cold!"

"Jesus, it's like ice!"

The fifteen castaways all toed the water and looked balefully at Joan. Several members' eyes glazed over as they enviously thought of David, the first castaway voted off the island. They just knew the pudgy, future cult leader was sipping margaritas in some tropical resort, courtesy of the BTBC, laughing at their misery.

The producer couldn't believe her shitty luck. What would it take to get these losers into the water? The storm couldn't have made the tropical waters that much colder.

"Helloooo? Can someone help me blow up my floaties?" Arturo's voice sang out.

Shannon looked at the hairdresser, who was trying to inflate the brightly-colored, plastic rings around his upper arms. "Come here," she called him over, rolling her eyes.

"Oh, Channon, thank you. I know these are not what you want your lips around, but…"

She slapped the Brazilian's arm. "Behave, Arturo."

"Get in the water!" Joan urged, making shooing motions behind them. The wind picked up, blowing sand in the contestants' eyes, eliciting more complaints.

Ryan sighed. Oh well, she needed a good cold dunking since seeing Shannon again. Without further hesitation, she plunged into the ocean and began stroking her way toward the Alpha Team's flag. Reluctantly, the other castaways followed her lead.

Standing on the shore, Joan was sure she could hear the castaway's teeth chattering. Rain began to pelt down, the drops large and cold. She wished for an umbrella. Or a paper one in a large drink.

Alpha Team made it to their flag first and began diving down to the treasure chest. In short order, they began moving it closer to the shore. Yun-kyung swam in front of the chest, carefully sweeping aside any animal or plant life that might be injured by the swimmers as they pushed it toward the beach.

Tony and Jason came up for air at the same time. "Think the chest has cigarettes?" Tony hacked, shaking his head and scattering salt water everywhere. "I could really use one."

"What about your patch?"

Tony pulled down the neck of his T-shirt, revealing three of the medicinal patches attached to his collarbone. "I think they're less effective when wet."

"Let's get going, girls," Marty growled when he came up for air.

Rolling their eyes, they followed him back underwater.

The Beta Team finally gathered at its flag. Joe nodded to Tanesha. "Okay, why don't we dive down first and see if we can get the trunk moved a bit."

She shook her head vigorously. "I can't."

"Why not?"

"Black hair."

"Huh?"

She indicated her head. "Black hair. I didn't bring conditioner as my luxury item. Do you realize what salt water does to it?"

Arturo sighed dramatically. "It is terrible! Terrible! I know!" He started to reach out to touch her hair, only to have his hand slapped away.

"Are we just going to dog paddle here forever?" Dawn asked, getting tired.

"I'm going back to the beach," Desiree announced and began slapping her stick thin arms against the water's surface. Shannon wondered how she managed to float without any body fat.

"Why?"

"Because Alpha Team already has their chest on the shore," Joe observed.

All seven pairs of eyes turned to shore, confirming their loss.

Bill nervously scratched his jaw. "Well, that and the Class II typhoon headed our way."

*   *   *

Shannon was impressed that Bill knew the correct meteorological name for the funnel-shaped cloud quickly headed in their direction. As she was pelted by the rain, wind and flying debris kicked up by the storm, however, she decided to focus less on vocabulary and more on finding shelter.

The Alpha Team and production crew had already disappeared. Shannon stared at the empty, abandoned treasure chest. *Bastards. This is just not fair. They have all the good team members.* Shannon suddenly felt like she was back in grade school with the freaks and geeks on the losing kickball team.

As if in sympathy, Shannon's calf cramped. "Jesus!" She took off, limping across the soggy sand toward the jungle, as the wind drove the rain nearly sideways against her, the droplets against her skin feeling more like BBs than water. At the tree line, her team scattered, running for shelter under the dense forest canopy.

In the distance, above the roaring wind, Shannon heard a high-pitched scream that she immediately recognized as Desiree's. She closed her eyes in irritation, hoping she'd last long enough on the island to get to cast a vote against that skinny bitch. Who the fuck cared how many calories plain white rice had? They were starving! If she wanted to eat buckets of it, she would!

Blending with Desiree's panic filled cries was a higher, more feminine sounding wail. She shook her head in amazement. Arturo. The man didn't have one damn drop of testosterone in his entire body, she was sure of it.

A loud crack drew Shannon's eyes upward as a gust of wind snapped the top off one of the tall jungle trees. Shattered limbs came crashing down all around her. But before she could move, a strong arm appeared out of nowhere, wrapped around her ribs, and yanked her away from the falling branches and into an alcove mostly sheltered from the wind and rain. Another hand clamped over Shannon's mouth as a cameraman passed a few feet in front of her, the light from his camera shining through the darkened forest like a search light.

Shannon's first reaction was to struggle against her captor. But when the hand splayed across her belly tightened its hold, molding their two forms together, and soft, wet skin rubbed against hers, Shannon came closer to melting than screaming.

When the cameraman had disappeared from sight, the hand slowly dropped from Shannon's mouth and the blonde felt something hard poke her in the lower back. "You had better not be Pete, the cameraman," she gasped. If Pete felt this good pressed against her, she was skipping counseling and going straight for the bottle. "And what I'm feeling against my back had better not be an indication of how glad you are to see me."

The body behind hers chuckled, jostling Shannon. "Pretty snippy, considering I just saved you from being crushed, aren't you?" a voice burred directly into Shannon's ear.

Damn, she feels good! Shannon couldn't suppress the shiver that chased down her spine, as hot breath tickled her ear and cheek, drying a small patch of skin. The moist heat disappeared from her back, and Shannon shivered again. She turned around to see Ryan smiling smugly, obviously quite pleased with herself.

Shannon's eyes went wide with disbelief and her fair eyebrows disappeared behind wet bangs. Her gaze zeroed in on Ryan's crotch and the obvious bulge. *OH. MY. GOD! The hottest woman on earth is…* Her mind refused to complete the sentence. But Austin Power's voice screamed out in her head, *"She's a man, baybee!"* Shannon squeezed her eyes tightly shut. *NOOO!!!!! Nietzsche was right!!*

Ryan's expression grew puzzled. *Why is she looking at me that way?* She followed the shorter woman's eyes down her own body. "NO!" she blurted out. "It's not…um…what you were feeling was my knife." Now that they weren't pressed together, Ryan had to raise her voice to be heard over the howling wind. She pointed to the bulge in her pocket, which had shifted into a rather unnatural position.

Well, unnatural for Ryan.

"See?" The tall woman pulled the knife out of her pocket, expertly flipping open the razor-sharp blade. Ryan couldn't help but eye it affectionately. "Want a closer look?" She enthusiastically thrust the knife in front of Shannon's face.

The blade was so close that the younger woman's eyes actually crossed as she tried to look at it. "Um…Wow. Yeah…That is…um…"

"She's a beauty, isn't she?" Ryan's throat closed around the words. Talking about her knife always got her a little choked up. She watched carefully as Shannon continued to stare at the blade. Years ago, Ryan had heard a woman proclaim that once you'd met someone who could love your cat, you would know you had met 'the one'.

Bullshit!

Ryan hated cats.

But a woman who could appreciate a precision-honed, life-saving instrument…

"She?" Shannon interrupted, as her hand drifted down to massage her cramping calf.

"Of course. *You* have a name don't you? Why shouldn't *she*?" *Tiffany. A pretty name for a pretty knife.* The survivalist hesitated to share the name, correctly believing it wouldn't be accepted gracefully.

Shannon didn't feel like debating Ryan's logic. She was still giddy over the fact that Ryan didn't have a penis, and didn't feel like stirring up trouble. Shannon bit her lower lip. How do you compliment someone's knife? "It looks reaaaaally sharp," she offered valiantly.

Ryan ducked her head bashfully. She didn't want Shannon to see the tears in her eyes.

"C'mon." Shannon grabbed Ryan's arm, limping a few steps deeper into the alcove. Sitting down, she carefully stretched out her leg and looked out into the jungle, where sheets of rain were pouring through the trees, creating huge puddles on the forest floor.

Now that she was alone with Ryan, Shannon didn't quite know what to say. 'Gee, your breasts look terrific in that skintight, wet tank top. I'd be happy to lick them dry,' just didn't seem like an appropriate icebreaker. But time was of the essence! How often could she expect to be trapped alone with tall, wet and sexy?

Shannon grimaced and grabbed her leg as her calf muscle seized up again. "Oww!"

"Let me." Not waiting for permission, Ryan dropped to the ground and pulled Shannon's leg across her lap. With sure hands, she began massaging the cramping muscle.

Shannon let out a low, throaty groan as Ryan's fingers dug deeply into the tender tissue. "Ohhh, that feels..." Green eyes rolled back in their sockets in pure pleasure.

Ryan swallowed dryly, willing her hands not to shake. "I'm Ryan."

Ryan's comment seemed odd until Shannon realized that even though they'd spoken on several occasions, they'd never been properly introduced. "I'm...ahhh...a little higher. I'm Shannon." The blonde flashed Ryan a quick smile before her face twisted in exquisite agony. "Right there!"

"Here?" Ryan pressed a little harder with her thumb, and was rewarded by Shannon arching her back and expelling a languid hiss of pleasure.

Every drop of blood in Ryan's body stampeded southward. *I must be strong. I must be strong.* Ryan opened her mouth but no sound came out. Swallowing, she tried again. "Is that better?"

Shannon nodded vigorously as she continued to twist under Ryan's relentless assault, her T-shirt working its way above her stomach.

Ryan stared openly at well-defined abs that bunched and released as Shannon moved. *Oh God!* Ryan's own belly clenched tightly as a wave of arousal washed over her. *Why was I being strong again?*

Shannon's movements began to slow as the muscle loosened and she blew out a deep, relieved breath. "Much better." Her face became serious as she reached out to grasp Ryan's hand, giving long fingers a gentle squeeze. "Thank you, Ryan. And not just for helping me with that cramp, but for before, too. I don't know if I would have been quick enough to get away from those falling branches."

Ryan dragged her gaze upward, settling on Shannon's eyes. "You're very welcome."

Shannon's stomach growled loudly. Before the blonde could apologize, Ryan leaned forward and pressed her ear to Shannon's belly.

The younger woman's breathing hitched at the unexpected, intimate contact.

"Sounds hollow." Ryan couldn't resist rubbing her cheek across skin that was even softer than it looked. "There are some banana trees a little northwest of your camp. The potassium will help to prevent cramping." She placed a soft kiss on Shannon's stomach before sitting up.

"Okay," Shannon croaked, licking suddenly dry lips. "Thanks again."

An awkward silence grew between the women, but neither woman was anxious to give up her physical contact with the other. Shannon's leg continued to rest on the taller woman's lap while Ryan's hand was held securely in hers.

"You're a writer?" Ryan finally asked warily. Was it possible Shannon was exactly what the castaway brochure promised? She had to find out once and for all before she could allow her heart to be completely lost to this woman.

Ryan had always scoffed at the notion of love at first sight. That was merely an invention of a government that wanted a herd of complacent, lovesick cattle to govern. But, if this is what it felt like to be Grade A Choice, Ryan was ready to be branded!

"Yes. Well, I want to be." Shannon's breathing paused as the hand on her leg began stroking her skin with a feather light touch.

"What do you write?"

Shannon's eyes were riveted on the fingertips dancing first along her calf, then her thigh. She wondered briefly if Ryan was even aware that her hand had begun to move. That touch was doing marvelous things to her senses, and Ryan's words simply rolled over her.

"Shannon?"

"Hmm?" she hummed dreamily. Shannon's gaze darted upward. "Um...I'm sorry. Did you say something?" A faint blush began to creep up her chest and neck.

"I asked what you wrote." Sky-blue eyes narrowed. Something was wrong. Why was Shannon hesitating? "Quick! What's a dangling participle?"

"What?"

"Answer me!"

Shannon's eyes went wide. Was this some sort of a pop quiz?

"All right then. What's a gerund?"

"What in the hell are you talking about?" Shannon snatched her hand back.

"And you call yourself a writer," Ryan snorted disgustedly, pushing Shannon's leg off her lap and jumping to her feet. "Uncle Sam's gonna have to do a lot better than you to trip me up, honey!" *Branded? What was I thinking?!* She took a step away but was stopped by Shannon's strong grip on the back of her shorts.

The blonde glared at the survivalist. Using Ryan's shorts for leverage, she pulled herself up. "Are you going to tell me what you're talking about, or do I have to guess?"

Ryan's face twisted into a sneer. "I don't have to explain myself to a spy!"

"You're insane!"

Ryan snorted again. "Like you're the *first* person to say that."

"Why would I be spying on you?" Shannon asked reasonably, letting go of Ryan.

"Because…" Ryan's mouth clicked closed. She chuckled evilly. "Oooo, you're good. You'd like me to tell you, wouldn't you?" Shannon was craftier than she had suspected. God, she wanted this woman!

Ryan gritted her teeth and called upon her iron will. She tried to tell herself that a million dollars was too much to risk for a bout of hot, sweaty, jungle sex with Shannon. Ha! Like that reasoning had a chance! *No. I can do this!*

The brunette turned to leave when Shannon shouted, "A participle is a verb ending in '-ing', and is called dangling when the subject of the '-ing' verb and the subject of the sentence don't agree. As in, um, 'Staring at the tall dark stranger with undisguised lust, the typhoon finally veered away from the island, leaving the writer wet and aching.'

"A gerund," she continued, with growing inspiration, "is a noun formed from a verb. As in, 'Aching seemed a small price to pay for the privilege of seeing the way her luscious breasts strained against the wet tanktop.'" Wow! And to think she had been regretting sleeping with her freshman grammar professor for all these years.

Shannon's words stopped Ryan dead in her tracks. She had no idea if what Shannon said was correct, but it did sound impressive and pretty raunchy. Ryan mentally shrugged. For the love of God, it was only money!

Ryan whirled around, and in two long strides pinned Shannon up against the alcove wall, first with her hands, then with the full length of her body. Their eyes locked for an instant before Ryan leaned forward and slowly traced Shannon's lower lip with the tip of her tongue, taking her lip into her mouth and sucking gently.

Shannon gasped, then groaned loudly at the feeling of Ryan's hot mouth teasing her.

Ryan responded with a moan of her own as she threaded her fingers tightly in pale, wet hair, crushing their mouths together in a frenzied attack of hot, slippery tongues, nipping teeth and soft, hungry lips. God! Shannon's mouth tasted even better than it had in her dreams.

"Stop!" Shannon commanded raggedly, tearing her lips from Ryan's, and pushing the darker woman away with the palms of her hands.

Ryan's nostrils flared as she stood panting in front of Shannon, clenching and unclenching her fists. "Something wrong?" she asked weakly, dreading the answer the way Tammy Faye Baker dreaded make-up remover.

"Yes." *SHITSHITSHITSHITSHIT!*

"I want to go first." With that, Shannon dropped to her knees in front of Ryan and slid her hands up the back of the taller woman's shorts. Giving Ryan's ass a good squeeze, Shannon pulled Ryan's hips to her face, using her lips and teeth to nip and kiss Ryan through her damp cotton shorts.

Ryan's entire body shuddered and she grasped Shannon's shoulders, hoping her knees wouldn't buckle.

Shannon was wetter than she had been before she came in out of the rain. Damn, this was good! Spurred on by Ryan's throaty moans, she began grinding her face into the survivalist's center while forcefully kneading Ryan's buttocks.

"Okay," Ryan managed to let out on an unsteady breath. The sweet looking blonde was a hellcat! Excellent! "You can go first if ya want."

"Mmm…Hmm…" Shannon mumbled, lowering her mouth to Ryan's inner thighs and dragging her tongue upward, sliding it under the edge of Ryan's shorts and swimsuit.

A light flashed in the jungle in front of the women's hiding place and Ryan bit her lip. "Shannon, that is so…"

Shannon turned her head toward the light. "What's that?"

"It's nothing. Nothing! Just ignore it." Ryan stroked Shannon's hair, doing her best to ignore the sounds of people approaching. *Anyone who comes in here dies! Tiffany will see to it.*

Shannon pulled her hands from Ryan's shorts and let the older woman help her to her feet. She didn't even have a second to steady herself before Ryan swooped down, giving her the deepest, wettest, most sensuous kiss of her life.

If Shannon had been a Southern belle, she would have swooned in Ryan's arms. If she had been black, she would have high-fived Ryan. If she had been Catholic, she would have felt guilty and crossed herself. But Shannon was a white Protestant from the West Coast so she did none of those things. What's a WASPy girl to do?

Ryan's lips moved to Shannon's throat, and her hands slid under the shorter woman's shirt. "We don't have to stop."

"OH GOD! Okay…" Shannon threw her head back, giving Ryan better access to her neck. "No." *Fuck!* "We do, Ryan."

"We don't. Whoever it is will go away."

The exact words from Rita's note flashed in Shannon's mind, shattering the moment. "You can't be gay!" she whimpered pitifully.

"My mother said the same thing." Ryan dipped her tongue in the hollow of Shannon's throat. "But she got over it. I certainly did."

The light passed closer to the alcove, shining across the wet rocks at the entrance.

Shannon shook her head 'no' but thrust her hips against Ryan. "You…You don't understand. I…um…yeah, it opens in the front…I can't be gay."

"Sure ya can, baby," Ryan muttered against Shannon's skin, unhooking her bikini top. "You're doing soooo well. It's easy. I promise."

Ryan closed her eyes in frustration when she heard several other voices joining Pete's.

Shannon heard the beginnings of a growl from Ryan and laid her hand against the taller woman's chest, rolling her eyes when Ryan's hand moved down to her big ass knife. "You can't kill them all, Ryan."

"Why not?"

Several castaways and cameramen found their way into the alcove at that moment, capturing on tape their rather intimate position and disheveled clothing. Pete thrust a camera in Shannon's face, only backing away when he received a withering glare from Ryan.

Shannon shrugged. "I'm sure there's *some* reason."

Tony stepped around the cameraman and began pacing wildly in the alcove. "I can't take this anymore! Give me a cigarette!" He stopped and faced Pete, a fellow chain smoker, twitching at the aphrodisiac smell of wet cigarettes.

"I can't, man. You know the rules."

"Fuck the rules! The rules said nothing about a fucking hurricane coming to kill us while we're here!"

"Actually," Bill piped up from his spot out of the rain, "assuming that wind speeds reach the requisite 74 miles per hour, this is a typhoon. Typhoons are the same thing as hurricanes but are called by a different name in Asia. During this time of year, you can expect an average of 3.4 typhoons to hit each of the islands in this chain. One of those would be devastating enough to–"

"Shut up, nerd!" Tony shouted and stepped threateningly toward Pete, grabbing a large fallen tree limb as he did so. "Give me a cigarette! Now!"

Pete looked over for some help from Ryan and Shannon, but found them to be otherwise engaged. Torn between taping some good girl-on-girl action and saving his own hide, he reluctantly lowered the camera and reached into his jacket pocket. He tapped out a cigarette and extended it to Tony.

"Keep it," Tony replied, taking the pack instead. Like Rain Man looking at fallen toothpicks, he could instantly calculate the number of cigarettes left in the pack: twelve. That might last him an hour.

*   *   *

Fifty-three minutes and eleven cigarettes later, Tony stood outside the tribal council area. The Beta Team had just sat down and was preparing to vote one lucky castaway off the island. Sucking on his cigarette, he started walking into the forbidden crew area. Stepping into it meant instant disqualification and a return to Marlboro Country.

He almost felt bad about abandoning his team. But, this way, it would keep the competition even. Now the Alphas would only be up one member.

*   *   *

"You are here to act on your solemn duty as a tribe," Joan intoned. "Tonight you must lose someone."

Tanesha rolled her eyes. God, she was tired of worthless white people! "Bring on the vote!"

"Do any of you have something you would like to share with your fellow tribal members?"

Bill dutifully raised his hand.

"Yes, Bill?"

"I was wondering what your meteorologists had to say about the probability of another Class II typhoon hitting the island within the next thirty days? According to a few preliminary calculations I made while we were hiding in our shelter, I believe that..."

Joan frowned. That geek was a bigger ratings killer than Al Gore in a Speedo. "Anyone else?" She paused for a millisecond. "No? Let the voting begin!"

Joe led the way to the voting booth. He picked up the marker and wrote down Desiree's name. Looking at the camera, "She really needs to go."

Tanesha was next. "Desiree is really the worst, but I want that skinny white bitch to stay here until her hair falls out." Her vote for Bill went into the box.

Dawn followed and wrote down Bill. Shrugging, she had no explanation.

Arturo wrote down Bill. "I want Desiree to stay so I can try out a new skin conditioner I am making from papaya extract here on the island. If it works for her here, I think she might endorse it when we leave." He clapped his hands together gleefully.

Shannon stalked into the voting booth. This was a simple decision. If she couldn't vote Joan or Pete off the island, Desiree would have to do.

Desiree came in next. She voted for herself. "I have a career to consider." Tears welled in her eyes. "I haven't been able to shave my legs for days!"

The camera panned down then jerked abruptly to the side as Desiree assaulted the cameraman. "Don't film them, you idiot!"

Finally, Bill entered the voting booth. He stared longingly at the marker, unconsciously caressing his empty pocket protector. And to think he had missed the annual Star Trek convention in St. Louis for this! His heart lurched painfully. This was the year they were finally going to admit the Spock-Scottie subtext, too! Bill quickly scrawled his own name on the paper, poaching the marker in the process. He felt much better now.

*   *   *

"I lost? What do you mean, I lost?!" Desiree shrieked.

Joan was confused. "No, you didn't lose. Bill lost. He has to go."

Bill had already left. He was running happily down the pathway to civilization. Shannon hadn't seen him move that quickly before. Well, except for the time he was worried about being eaten.

"Which of you didn't vote for me?" Desiree wheeled around and pointed a long, skinny finger at Shannon. "Did you vote for me?"

"I most certainly did."

"Did you?" she asked Arturo.

"I am so sorry, chica. But, no."

Desiree launched herself at the Brazilian.

Shannon sighed. The BTBC wouldn't be in last place for long with this type of programming. Look at what WWF Smackdown has done for Fox.

<Fade out>

Castaway Farewells (Bill and Tony)

"Time to shoot your goodbye clip, Bill," Pete said patiently. "Put the computer down."

Bill sat in one of the production huts, lovingly caressing his laptop. It had been there waiting for him, during those long, lonely 12 days. Just out of reach! But now Bill felt his world slowly righting itself as he clutched his baby. "No."

Pete rolled his eyes. "Put it down, man!"

"I will not." Bill pushed the 'on' switch. Closing his eyes, he groaned in ecstasy as he listened to the familiar, erotic hum of his machine booting up.

Pete looked on in rapt fascination as Bill cooed and stroked the machine as though it were a woman. Not that Pete could blame him. Hell, it was probably as close to a woman as Bill would ever get.

Bill looked up into the camera with tear-filled eyes. "None of you appreciates me the way my baby does. You are all illogical." With that, he laid a sloppy wet kiss on the computer screen, turning his back so he could enjoy his reunion in private.

Bill didn't need to 'survive' on the island. He knew that someday, his kind, would take over the world.

<Fade out>

            *   *   *

Tony sat in the Talk Back Hut and stared at the camera. Once they found him in the crew area sucking on two cigarettes with a third smoldering in his hand, he was instantly disqualified. Joan then hauled him, literally, by the ear to say his goodbye to his fellow castaways.

Taking a long drag, he savored the taste of the nicotine. So what if they controlled the amounts in the cigarettes? As long as they put in more, he didn't care. Until he got his own nicotine levels stabilized, he was still wearing two patches.

"Well, Alpha mates, sorry, but I had to go. There's no such thing as paradise without a good smoke. In fact, now that I hear all this Elian crap is over, I hope we lift the embargo against Cuba. Aren't good smokes important? I mean, democracy, shit, you can find that anywhere. But, a good cigar? Ask Clinton, good cigars are hard to come by. And useful."

He took another drag, his face taking on the look of a man in ecstasy. "So, good luck, castaways! I'll be seeing a lot of you by the pool real soon!"

<Fade out>

Panelist's Article: This Series Has Great Potential by Maggie Goodheart

Remember Agatha Christie's bestselling 'Ten Little Indians', where a group of guests were trapped in an isolated setting, their numbers steadily declining one by one? There's no murderer on Paradise Island of course (though it might increase the ratings if there were!). But the elements that make for a gripping and tense story are there: hardship (survival conditions), high stakes (a million dollars), rivalry (competing teams), and diverse personalities (16, not counting the camera crew), all causing friction resulting in sparks (and hopefully a few romantic flames?).

It's a recipe for fireworks (which can also be found, coincidentally, in my latest novel: "Blue Touchpaper", currently available at all good book stores.)

Will the story that unfolds be comedy, romance, tragedy, or a little of everything?

This novelist waits eagerly to find out.

EPISODE FOUR

Go Fish!

Shannon sat leaning against a tall palm tree at the beach's edge. She dug her toes into the warm sand, rereading her latest journal entry. With a satisfied nod, the blonde looked up from the thick tablet, her gaze drifting out over the sparkling blue water.

Then it hit her. The smoky smell of cooking fish. She closed her eyes in ecstasy as she began to salivate, and her stomach growled furiously. God, what wouldn't she do for some of the Alpha Team's food?

Maybe she could offer her body in exchange for sustenance? Oh, yeah. That might work. But she would only give herself to their leader, Ryan. It would be a sacrifice, but Shannon was just that kind of person.

Sacrificing. Of course, that usually required a virgin, but that state was fortunately only a distant memory for Shannon. She wondered if Ryan would care.

Ryan would undoubtedly require that she perform some hideous, vile act. Something that even Hugh Grant would refuse to do. But, oh yes, Shannon would persevere. This was, after all, for the greater good. She was going to bring some fish back for her team, too. But only after she satisfied her undeniable, insatiable craving to feast on the succulent, tender...

"You're thinking about her again, aren't you?" Arturo accused, dropping down onto the sand next to Shannon.

Shannon's eyes and mouth flew open.

"Talk to the hand, girlfriend." He thrust his palm in front of her face. "Don't bother denying it, Channon. You're drooling."

Shannon's hand shot up to the corner of her mouth. Green eyes turned to slits. "Very funny."

"Rambo Ryan's reality check bounced, girlfriend. A sweet thing like you should stay far, far away from her. She's on the boat to Loco Island."

"She is not! And who says I'm so sweet?!" Shannon added indignantly.

Arturo just smirked.

A strong gust of wind drew Arturo's and Shannon's attention back to the scent of roasting fish.

They both groaned.

"I can't take it anymore!" Shannon wrapped her arms around her empty stomach.

Arturo nodded. "Anything, chica. I will do anything for some real food."

"Then we must be prepared to make the *ultimate* sacrifice." Shannon tapped her chin with her pencil, a predatory look crossing her face. "We've got to offer something far more alluring than our bodies. Something no person in his right mind could refuse."

*   *   *

"Toilet paper," a wide-eyed Marva said in a hushed, wistful voice. Her fingertip reverently grazed the note in Ryan's hands, which was written on several squares of pristine white, exquisitely-quilted, baby-powder scented tissue. "We have to do it, Ryan!"

Ryan's heart nearly burst with pride as she read over Shannon's offer. Damn, but Shannon was good! Too good for the CIA. But who then?

The United Nations? Scotland Yard? Interpol? KGB, IRS, FAA, FTC, ESPN, NRA, QVC, FHA, or IRA? Ryan began to get dizzy.

Marty looked from the tissue to the fishing pole and back again. Even a manly man, such as himself, knew a bargain when he saw one. "It's an offer we can't refuse," he admitted gravely.

Though she thought it impossible, Ryan's ardor for the pretty blonde increased two-ply.

*   *   *

"Time to earn those butt wipes! All those with breasts—go with Ryan." Marty looked over the other castaways distastefully. "I'll take," he couldn't bring himself to call these candy asses men, "the rest," he grunted.

Marty didn't want to waste his time teaching the women how to fish. What would be the point? The sooner the women were voted off the island and sent back to their men, the better. "C'mon, ladies, daylight is burnin'." When Arturo happily pranced over to the men's group, Marty gave the hairdresser a shove toward Ryan and the rest of the females. "*You* don't need breasts to be a girl, Tinkerbell."

Arturo burst into tears, running over to the sympathetic arms of Dawn and Marva. "Pig," Dawn spat at Marty.

Marty made a point of staring at Dawn's painfully flat chest. He opened his mouth only to have Tanesha step forward and grab him by the collar, pulling his face right up to hers. "Keep your hands on your own team, honky! He may be a limp...."

Russell cringed at the word 'limp.' Damn! Why did he let his secretary send in his biographical information to the BTBC? Unreasonable bitch! But he knew that someday she would forgive his roaming eyes. And other body parts. He only hoped she'd be able to forgive her sister. And roommate. And therapist. And daughter. And the rest of her daughter's cheerleading pals.

"I've been silent long enough!" Yun-kyung shouted, attracting everyone's attention. "I cannot stand by while you commit cold-blooded murder of these helpless creatures! Some of them may be on the preparatory list as alternates for possible future consideration as protected species!"

"Shut up, Chung-King!" someone yelled at the ranting veterinarian.

"It's Yun-kyung."

"Whatever, King Kong. We're starving! I'd kill Bambi myself!" Tanesha stated unrepentantly.

Dawn licked her lips. "I want him with gravy!"

"Ooo, and I'd make homemade biscuits and peach pie for dessert," Marva added helpfully.

The women's words were met with a round of appreciative moans.

"And how would you like to eat your meat, Channon?" Arturo asked saucily.

Shannon raised an eyebrow but decided to play. Her green eyes focused solely on Ryan as she answered Arturo's question. "I like mine wild. Raw even," she said in a soft, sensual voice, hoping she wouldn't blush.

Ryan's jaw sagged before she swallowed hastily. "Oh, so would I." Swaggering a step closer to Shannon, Ryan lowered her voice to a purr. "In fact, my," she paused, "*mouth* is watering right this second. I can just imagine the bold," Ryan's eyes slid closed, "sweet..."

"Isn't this wonderful?" Molly exclaimed, completely oblivious to the sparks between Ryan and Shannon, which now had most of the castaways squirming. "It's only by overcoming strife and working together that we will free our inner children, becoming who we were meant to be...in this lifetime."

"Quiet, you hairy-legged hag," Marty groaned impatiently. "I'd like to kick your inner child's ass!" Damn! And it was just getting good, too. This was better than cable!

Desiree's head snapped up, and a look of pure panic crossed her face. "It's okay," Dawn soothed. "He was talking to Molly, and her legs were hairy *before* she came to the island."

For some reason, that seemed to pacify Desiree, and the woman returned to her near-catatonic state, muttering something about waxing. Day after day of sun, heat, and a lack of hygiene and makeup products had finally taken its toll. Soon she would have only one eyebrow!

"You were talking about food." Marty's eyes begged Ryan and Shannon to continue. They were both gorgeous and maybe they'd kiss! If God were truly a man, there would be tongue.

"Enough!" Ryan exploded. She needed some time alone with Shannon, and she needed it yesterday. In a matter of minutes, she had passed out bamboo poles and fish-bone hooks, given a cursory fishing lesson, and paired up each castaway, instructing the pairs to space themselves evenly along the beach.

Yun-kyung, refusing to take part in the savagery, stalked off to go shell collecting instead.

*   *   *

"Jesus, this is vile." Shannon made a face as she speared the plump grub onto the end of her hook. The white creature was the size of her thumb and continued to writhe and twist as she pushed it farther up the sharp bone.

Ryan grinned proudly. She *knew* it wasn't a good idea to mention what excellent roughage these little guys would add to Shannon's diet. Ha! Her brothers were so wrong. She did too know how to talk to a woman! "Yeah, I guess they are kind of gross."

Shannon looked up from the grub, clearly surprised. "Really? I figured I was being a wimp, and well…that you were used to this kind of thing."

"Nah." Ryan frowned. "Just because I'm used to it, doesn't mean I don't know what's gross." Some gross tasks were simply necessary. Like sucking the venom out of an especially hairy buddy's ass after a snakebite. Ryan shuddered. It was nasty but had to be done.

Shannon tossed her line into the surf, glancing at the other castaways spread out down the beach. The nearest pair was well out of earshot. The cameras had started filming at the other end of the beach first, allowing her and Ryan a modicum of privacy. "Tell me about yourself, Ryan," Shannon prompted casually, keeping her eyes trained firmly on the water. *Please don't get all nuts. I don't want you to be nuts. I don't even like squirrels.*

Ryan immediately stiffened. "What do you wanna know?"

Okay, I can live with cautious. Cautious is not *crazy.* Shannon laid a reassuring hand on Ryan's arm, running her fingertips down the soft skin until she reached Ryan's wrist. Her eyes never left the sea. "Anything you'd like to share with me."

Ryan's chest tightened, and her palms began to sweat. She wanted to talk to Shannon. But it had been just her and Tiffany for so long! *Please don't be a spy. I don't want you to be spy.* "I need to ask you something. Okay?"

"Sure." Shannon adjusted her fishing pole and turned, only to find herself captured by an unwavering pale gaze that reached down deep inside her, grabbing her heart and shaking her. Hard.

"Are you working for the Feds?" Ryan intently studied the verdant eyes gazing into hers. This close she would feel the lie. She was sure of it.

Shannon felt a flash of anger at whoever or whatever had made Ryan so wary. *She's serious about this.* The smaller woman held Ryan's gaze and answered unequivocally, "No." A pause. "I even paid my taxes late last year," she added with a smile. *C'mon, Ryan.*

Ryan remained unmoved. Physical attraction was one thing. They'd had that from the first moment they laid eyes on each other.

But an honest friendship? Could she tell Shannon everything? About her parents' so-called accident? About her hidden community in the Kentucky hills?

Shannon's heart rate picked up. "Don't you believe me?"

Ryan suddenly found the extra fish hook, in her hands, extremely interesting. "I…ah…I think so." *Liar! You know you do. Tell her!*

"Good enough." Shannon nodded happily, her face creasing into a dazzling smile that crinkled the soft skin around twinkling eyes. "For now."

With her next breath, Shannon allowed her heart to lay claim to Ryan. Hell, she worked in television. She was used to crazy.

When Ryan looked up, her own heart skipped a beat, her grin unconsciously mirroring Shannon's. Oh yeah. That attraction part was so very covered. "For now," she agreed, grasping the blonde's smaller hand tightly in hers.

Shannon leaned back against Ryan, hoping to capture more than fish this day. "Wanna hear my idea for my new book?" She easily shifted the conversation to what she figured would be safe ground. Ryan needed a little time. She could live with that, as long as it wasn't *too* long.

Ryan scooted closer, tucking a strand of golden, blowing hair behind Shannon's ear. "I'd love to."

*   *   *

"No way! They do not do that!"

"Oh yes, they do," Ryan insisted, casting their line into deeper waters and handing the pole back to Shannon. It had been over two hours and they hadn't had as much as a nibble. She knew that she and Tiffany could go for a little swim and get something. But this *was* supposed to be a fishing lesson. And she really didn't want to leave Shannon's side.

"There's a master list kept at the FBI headquarters and every time you click on a website it's recorded there and categorized," Ryan continued.

"They keep track of *everything*. Credit card purchases, the books you check out from the library, your bank statements, who you talk to on your phone…"

Shannon frowned. "And why exactly would they do that?"

Ryan blinked. She opened her mouth, then clicked it shut. Damn! Why does she keep asking these logical questions? "Well, to keep track of us, of course."

"For whom?"

Blue eyes rolled. "Duh!" Ryan snorted. "Who else? The Attorney General." Didn't Shannon keep up with any of the better news resources, like 'Guns & Ammo', 'Mercenary Today', and 'Soldier of Fortune'? Ryan shook her head as if to clear it of the ridiculous thought. *It's not like she's crazy or something!*

Shannon set her pole down next to her and crossed her arms over her chest. "Are you trying to tell me that Janet Reno cares that I surf the 'Charlie's Angels Homepage'?"

Ryan burst out laughing. "Which Angel do you like?"

Shannon blushed, then scowled. "Like I'd tell you now," she grumbled petulantly.

"Come on," Ryan prodded, beginning to tickle the younger woman's ribs.

"Okay, okay!" Shannon began half-heartedly slapping away Ryan's hands. "I like…"

Both women's heads shot up as Shannon's pole lurched forward on the sand.

"Is that a bite?" Shannon was already starting to salivate as she tightly gripped the long bamboo rod.

"Yup," Ryan confirmed. "Whoa!"

The rod jerked forward again, this time taking Shannon with it, dragging the smaller woman several feet across the beach.

"Shit! Hold on!" Ryan covered Shannon's hands with her own, and pulled the blonde back tight against her chest, so they could wrestle the fish together. "Oh, baby! This is a big one." The survivalist's face lit with a look of undisguised glee that only came with a good hunt or knock-out sex.

Shannon wanted both.

"MURDERERS! Remember Orca!!! Free Willy!!!" Yun-kyung bellowed. "The shark in 'Jaws' was just misunderstood!" The Asian woman was running down the beach with the other castaways, a frazzled-looking Pete trailing her.

"What in the…?" Ryan looked on in shock as Yun-kyung splashed through the surf, grabbing their taut fish line. "Let go of it!" Ryan growled.

"NEVER!" cried the animal activist. Yun-kyung whipped out a slender shell she had spent the afternoon sharpening against a rock. Using the shell as a knife, she cut Ryan and Shannon's line.

Shannon stared in horror at the severed line. "BITCH!" she screamed, dropping the pole, and lunging after Yun-kyung who was now trying to swim away.

Ryan, joined by the other castaways, looked on with interest as Shannon caught up with Yun-kyung and began dragging her back to shore, stopping occasionally to slap her and hold her head underwater.

Pete, the cameraman, shut off his camera and laid down on the beach in front of Ryan, waiting for his impending heart attack. He was worried that all this exercise had dislodged a french fry in his heart. Humans weren't meant to do so much running around. It was plain unnatural. "Are we going to let Shannon kill her?" he gasped, hoping the answer was 'yes'. He wanted to at least take *someone* with him.

Ryan raised an eyebrow at Pete, who quickly shut up. God, she loved a woman who could kick ass and take names!

∗   ∗   ∗

Joan found the castaways in a particularly foul mood later that afternoon. She had spent the morning at the crew camp trying to pretend she wasn't there. Why had she taken this God-awful assignment? Had all the years in television finally eroded every last bit of her self-respect and integrity? Considering that she had had lustful thoughts toward Pete last night, the answer had to be a resounding 'yes!'

Making matters worse was the note she'd received, from Bender himself, instructing her to make the challenges 'more interesting' and to 'pump up the danger level'. Apparently, living on a deserted island surrounded by goddamn sea snakes wasn't enough. *Prick. Don't see his fat ass out here anywhere.*

Today's challenge should do the trick. The premise was simple. The first team to navigate their way through the jungle path to a designated clearing would win. Unbeknownst to the castaways, the jungle path was filled with traps. In addition to receiving immunity, the winners would be given a wild boar to roast. Of course, they would have to figure out how to kill the damn thing first—which should help satiate Bender's bloodlust. *Note to self: Call Granny and tell her to stop watching the show.*

Joan sighed. What the hell, they were insured. The contestants they had chosen wouldn't be missed by anyone—she was sure—should something really awful happen. The original sixteen castaways were much better. But then Bender had to get his Texas-sized ego involved. And now the show was just all shot to hell.

The two teams stood waiting for her just beyond the jungle clearing. The remaining six members of the Beta Team weren't looking particularly good at this point. Desiree had better hope to God no paparazzi photographer was within a hundred miles of the island. Her red hair looked like it could come out in clumps, her skin was blotchy and her eyes glassy. She kinda looked like a Tyson chicken. With hair. A picture of her now would certainly destroy her career. The rest of the castaways just looked really hungry. And horny.

Disturbingly horny. Joe and Dawn were giving each other looks that would make sheep on some Arkansas farms nervous. And Shannon was giving the exact same look to Ryan. Christ! Were all the 'nice girls' turning out to be sluts?

The Alpha Team looked to be in a bit better shape than the others—they all appeared to have eaten a meal or two while on the island. But for some reason, Yun-kyung was standing far away from the team. Her T-shirt was ripped and she was missing one shoe.

No one was talking, but something had obviously happened. Joan frowned. She'd have to wait until that evening to look at the daily footage and figure it out. Thank God for editing.

"All right! Is everyone ready for the next challenge?" Joan enthused. These people were rating-killers. Worse than the Synchronized Swimming competition the Olympics committee had included in medal competition this year. Or having Dennis Miller announcing the NFL play-by-play.

"So, whichever team loses the competition has to vote someone off, right?" Shannon asked carefully, trying to give Ryan a hint with her tone. Her eyes traveled between Ryan and Yun-kyung. *Come on, Ryan, you believe in secret messages. Decode mine. Oh, yes, decode mine. I have a couple of bumps and ridges I'd like you to read.*

"Yes. Immunity goes to the winning team."

Marty crossed beefy arms over his chest. "What else does the winning team get?"

"Dinner."

Groans all around.

Ryan smelled a rat. Not a physical rat, but a big, old, government rat. There's no such thing as a free meal. This was especially true in the government-subsidized media. Her gaze drifted to Shannon. Hell, it never left Shannon, except when she had to blink. The luscious blonde was looking a bit on the thin side. Ryan's eyes narrowed. Perhaps it would be best for the Beta Team to win this round.

Besides, she had a score to settle of her own. She didn't like anyone interfering with her survival lessons. Especially not when they centered on a certain delectable writer.

Yun-kyung coughed, expelling the last of the seawater from her lungs. Who knew Shannon was so athletic? And she had been more than a little pissed off that no one had come to her rescue. Killers. Butchers. The whole lot of them. She had been very carefully going into the jungle every day and picking up fruit that had fallen from the trees. Mother Nature had provided for her here, as she did at home. There was no need to pick, pluck, or pierce her meals. Once she ate around the rotten parts, the fruit was pretty good. And best of all, her diarrhea was now down to twice a day!

Ryan caught Shannon's eyes. "Is your offer still good?" she asked softly.

Fuck yes! Which offer? The offer where I take you into the jungle and we have hot monkey sex? Or the offer where I take you into the ocean and we have hot monkey sex? Or the offer where we climb a tree and have hot monkey sex?

"Shannon?" Ryan asked when she didn't get an answer and the object of her affection looked like she might pass out.

"Absolutely." She puckered up for a kiss. The traditional way to seal an offer was a handshake, but she had never been a traditional girl. She also didn't give a rat's ass that the cameras were there. She had been wanting a kiss all afternoon. Now seemed like as good a time as any to get one. *Fuck Bender. Well, not fuck Bender. But, rather, to hell with Bender. There. That sounded better.*

"Great. See you at the finish line."

Finish line? Shannon was confused. She was sure they were talking about sex.

"I really must protest!" Yun-kyung said, struggling to her feet. "This brutal carnage must stop!"

Joan looked at her with bug eyes. "Brutal carnage?"

"Yes!" Gaining momentum, she jumped over to the vegetation. "Some of these plants might one day become endangered! Here we are, just crushing them underneath our heels! The Conservationists of the World group will want to hear about this!"

"C.O.W.?" Russell echoed, laughing at the image. That's how he envisioned all of those whacko, short, stout, hairy-armpitted, lesbian activists. They all looked the same. Was it any wonder they couldn't get a man?

Marty spat. "My God, you're a tree-hugging lunatic!"

"And this constant devouring of meat! PETA will back me up on this! Vote me off! Throw me off! But you cannot silence the voice of the animals!"

"Animals have voices?" Desiree asked, looking very disoriented. Oh wait. Never mind. She remembered 'Dr. Doolittle' now.

"We really need to start the competition," Joan interrupted. She had to jump in and stop this before Yun-kyung started singing "The Lion Sleeps Tonight" and really making a mess of things. "Go!" Joan shouted, signaling the beginning of the competition.

All of the contestants exchanged looks, taken by surprise at the start. With the enthusiasm of lawyers attending ethics training, the teams took off into the jungle.

The teams weren't one hundred yards into the race when the ground collapsed beneath Yun-kyung and she fell into a pit. The Alpha Team and camera crew gathered around the hole and stared down at her.

"You okay?" Marva called to her. She didn't like the vet, but Marva was a good person deep down and wouldn't want her to be hurt.

Yun-kyung moved and a squishing sound was heard by the people ten feet above her. "What is in here?"

"It's elephant dung," Pete helpfully supplied. "We had it imported."

"Is there no end to the abuse?" Yun-kyung wailed, clasping her hands to her head and swaying in pain.

Shannon and the Beta Team raced past the Alpha Team, Arturo squealing with delight as he pinched Marty's ass. "Let's go, let's go, let's go!" Shannon chanted, trying to motivate her team.

Ryan smiled. Shannon was a goddess. She was going to worship at her altar. Soon. Very soon. Very, very soon.

"So, what should we do?" Marva asked Ryan.

The survivalist shrugged. "I guess we'll just have to concede this challenge."

Jason looked over at Joan who had come over to see what the commotion was about. "Can we go ahead and vote? Because I really don't want to have to find a way to get her out of that shit hole."

Pete shrugged. "It sure as hell ain't in my contract."

Joan groaned. *Second note to self: drink a lot of tequila and sleep with someone tonight.*

<Fade out>

Castaway Farewell (Yun-kyung)

Yun-kyung tried to get up from the chair, only to be pushed down by Joan. "You have to say something."

The veterinarian glared at the camera, the love she reserved for flora and fauna not exhibited toward the homo sapiens behind the lens. Pete thought about that for a moment, he didn't like anything that started with "homo." Though he did like Ryan and Shannon, and he was pretty sure they were homo-something after that display in the alcove the other day.

"This is outrageous!" Yun-kyung barked at the audience. "We will not stand by idly and allow you to continue to harm the plants and animals indigenous to this beautiful island!"

Pete noticed one of those indigenous animals making its way across the floor of the hut. He took a step back, trying to appear nonchalant.

"When PETA hears about this, they will just shit! And it'll be a big dump, too, like the one you threw me into! It is against an elephant's human rights to have his feces removed like it was just some garbage!"

The indigenous animal was now only a foot away from Yun-kyung. Pete, in turn, was now only a foot away from the door to the hut.

"I will be back! You may throw me off the island, but I will be back! Trying to protect the animals you so cruelly disregard!"

Joan looked down and noticed the very large scorpion crawling up Yun-kyung's leg. "Uh!"

"What?" Yun-kyung growled.

"Nothing," Joan replied, smiling sweetly and moving away.

It was then Yun-kung felt the extra legs on her own. "Holy shit!" She shook her leg and the small animal fell to the ground, only to be instantly crushed by the vet's heel. Mortified, she looked up and confirmed that Pete had caught the whole incident on tape. "I'll be going now."

<Fade out>

Panelist's Article: Oopsie Poopie by Poopsie Gebilhiney, Ph.D.

"This is Professor Poopsie Gerbilhiney, Ph.D. Thank you for the opportunity to comment on the anthropological aspects of the Castaways' social hierarchy. Having viewed the first two episodes that aired, I would like to submit my early findings via recording, to be transcribed by your staff at a later time. I am currently on an expedition to a settlement in the Amazon jungles studying a small tribe of natives who were suddenly exposed to artificial flavoring and food preservatives when a cargo plane full of Fruit Loops crashed into their territory.

"The dawning of mankind witnessed the evolving of a specific socio-economic structure which I find amazingly duplicated by the two Castaway teams. I must admit that I fully expected to see a 'Lord of the Flies' society emerge, and, to some extent, I have not been disappointed. However, and this may be due to the presence of television cameras which cause people to forget their more natural behavior in favor of displaying a more self-serving image, I have only seen it to a small degree.

"There is always one who emerges as a leader of sorts. Notice how the Alpha Team who obviously looks to the one called Ryan in that role. She clearly displays a dominant posture, a sort of alpha female, in relation to the rest of her team. Notice how they naturally migrated to the one who was taller, better-looking with a nice body...great tits! Oh, Emily, make sure that last comment gets erased from the tape before you send it. Thanks, sweetness. Hmm? Not right now, honey. I know it's been weeks. Well, I'M NOT THE ONE WHO ALWAYS HAS A HEADACHE! What? Oh, excuse me...I told you to use the netting. But you don't see me letting a few mosquito bites stop me from...Hey! Is this thing still on? Well, make good and sure that you edit this tape before you mail it off...and I'll see if I can't scratch your itch later, huh?

"As I was saying, I found the early return to the more basic roles and behaviors of our earliest ancestors to be quite compelling. Rewind the tape for me. Thanks, Doll. Notice the short blonde on the Beta Team. Her return to primitive conduct when she scratches her back against that tree. Oh, yeah, shake it baby…Ahem. The more traditional tribal roles are being filled and will continue to be redefined as the teams grow smaller and smaller throughout the life of the competition. Hannah! What? Emily? Oh yeah, Hannah was my last assistant. Great ass! Come back here! Okay, I shouldn't have made that crack about the blonde.

"Uh…um…Feel free to call on me for more insights into the anthropological implications of the Castaways, but for now…I gotta go! Hannah…uh…Emily? Sugar! I didn't mean it! Come back Sweetie! Honey?"

EPISODE FIVE

The Spy Who Loved Me

Shannon and the rest of the Beta Team stood around the tribal council pit, waiting for Joan and the Alphas to arrive so they could begin their next challenge. The blonde didn't know what it would be, but frankly, she didn't give a rat's ass. All she knew was that she couldn't go one more day without knowing Ryan.

In the biblical sense.

God, how she longed to peel off that tight black tank top with her teeth; taste that luscious, incredibly soft skin; attach her mouth to a rock-hard...

"Ms. Muldoon?"

...nipple. Suckling softly at first, then with increasing pressure...

"Shannon."

...taking in as much of that gorgeous, round breast as she possibly...

"SHANNON!"

"WHAT?" Shannon roared, opening her eyes to see Pete, the cameraman, shifting nervously in front of her, a piece of paper gripped tightly in his sweaty hand. Why was someone always interrupting her?

Pete gulped but remained silent. Ever since Shannon had kicked Yunkyung's butt, Pete had given her an exceptionally wide berth.

Smart man.

Arturo rolled his eyes knowingly and addressed the rest of the Beta Team, who had stopped their individual conversations to stare at Shannon. Well, actually they'd been staring before Shannon yelled at Pete. But she didn't need to know that.

A few more minutes of watching the young blonde—with her eyes closed, lips parted, and breath coming in short pants, thinking God only knew what—and Joe was going to need a cigarette to top off the experience.

"Everyone back to their business!" Arturo began making shooing motions with his hands. "*Next* time you see Channon's eyes closed or glazed over, and her mouth hanging open, go away until she cries out, 'God, yes, Ryan! YES!'" He thrashed his head from side to side for effect. "YES! YES!" When Arturo finished gyrating and screaming, he raised a mischievous eyebrow at Shannon. "Then we'll know it's safe to approach her."

Shannon shot the hairdresser an evil glare. "I hate you."

Ignoring Shannon's words, Arturo put his hands on his hips but his eyes softened. "You need to get over this obsession, girlfriend. I am so sorry to have to tell you this. You know that I would *never* tell tales out of school." At the sound of several snickers, Arturo whirled around and scolded his teammates with two quick snaps of his fingers, hissing like a snake.

Turning back to Shannon he said, "I heard your chica loca, Rambo Ryan, talking about some other woman that she loved above all others. Her name was Tina or Tammy or something like that. I am so sorry, Channon. But if it makes you feel better, and it would me, I am sure that this other woman is not a natural blonde."

Green eyes narrowed. Sure, Arturo was a bitch and all. But he wouldn't lie about this. Shannon sadly nodded her thanks. *I can't believe that Ryan is already seeing someone! And to think, I was going to do things to*

*her that are illegal in twenty-two states, including the entire Bible Belt!
What a slut!*

"What about Tanesha instead?" Arturo suggested gamely. "Surely she is cut from the same cloth as your Rambo Ryan. And with just one look, she makes me go limp almost as quickly."

Shannon shuddered, the thought of Arturo's limpness affirming her sexuality in a way that words never could.

Dismissing the hairdresser with a disgusted look, Shannon adjusted her ponytail a little higher on her head, wiping the loose strands of hair from her sweaty neck. Sure, butch chicks loved the long hair. But was it *really* worth the trouble? "What is it, Pete?" she finally asked, noticing the chubby cameraman was still waiting.

"I'm supposed to give you this."

Shannon looked down at the note still crumpled in Pete's hand, recognizing the paper from Rita's last message. "Keep it."

Pete's eyes widened. "But I'm not allowed to film you until *after* you read the note!"

"Good."

"You don't understand!" Pete affected his saddest expression, the one that always made his girlfriend give him the rest of her onion rings even when she hadn't finished eating them. "I'll get fired if I don't film everyone," he whined pitifully.

Rolling her eyes, Shannon yanked the note from his hands.

Sucker! "Thanks…" Pete's words were cut off by the arrival of the Alpha Team. "Gotta go." He lifted his camera and trudged away, noticing that it felt a little lighter than usual. He sucked in his gut proudly. At this rate, there would be something other than skin and fat on his arms to show his girlfriend by the time he got home!

Shannon closed her eyes in irritation. What did Rita want now?

Dear Shannon:

OH MY GOD! Just what in the (deleted by government censor) do you think you're doing? Do you know
all the trouble you've caused? Enough with the 'bedroom eyes'! You've always been able to control yourself
before. And I've known you for....Well, I don't
remember exactly how long. I get you confused with
that other secretary.

Shannon began cursing under her breath. Rita's other minion was a
62-year-old black man from Haiti named Anton, and neither he nor
Shannon were secretaries!

Anyway, you are in deep (deleted by government censor)! BTBC is now being targeted by Jerry Falwell, Oral
Roberts, Pat Buchanan and Janet Reno (Although, I
don't really understand that one. Especially when it's so
obvious that she's as (deleted by government censor at
the request of the U.S. Embassy) as a three-dollar bill).
And don't even get me started on that crazy (deleted by
government censor) with her own talk radio show. But,
at least she takes bribes.

Our sponsors are up in arms. Mothers are writing in
droves, afraid that their teenaged daughters will turn
queer just because the girls' worthless, pubescent
boyfriends don't look at them the way Ryan looks at
you! (BTW, when you get home you'll have to tell me if
her tits are real—I think I'd jump the fence for those.)

Bender is beside himself. Yesterday, he actually went
to his real life 'girl next door' and asked her if she was a
homo too. If I have to sleep with him just to calm him

down, you can look forward to wearing that home monitoring system my lawyer talked the judge into after my fourth, no fifth, DUI. You think you're on a short leash now, Missy?!

In order to save face, I'm ordering you to do something that screams heterosexual. Since there isn't time for you to marry one of the castaways and then refuse to sleep with him, I want you to have sex with one of the men...on camera. And Arturo doesn't count. We'll edit out what we can't sneak by the censors later.

Your superior (And, yes, I mean that in a philosophical way, too),

Rita
P.S. Telegrams to Bum (deleted by government censor), Asia are $11 per word. This is coming out of your severance pay.

Shannon's mouth dropped open in shock. "She expects me to do porno?!"

"Whatcha lookin' at?" Ryan peered over Shannon's shoulder.

"Jesus!" The blonde nearly jumped out of her skin. Did Ryan have to sneak up on her that way? "It's nothing," she assured quickly, wadding up the note and sticking it in her pocket. *She won't understand! She's already as paranoid as Bill Clinton on Father's Day!*

The survivalist's eyebrows disappeared behind windblown bangs, and her heart began to thump double time. Pale eyes went icy cold before closing tightly. "What are you hiding, Shannon?" she asked evenly, her voice giving no hint of the fact that her heart was twisting in her chest. *I believed in you! You promised you weren't a spy!*

"What are *you* hiding?!" Shannon poked her finger at Ryan's chest. "Hmm? Who is she? A girlfriend?" The writer swallowed past a lump in her throat, and her voice cracked a little when she whispered, "Or…is she more than a girlfriend?"

Ryan blinked. *What the hell?* "I have no idea what you're talking about."

Shannon opened her mouth, but Ryan kept right on talking. "We need to talk, Shannon. Remember that little cove we passed on the way to the second challenge?"

Shannon nodded mutely. How could she forget? It was only the single most beautiful place she'd ever laid eyes on.

"Meet me there tonight at midnight."

"Okay," the shorter woman agreed softly. *Dammit. I was supposed to say no! She's going to break my heart! And I'm letting her.*

"All right, castaways," Joan's voice rang out over the general hum of conversation. "Gather around the council table." The host moved to the long wooden table, subtly shifting her position to present her best side to the camera. *Never the left side, asshole!*

The Alpha and Beta Teams sat down on wooden benches on opposite sides of the table.

Pete, the cameramen, sat two buckets in the center of the rough wooden slab, holding his breath the entire time and praying the lids wouldn't fall off. Fuck! Joan was one soulless bitch!

"Okay, teams," Joan began, hoping there really wasn't a Hell. If there were one, she knew exactly what she'd be doing for all eternity. She shrugged mentally. Whatever. It was still better than public television.

Taking a deep breath, Joan launched into a quick explanation of the challenge. "Each team must eat all the contents of its bucket. A coin toss has determined that Alpha Team gets to select which bucket it gets. Don't forget, each team member must eat at least one of what's inside. The first team to consume everything in its bucket wins immunity…" Joan paused, glancing at Marva and Joe, knowing this would be of special interest to them. "…and a ten minute phone call home."

Joe leaned forward, staring at the buckets. He **needed** to call his son. That bastard accountant his ex-wife had married had probably taken the boy to Disney World three times since Joe had been gone. He needed to begin the deprogramming!

Marva eyed the buckets with predatory intent. There was no way she was going to give up a chance to call her little pumpkinseeds. She didn't care what was in those filthy buckets. Mama was gonna come through for her babies!

"Alpha Team, which bucket do you choose?"

"We'll take the green bucket," Molly immediately answered. "Green is the color of Gaia, giver of all life!"

"Yeah…Yeah…we'll take the brown bucket. Brown is the color of shit. Can we get on with this?" Joe asked impatiently. His eyes suddenly widened. "It's not *actually* shit, is it?"

Joan scowled. They'd have to bleep out both of those references. "Of course not, Joe," she said patiently. *They wouldn't let us feed you shit. I checked.*

The host smiled broadly and motioned for the cameras to get a close-up of the buckets. She pulled the Beta Team's lid off first.

Gasps all around.

The bucket was a third full of enormous, hard-shelled, black beetles that were crawling all over each other in a writhing, pulsing mass.

Tanesha paled. "Sweet Jesus."

Arturo turned on his heel and took off running.

"Damn!" The athletic recruiter sprinted after the hairdresser. *The brothers are definitely wrong*, she thought as she navigated the rough jungle floor, leaping over downed trees and tangled vines, *white people can too run. They only need to be properly motivated.*

Dawn looked at Joe with round, trusting eyes. "With Desiree gone, we can do it, Joe."

The redheaded model had finally gone berserk the day before and tried to kill Joan with a coconut. It was an amazingly effective way to get kicked off the island, and the remaining castaways tucked the idea away in their brains for safekeeping. Or just for fun. Who needed TV?

Joe looked back at Dawn adoringly.

Joan fought the urge to gag. "Now for the Alpha Team's bucket." She picked up a large stick and used it to knock off the lid.

Jason frowned. That was so *not* a good sign.

Before looking into the bucket, Ryan pulled Marva aside for a quick pep talk. Grabbing the housewife by the shoulders, she said, "Whatever is in that bucket is standing between you and your children."

Marva's eyes narrowed.

"Do you want the neighborhood kids to tease your children because their mama was too much of a wuss to do her best?"

"NO!"

"Then go get 'em!" Ryan pushed Marva toward the table as both teams peered into the green bucket. It was filled with huge, black, crawling spiders, whose hairy bodies were the size of silver dollars.

"Oh, thank God we got the beetles," Shannon muttered backing away from the bucket of spiders. She glared at Joan, the network whore, who was smiling wickedly.

"Go!" Joan shouted.

No one moved.

"I said, GO!" *Oh no. Not again.*

Joe scratched his bristly cheeks. He had lived through five years of marriage with a manicurist from Queens. Shrugging, he reached for the bucket. He'd lived through worse. Grabbing a handful of beetles, he stuffed them into his mouth all at once.

Dawn immediately mimicked him and began crunching away.

Ryan pulled out Tiffany, and stuck her down into the green bucket without looking, spearing a large spider. The survivalist pushed the enormous arachnid into her mouth, sucking down the wriggling black legs like errant spaghetti noodles.

Pete passed out.

Tanesha burst through the bushes with Arturo in tow. Shannon and Dawn held the kicking and screaming hairdresser down, while Tanesha force-fed him a single beetle.

Pandemonium broke out as the castaway's natural inhibitions fell by the wayside and they dove into their respective buckets with abandon. Marva and Joe led the charge.

Joan looked on, smiling through the horror. This was repulsive! This was hideous! This was television at its finest!

After several moments, Ryan leaned forward and stabbed the last spider. This would be another victory for the Alpha Team.

"Wait," Marty screamed, wiping a few half-eaten spider legs off his stubbly chin. "Earth Mama hasn't eaten one yet!" He pointed an accusing finger at Molly.

"Get over here!" Jason roared, sure that his last spider was trying to crawl its way back up his throat.

"I can't!" Molly whined. "My...my inner child is afraid of bugs!"

Marty grabbed Molly by the arm and dragged her to the council table. "Fuck your inner child!"

"And your little dog, too!" Jason chimed in, as he began trying to pry apart the thrashing woman's lips.

Ryan was about to administer a pressure point technique she'd learned from a Chinese spy named Ma Loa when Joan called, "TIME! The Beta Team has won!"

"NOOOO!!!!!!!!" Marty screamed, dropping to his knees.

Shannon and Dawn let go of Arturo and crawled over to the bushes to retch their guts out.

Joan smiled wryly, drawing the cameras toward the vomiting women. "Just another day in paradise."

*   *   *

Shannon's stomach was feeling normal again by the time she snuck out of the Beta Team's encampment and headed for the cove. She had finally barfed up the last of the beetles; at least she hoped she had. God, that was vile! She would be sure to put some rat poison in Rita's coffee when she got back to the office.

She was surprised at how easy it had been to sneak out of the camp. The camerawoman who was normally stationed nearby was missing, most likely in the jungle taking care of business.

She was gonna take care of some business too. Filled with happy thoughts, Shannon fairly skipped through the jungle.

*   *   *

Ryan waited impatiently. She had barely managed to sit through tribal council long enough to vote Molly's wimpy ass off the island. Tonight was the night. She was going to get better acquainted with the little blonde or she would die trying. No, that didn't sound quite right. Ryan paused, and thought it through again. She would get better acquainted with the little blonde, or she would…

Hmm.

She pulled out Tiffany. Carefully opening the beautiful blade, she gazed at the stars and moon reflected in the shining metal. "You are so beautiful," she whispered reverently. "We've been together so long, just the two of us. Remember that time we were being followed by the FBI? You are so sharp, I was able to puncture all their tires and they couldn't follow us any longer. Or that time our phone was being tapped by the ATF? But you took care of that in a jiffy. Slice, slice, and nosy Uncle Sam was shit out of luck."

Ryan sighed. Was there room in her life for another love?

Especially one that was getting secret messages? Shannon had said she wasn't a Fed. But isn't that what they all say? They never admitted to it. Hoover never admitted to wearing dresses and pantyhose. But that didn't make it any less true.

What would she do if Shannon were a Fed?

Feds had taken her family away. Oh, sure, the police had said it was an accident. *An accident, my ass!* Her parents had led the fight against microwave technology. Not microwave transmissions, but microwave ovens. *Sure, everyone says they're safe. But they're not. This is the same industry that had to prove it was keeping dangerous microwaves within the oven before it could sell them. Nobody cares about what they do to the food! The government is in the hip pocket of the microwave oven manufacturers.*

Ryan's parents had fought against the evil industry, but had been found dead in their car one morning in Death Valley. The official autopsy report said they had been baked alive.

The government had a cruel sense of humor.

Since then, Ryan had taken her younger brothers and built a completely technology-free home in the Kentucky foothills. No microwaves, no phones (except for her modem line), no electricity (except for the small generator that powered her television—a girl has to have some vices), and no running water. Though, lately, Ryan was beginning to miss the joy of indoor plumbing. If Shannon came home with her...

Don't put the cart before the horse. Not that she considered Shannon a horse. Though horses did have long, flowing manes like Shannon.

"Ryan?"

The survivalist jumped, startled out of her thoughts. Turning, she saw the luscious blonde standing behind her, bathed in moonlight. *Just as beautiful as Tiffany!* "Hi," she mumbled, suddenly shy.

"What are you doing with that knife?" Shannon gestured toward Tiffany, who was still standing erect and tall in Ryan's hand. "And who were you talking to?" The writer looked around the beach for the slut, who was seeing 'her' Ryan behind her back. If it was that Marva chick, though she'd hate to do it, Shannon was going to bitch slap her silly. She

could take her. Shannon had already proven it by her trouncing of Yun-
kyung earlier.

Ryan looked down at Tiffany then carefully folded her up and put
her away, caressing her gently as she did so. "Nothing. No one."

"I heard you talking to someone," Shannon insisted, folding her arms
across her chest. Well, actually she folded her arms and pressed them up
underneath her boobs to make them even more prominent. She knew
it would get Ryan's attention.

"Huh?" Ryan replied, watching Shannon's boobs lift.

"I heard you talking to someone."

"No one."

"Fine. I'm outta here," the writer huffed, turning on her heel, and
beginning the long walk back to Beta camp.

The survivalist stood rooted to her spot, torn between blurting out
the truth and her fear of rejection. What if Shannon didn't understand
the love she had for her knife? What if she ridiculed Tiffany? What if she
made her choose between the two of them? Ryan couldn't even begin to
know how she would make a decision like that. Finally, as she watched
Shannon walk away, she called out, "Tiffany!"

Anger flooded through Shannon at the sound of the slut's name
coming from her beloved's lips. Tiffany? Tiffany? What type of candy-
ass name was that? Bet the bimbo had huge, fake tits and a bleached-out
brain. Shannon executed a perfect military about face and marched
back over to the tall brunette. "Where is she?"

Ryan hung her head.

"In the sand? You have her buried in the sand here?" Shannon was
like a rabid gopher, dropping to her hands and knees, scooping sand out
of the way.

"I'd never let sand get on her!" Ryan bent down beside the blonde,
although she enjoyed the view for a few moments before doing so.

"Then where is the tramp?" Shannon bellowed. "What do we have to
do? Arm wrestle for you? Defuse a bomb? Undo a wire tap?"

God, would Shannon really do all those things for her? "She's not a tramp, she's my knife." Having revealed her secret, Ryan pulled the knife out of her pocket and presented it to Shannon. She indicated the plaque on the side where 'Tiffany' had been lovingly engraved. "See?"

"You named your knife 'Tiffany?'"

"Well, she's a girl." *Why is that so hard to believe?!*

Shannon shook her head, trying to rid it of all of the sarcastic comments. Ryan was already spooked enough. "That's who you were talking to? Your knife?"

Ryan didn't like the tone she heard in Shannon's voice. Pale eyes narrowed. "Yeah."

"And her name is Tiffany?"

"Yeah."

"Are you dating someone else? I don't want to get involved in another lesbian psychodrama. Jesus! There are enough of those to last a lifetime without me contributing."

"No, I'm not dating anyone else. There aren't even any women where I live!" Only her brothers, a couple of grizzly old guys, and some livestock. The latter were good enough for the men, but she had higher standards.

Wow. A world without women? Did such a place exist? She'd never have to worry about Ryan straying there.

"Since we're laying our cards out on the table, what about that note you received? Who are you working for? The FBI?"

"No."

"The CIA? KBG? NAFTA?"

"No. No. Isn't NAFTA a trade agreement?"

"Don't try to confuse the issue!" Ryan growled. "Who was the note from?"

"The BTBC," Shannon confessed, getting incredibly turned on by Ryan's forceful demeanor. She hoped the tall survivalist would throw her on the ground and make love to her. Or push her up against a tree and make love to her. Or take her out in the water and make love to her. Or...

"The BTBC?" Ryan repeated. "The Bureau to Begin Cloning'? The Bankers' Total Bureaucratic Control? Ban the Burgeoning of Capitalism? Be the Best Cuban?"*Damn!* She had never heard of this group. They must be wily to have escaped her notice.

Shannon reached out and put her hand on Ryan's. "No, the Bender Television Broadcasting Channel. The people who sent us here."

"Why are they writing to you?"

Shannon swallowed. *Time to be honest; she told you about her knife. And your secret isn't nearly as weird.* "I work for them."

"You're a plant!"

"Not really. They fired me!" That was, technically, true.

"Bastards!" Ryan commiserated. "So, why do they still send you notes if they fired you?"

Shannon frowned. She hadn't anticipated that question. *Think. Think. Think.* "They want me to stop wanting you." Reluctantly, Shannon went with the truth again.

Ryan knew it! Soon the media companies would be ruling the world! They get inside your brain, tell you what type of car to drive, what type of soap to use, how to run your life. Thirty seconds of mental programming played multiple times every day. That was why Ryan always left the room when the commercials were on. The subliminal messages couldn't be good for her. And she had found that her aluminum foil hat didn't block out all of them.

Ryan soon focused on the important part of what Shannon had just told her. "You want me?"

"God, yes," Shannon sighed. She wanted Ryan the same way Elizabeth Taylor wanted diet pills and booze.

"Good enough for me." Ryan reached out and pulled the smaller woman tight against her body. "I want you, too." She captured Shannon's mouth with her own, once again marveling at how good she tasted. Tongues dueled for supremacy as they clawed at each other's clothing like cats in heat.

Shannon remembered something on the Nature Channel about why cats howled when mating. She really hoped her cat analogy ended with the shredding of the clothing.

Soon, naked as the day they entered the world and the time Shannon went to a Dixie Chicks concert, the two women lay down on the beach. Shannon immediately felt sand in the crack of her cheeks. She squirmed against Ryan atop her, trying to dislodge it. God, it was really miserable.

This served to further inflame Ryan's ardor, and she began licking the succulent neck presented to her. Her large hands covered Shannon's breasts, kneading them like a newborn kitten.

Shannon began purring, deciding that the cat analogy still worked. She also continued to twitch. She reached one hand under her body and began trying to wipe away the sand there.

"Oh, baby, you like it that way?" Ryan asked, her voice rough with excitement. She reached under Shannon's body.

Shannon squealed when she felt Ryan's hand join hers. "What are you doing?"

"Taking over," came the reply, before Ryan's mouth closed over her breast.

The tongue almost caused Shannon to forget about the hand at her ass. "Whoa!" she cried out, bucking up against the larger body. "Ohh…" she sighed after another moment.

"How's that?" Ryan asked.

"Don't stop! If you stop, I'll kill you!"

Ryan felt herself fall a little bit more in love with Shannon at that threat. "No stopping, I promise." With those words, she began feasting on Shannon's body the way women in Weight Watchers munch on donuts, cake and candy. Although, she wasn't moaning quite as loudly.

The slow burn Shannon had felt whenever she was in the survivalist's presence flared into a raging fire. Every touch of Ryan's tongue nearly sent her over into ecstasy. Apparently, the reason Ryan was a woman of few words was because she had much better uses for her tongue. Shannon vowed never to let Ryan speak again.

Ryan painted erotic patterns over the writer's breasts. She stopped and suckled like a hungry newborn at each, drawing the pink nipples deep inside her mouth. Shannon's skin tasted incredible. *Mmm…she must be using coconut oil.*

Shannon thrashed her head from side to side, but instantly regretted her actions as sand poured into one of her ears. She turned her head to drain the sand, but it didn't work. Lifting her neck, she banged her head on the beach several times to no avail.

At the movement, Ryan looked up from her position. Was this some new kama sutra kinda thing? It looked painful to her. Oh well, as long as Shannon wasn't complaining, she wasn't going to stop what she was doing.

She moved up to enjoy Shannon's mouth once more, when she felt something hit her back. Ryan raised her head and looked around, trying to figure out what it was.

"More!" Shannon complained, grabbing Ryan by the hair and guiding her back to where she had been.

Ryan willingly complied until she felt something else hit her. "What in the hell?" she growled, pushing up and once again surveying the area.

Two quick jabs to the crooks of Ryan's arms caused her to fall back on top of Shannon. "I said more!"

Ryan was about to comply, when she saw something move out of the corner of her eye. She grabbed Tiffany from her discarded shorts and lunged to the right. With her outstretched hand, she caught hold of a furry piece of rope.

"Where the hell are you going?" Shannon bellowed. She didn't care if the Four Horsemen of the Apocalypse were headed for them, she needed to get off, and she needed to get off now. This required Ryan's participation. Tears stung her eyes. She was tired of flying solo!

Ryan pulled on the rope, only to come face to face with a rather pissed off monkey. She let go of his tail and he screeched when he saw the look in Ryan's eyes and his own reflection in Tiffany. The monkey dropped the nuts he had been hurling at Ryan and took off for the jungle.

"Apparently he thinks hot monkey sex should just be for monkeys," Ryan laughed, crawling back over to the blonde.

Shannon didn't bother with a reply. She was past words. Talking was overrated.

Ryan found herself pushed down to nestle between Shannon's spread legs. She idly noted that her new lover was a natural blonde, then slid her tongue inside the smaller woman.

"God! Yes!"

God has nothing to do with this, baby, Ryan thought smugly.

Shannon began moaning, loud and long. Ryan teased her, moving in and out, flicking across the areas where Shannon most needed her presence. The writer's hips bucked, anxious to present everything to Ryan's talented mouth. "Yes! Yes! Yes!" *Damn, Arturo had me totally pegged!*

With her right hand, Ryan reached up and squeezed one of Shannon's nipples, the pressure sending the woman closer to the point of no return. She continued to feast where she was when she heard Shannon's voice.

"Not...not...quite so hard on my left breast, dear..."

As Ryan's left hand was helping to support her weight, she wondered who—or what—was causing her new lover distress. A quick glance confirmed her fear. Moving quickly, she grabbed the hermit crab and threw him down the shoreline. *Making love on the beach is highly overrated.*

Wanting to bring this gig to a close, and, truth be told, to get closer to Shannon's reciprocating, Ryan picked up her speed and soon heard Shannon's scream of ecstasy. At the sound of her piercing cry, all the birds in the nearby trees took flight, fearing an impending attack. Then the jungle went silent.

It took all of Ryan's self-control not to react to the war cry. Screw Tarzan! That yell had just made Shannon the Queen of the Jungle.

Her queen.

Ryan wondered if Shannon was always that loud. If so, she was going to have to build her brothers another cabin. Quite a distance away.

For the first time in her life, Ryan was in love with something that didn't require sharpening. Although, she wholeheartedly looked forward to oiling Shannon regularly.

<Fade out>

Castaway Farewells (Desiree and Molly)

Desiree sat in a chair in front of the camera, looking haggard and far too old to be a supermodel. Joan stood in the corner of the hut with several technicians between her and Desiree. She wasn't taking any chances with the loony, red-haired bitch. If the model's bony, useless arms had been a little more powerful, those coconuts she pelted Joan with might have actually hurt.

Desiree smiled for the camera, and Pete winced at her yellow teeth. Damn, that was going to look ugly on a big screen TV!

"I want my public to know," Desiree began, "that I don't really look like this."

Pete rolled his eyes.

"This is all an optical illusion created by makeup artists. You know, a before and after comparison. This is before. WAAAY before." She reached up to primp her hair, only to have a large clump come off in her hand. Desiree stared at her palm in horror before discreetly brushing it off on her shirt.

Pete sniggered. Now it looked like she had long chest hair growing through her white, designer T-shirt.

"But no matter how you look, I want all you teenaged girls in America to know that it's not how you look on the outside that really matters. It's the makeup you buy to cover up your ugliness that's important. Unless, of course, you're fat or have too many zits. Then you should just stay in the house so no one can see you."

Joan and Pete both shook their heads. There went Desiree's cosmetics contract. The camera's red flashing light went off.

Desiree stood up, still dusting off her hands. "See, you Hollywood bitch," she hissed at Joan. "I told you I could work a capella!" She turned to Pete. "That's French Canadian for 'without teleprompter' for you idiots."

<Fade out>

*   *   *

Molly looked at the camera, tears glistening in her eyes. She clutched at her harmony beads. Considering how worn smooth they were, it was unlikely that they had ever been of any help to the New Ager. "I don't think it's nice to threaten someone's inner child. I mean, we must protect the sanctity of the innocence within. Innocence is all we have when we come into this world. And all we can hope for when we leave."

She paused and mouthed one of her favorite calming chants. She had recently set it to the tune of 'Only the Good Die Young' and she really liked the new up tempo feel it had. Feeling better, she continued, "I hope that those remaining on this island will see the beauty that surrounds them. This is a place where you can harmonize with nature, realize your inner peace, transcend the ordinary, and embrace those around you."

Molly frowned. "Some more literally than others.

"I'm off now. I'm going to sit by the hotel pool and contemplate my place in the universe. Right next to the bar." She hadn't meant to say that out loud.

<Fade out>

Panelist's Article: Dear Dr. Maura...by Dr. Maura

First, I would like to thank BTBC for allowing me to participate in this forum. I want to make sure that normal people, the people who listen to ME, have a say in this disgusting show. There are enough freaks contributing to the delinquency of our children. This will tilt the balance a little more to the right.

I saw the seven deadly sins committed in the first episode of Castaways and most of the Ten Commandments broken. I am not sure what is worse: the fact that they are attempting to portray lezzies as normal people or the fact that they suggest it's okay for our kids to grow up and scratch, claw, sell their souls, and stab each other in the back solely for the love of money.

Well, actually, that IS okay. In fact, it's the American way.

But it is SICK and totally unnatural for anyone to have sex with another person unless they are trying to procreate. People should only procreate while under the protection of the holy union of matrimony with someone of the opposite sex, of course. Otherwise, it is just completely amoral and sick.

As a matter of fact, so as not to go against God's wish that we go forth and multiply, I have decided to advocate that ONLY women of child-bearing years should have sex (with men, of course). Everyone else needs to just stop. I was able to stop having affairs so I know it can be done. In fact, my husband and I haven't had sex in....well that is of no importance. Back to the series...

Sigmund Freud, the father of psychoanalysis and the author of 'Totem and Taboo; Some Points of Agreement Between the Mental Lives of Savages and Neurotics', agrees with me. Of this I am sure. Well, pretty sure. I'll know better once I have someone read the book to me. But I know that if he were alive today he would say that everyone and everything associated with this series is just sick...sick sick sick. The gay and lesbian groups have taken over the airwaves. Next thing you know, they will be in Congress, in the Senate, and maybe even having children together. Sick, I tell you, sick!

EPISODE SIX

Hair Today, Gone Tomorrow

Today the two teams would combine. The rest of the competition would be spent together at the Alphas' camp, where the Betas were heading now. Arturo walked several steps behind Shannon, but she could still hear his heavily accented, taunting song. "Cheena of the Jungle and Rambo Ryan sittin' in a tree. N-A-A-K-E-D-D."

"That's not how you spell it." Shannon stuck out an impudent tongue at the hairdresser.

"Oooo, you slut, chica. Does Ryan, Warrior Princess, know you'll whip that out for anyone?"

"You're just jealous that Marty would gouge his eyes out before hooking up with you."

Arturo made a hissing sound, and shaped his hands into claws.

A hush came over the island's wildlife as the writer walked by. Even the insects were respectfully silent. Green eyes narrowed. "Jesus, I wasn't *that* loud," Shannon shouted.

Arturo just snorted. "Tell the truth. How many times have you been evicted, chica?"

"None!" Okay, twice. But that was none of Arturo's business. And those experiences paled in comparison to what she had shared with

Ryan. Shannon was amazed she'd remained conscious through so many orgasms. A few more encounters with the amazing survivalist, and Shannon was sure she'd be able to come on command. Like a well-trained puppy, only with boobs, sex toys, and a multifunctional, padded leash.

The blonde's eyes rolled back as she began reliving the night in the cove. But the grin slid from her face when she remembered how the evening had ended. While Shannon had achieved a level of satiation previously unknown to man or beast, Ryan had been left wanting. She cringed. All right, 'homicidal' might be a *teensy* bit more accurate.

Joan had called an impromptu, emergency castaway meeting. When she couldn't find Shannon and Ryan, the host had ordered a massive search. Arturo had literally stumbled onto Ryan and Shannon a few moments ahead of two cameramen. Without his warning, Shannon would have been caught up to her eyeballs in—well, Ryan, actually.

Joan, the network whore, had only called the meeting to bitch about Russell, who had been disqualified for boffing an exceptionally unattractive camerawoman in exchange for Kraft Macaroni and Cheese. Shannon felt a sudden surge of empathy for the professor, who had clearly hit rock bottom. But, damn, it *was* the cheesiest!

Before Ryan had left for the Alpha camp that night, she had let out a tortured moan of pure sexual frustration that had haunted the younger woman's dreams. It was more than Shannon could bear. Well, she *could* bear it; but only after several itchy, but ultimately satisfying, trips to the bushes for some quality time with herself. But how long would that be enough? She needed Ryan like Elvis needed fried chicken. It was a medical addiction!

Shannon unconsciously licked her lips. God, she would have Ryan in ways that would make even Rita blush.

No, wait. That was impossible.

Juggling her toilet paper stash and journal, Shannon began fanning herself, wondering if the jungle seemed unusually hot to anyone else.

When the Betas rounded the corner, the Alphas' camp came into view. Shannon and her team stood there in slack-jawed, wide-eyed silence, taking in the scene before them.

The Alpha camp was fantastic. Marty and Jason were resting comfortably in slowly swaying hammocks made from woven palm fronds. And they were drinking something frothy out of coconut shell cups.

Marva was basting some unidentifiable, but undeniably delicious-smelling, hunk of meat, which was mounted on a wind-powered rotisserie and slowly spinning over an open flame. Several chairs, whose bottoms were padded with soft, grass-filled cushions, flanked a tree trunk table. And the bug population was almost non-existent, due to the citric-laced torches that lined the camp's edge and bathed it with a clean, fruity scent.

Overcome with curiosity, the writer walked over to the corner of the camp and pulled on a dangling vine that extended from a black tarp. A fine spray of water instantly poured to the ground. Shannon stuck her hand in its stream. "OH MY GOD!" she shrieked. "It's warm!" She looked at her hand in amazement. "And clean!"

"Of course it's clean," Ryan said with a scowl. Did her woman think she was some sort of savage? "We have a screen on top to keep the leaves out, and it's heated by the sun."

Shannon marched over to Ryan, not bothering with a greeting. "Have you been living like this the entire time?"

"Don't be silly. We didn't finish the enclosed latrine until the second day. And cutting down the bamboo for the running water took a little time as well."

Marty yawned. Stretching his arms out in front of him, he cracked his knuckles. "Yeah, that one day we had to crouch in the bushes to shit was pure hell."

"Running water?" Shannon echoed. A glance to the right revealed the water fountain they had constructed. Shannon grasped Ryan's forearms, willing her hands not to shake as a slow, angry flush worked its way up her chest and neck. "And you have a bathroom?" she ground out, still not quite believing what she was seeing and hearing. They were living like the Swiss Fucking Family Robinson, while her team had been in hell!

Ryan's eyebrows drew together. What was Shannon talking about? "Of course we have a bathroom. It's really not safe to…"

SMACK!

"Ouch!" Ryan winced, rubbing her upper arm. "Where are you going?" she called after the furious writer, as Shannon tore out of camp in a barely controlled rage.

Marva gasped and shook her finger at Ryan. "Don't tell me you didn't help them with their camp? Even after you and Shannon…." Her eyes filled with disappointment in her jungle hero. "Oh, Ryan, how could you?!"

"Huh?" Ryan looked confused. "I figured they must want to sleep in curled up balls…in the weeds…along the beach…under the stars. I mean, why else would anyone…"

SMACK!

"Ouch!" Ryan grabbed her other shoulder. "Why is everyone hitting me?" she yelled, as Marva stalked after Shannon in a show of female unity.

Dawn stood in front of Ryan, but was too afraid to hit the survivalist. She just looked at the taller woman disapprovingly. "I can't believe you did that to Shannon! And she really likes you, too!" Dawn disappeared down the beach.

Arturo pranced over to Ryan, tsking loudly and shaking his head.

"Touch me and die, girly-boy," Ryan snarled.

Twinkling brown eyes traveled the length of Ryan's body before Arturo lifted a sassy eyebrow. "Men!" With that, the hairdresser skipped out of camp, eager to begin dissing butches in general. They were so thoughtless, and never conditioned after shampooing!

Ryan whirled around to face Tanesha. The athletic recruiter was sprawled in one of the empty hammocks, drinking a mango smoothie and looking terribly bored by the entire exchange. "Well?" Ryan demanded.

Tanesha thought for a moment. "Well, I'd say you are one cold-hearted, honky bitch for letting your woman live like a dog while you're," she gestured broadly, "…here." The black woman shrugged. "I'd stab a brother in the nuts for less."

The men all crossed their legs.

Ryan flopped down next to Tanesha; the word 'stab' had immediately brought to mind her beloved. She knew that Shannon would end up being more unreasonable than Tiffany! Although, Ryan mentally conceded, Shannon's great breasts *did* make up for a lot.

Tanesha chuckled, noticing the same dazed, desperately horny look that Shannon got at least three times daily. "Don't bother thinking about what you can't have, girl. Winged monkeys are gonna fly outta your ass 'fore you get any again."

The men grunted their agreement. Marty sat up and slapped Ryan on the back. "Welcome to the dog house. There are a lot of tits and ass magazines…"

"And home movies…" the engaged law student added, helpfully.

Marty nodded approvingly. "…to get you through these times. Too bad you don't have any here." He smirked. "These items are indispensable in your war against the weaker…"

Ryan's hand shot out, grabbing Marty by the throat and cutting off his oxygen supply.

"I…mean…fairer…fairer sex," he croaked as he began to lose consciousness.

*   *   *

"We have to do what?" Dawn asked Joan, shielding her eyes from the sun as she looked up into the trees, where five bundles were suspended at least 20 feet off the ground.

"Your challenge is to get the bundles out of the trees, alone or in pairs." The host looked into the camera and tediously reminded the slower viewers of the rules once again. "There are no longer two teams. The castaways will now compete individually for luxury items and immunity tokens. In each of the bundles is a luxury item. In only *one* bundle there is an immunity token. Whoever wins the immunity token cannot be voted off the island, but he or she can vote against the others. Starting tonight, two members of the island will be voted off at each tribal council."

Joan's gaze landed on each castaway, lingering so the camera could follow her movements. "You have 10 minutes to be back on the ground with your bundle. GO!"

Ryan fingered Tiffany anxiously. *Soon, baby.* With one toss she could free the booty. But what if the fall damaged what was inside? No. Better to try and lower the items to the ground. Alert eyes scanned the foliage for hidden devices, especially Venus flytraps. They contain microprocessors that attach themselves to human skin and collect an involuntary DNA sample for the FDA. She'd found one of those yesterday. Marva had tried to convince her that it was just a dead fly in the plant. Ryan snorted at the thought. Oh, to be that naïve again!

After a quick inspection, Ryan grabbed Shannon's hand, even though the younger woman was still refusing to speak to her. "C'mon, I need a partner." When Shannon wouldn't look at her, the survivalist gently cupped the blonde's chin, forcing her gaze upward.

Their eyes locked, and Shannon fought the urge to drown in those gorgeous baby blues. Sighing inwardly, she gave up almost immediately. *It's way too late for that. You're already gone and you know it, Shannon.* "Okay," she agreed softly.

The other castaways paired up, except for Marty, who mumbled something about not needing some candy ass' help to win. One member of each pair climbed up a tree as far as possible, then stopped to help the other. Joan frowned. They were working well together! This was boring!

"I said, I didn't do it!"

Breathing a sigh of relief, Joan pointed to Tanesha and Jason, who were working their way up the middle tree. The cameramen went scurrying.

"Liar!" Jason groaned. "Who else could have stepped on my head? We're the only ones in this tree!"

"Maybe you hit your own head, ignorant cracker! I'm innocent."

"Like O.J. Simpson, you mean?"

Dark eyes turned to slits, and Tanesha's voice became a menacing growl. "*Just* like that."

"Figures. Only a brainwashed spear-chucker would be idiotic enough to really believe that!" *Oops. Did I say that out loud?*

And with a glorious flush, Jason's future political career went swirling down the crapper. God bless television, videotape and instant replay.

Joan smiled so broadly, she began to worry that her chin and cheek implants might have shifted. Oh, baby, this was nearly as good as that tape she had of Ryan and Shannon making out. And she was going to retire on *that* bad boy once it hit the black market!

Ryan paused in her climbing efforts. "O.J. *was* set up. And the entire trial was done on a Hollywood sound stage. Just like Neil Armstrong walking on the moon. Duh! Everybody knows that!" she whispered to Shannon, as they watched Jason and Tanesha with interest.

Shannon remained silent, trying to pretend she hadn't heard Ryan's last comment. Had the brunette ever considered Prozac?

"Oooo…" All the castaways and crew groaned simultaneously as Tanesha kicked Jason's head several times in rapid succession. That had to hurt!

Despite the fact that they were still brawling, Jason managed to grab hold of the bundle, only to have Tanesha tear it from his arms and send it flying through the air and into Shannon. The force of the swinging object sent Shannon crashing into the bundle she and Ryan were trying to claim. The blonde grabbed wildly, reaching for anything that would keep her from careening to the ground, but her hands slipped on the cloth surface. She closed her eyes, preparing to fall, when her head jerked back violently. It took several dazed seconds before Shannon realized her hair had tangled in the ropes, and that she was now hanging suspended in the air, alongside the small pack of luxury items.

"Son of bitch!" Ryan cursed, her stomach in her throat at the sound of Shannon's cries.

"One minute!" Joan called, sure she would need a change of undies after this excitement.

"FUCK!" Unable to reach Shannon, Ryan scurried down the tree and surveyed the situation from the ground, flipping Joan off when the host pointed to her watch.

She had no choice. Ryan pulled Tiffany out and took just a second to lay a tender kiss on the shiny blade before sending her sailing toward Shannon. The spinning knife sliced through the ropes, and Shannon's mane, like hot butter. Tears stung Ryan's eyes as she watched poetry in motion. She would retrieve her baby after she saved her love.

Shannon landed safely in Ryan's arms, and a second later the bundle came crashing down on them both, buckling Ryan's knees.

"TIME!" Joan looked at the pile on the ground that was Shannon and Ryan. "CUT!" she directed Pete while smiling wickedly. "No pun intended, Shannon."

Arturo nearly fell out of his tree as he clasped his cheeks with both hands, crowing with undisguised delight, "I smell a makeover!!"

*   *   *

Arturo stood behind Shannon and surveyed his work one last time. "Oh, chica, you look good enough to eat. Si, Ryan?"

"Oh, yeah," the survivalist lustily replied.

"I'm not talking to you!" Shannon huffed, turning on the stump, presenting her back to Ryan.

Ryan frowned. Why didn't her beloved understand? Why must women be so temperamental? That was the best thing about her Tiffany. Tiffany was beautiful, but without all the complications. Of course, Shannon had several advantages over Tiffany, most importantly, the ability to not cause internal bleeding. Not that Ryan had experienced that particular benefit yet. Even *she* wasn't rugged enough to go there.

"Go away!" Shannon groused.

Pushing herself up to her feet, Ryan ambled into the jungle.

Marva sat by the fire, watching the dejected brunette wander off alone. This was no good. If Ryan was upset, then there went their food supply. That woman could hunt and skin anything. Marva wanted to win the million dollars, but she would prefer to avoid developing an eating disorder while doing so. She turned to Dawn, who was sitting beside her. "You realize our best chance for dinner just went into the jungle—depressed?"

"That's not good." Dawn was getting hungry. Her hand went to her stomach unconsciously.

"You know who caused it?"

Dawn looked over at the hairdresser, who was still primping Shannon's new hairdo. "Shannon?"

"No!" Marva shook her head emphatically. "Jason and Tanesha!"

"They did?" Dawn was confused. She thought Ryan was upset because she wasn't getting any. That was the phrase she had learned from Joe recently. She'd been learning a lot, actually.

"Yeah. They started fighting, and that's what caused the accident. Now Shannon is upset, because Ryan had to cut her hair to save her."

"So? What can we do?"

Marva's eyes took on an evil, determined glint. "Let's toss Tanesha and Jason at tribal council later."

Dawn thought about it for a moment. In the jungle, it was eat or be eaten. Or both, in Ryan and Shannon's case. If she didn't join this coalition, the next one might be voting to get rid of her. "Okay." And she was tired of Jason being referred to as the Ivy League Graduate Student by the camera crew. Fuck that. The University of Iowa might not sound very prestigious, but it was good enough for her family.

Marva nodded. Only a few more votes to round up, and tonight's tribal council meeting would be fine. She sighed and looked at where Ryan had disappeared into the jungle. Then all that would be left would be mending broken hearts.

Not a problem. She was a mother.

*   *   *

"I need to do what?" Ryan repeated, her voice petulant, sounding like Anita Hill at Clarence Thomas' confirmation hearings.

"Woo her."

"Whoo?" Ryan scratched her head. "Like a train? Whoo-whoo?" That didn't make much sense. What did trains have to do with her and Shannon? Was this some of that Freudian stuff she had heard about once, that the government used to make you hate your parents? She remembered it had something to do with trains and tunnels.

Marva counted to three. "No. 'Woo,' as in romance her."

"Romance?"

"Stop repeating me," Marva chastised. "Look, Ryan, Shannon is hurt. When women get their feelings hurt, they like to be romanced. And Shannon is going to require a lot of romancing right now, I'm afraid."

"You mean like candles and flowers and shit?"

Marva smiled, pleased that she was getting through. "Well, not the shit part."

*   *   *

Tribal council hadn't gone so well. Fortunately, Marva's coalition had held strong. Three votes for Jason. Three votes for Tanesha. One vote each for Marty, Dawn and Ryan.

Marva figured Tanesha had voted for Marty, Jason for Dawn and...unfortunately, Shannon for Ryan.

Trouble in Paradise.

Marva sincerely hoped it would get better soon. She was getting hungry.

*   *   *

In the morning, Shannon awoke to a horrific stench. She opened her eyes to find several glassy eyes staring back at her. Immediately alert, she began scrambling away from the huge stack of dead fish piled next to her bed. *What in the hell???* Had the entire ocean washed up next to her pillow during the night?

Then she noticed the message cut into the scales of the top fish: I'm hooked on you.

Ryan.

If Ryan thinks a pile of slimy, scaly, nasty fish piled by my nose, no less, will make up for the removal of my golden fleece...well, she has another thing coming. Shannon rolled over and tried to go back to sleep.

"Breakfast!" Marva exclaimed. *Yes!* The pep talk had worked. The way to a woman's heart was through her stomach. At least, that's what she had assured Ryan last night. Happily, Marva gathered up the fish and began preparing them for the morning meal.

Ryan watched as her first peace offering was rejected. "Stupid, Ryan, stupid. You sent her a mob sign: sleep with the fishes. She must think you threatened her!" She dropped down to the sand and began trying to figure out her next move. "Okay, what do women like? Debugging equipment? Bulletproofed vests? Their very own gas mask with washable filters? Flowers!"

The survivalist raced off into the jungle to find some flowers that weren't full of bugs. Of the government kind.

*   *   *

When Marva saw Ryan coming back into camp, she ran over and greeted the tall castaway effusively. "Thank you for breakfast, Ryan!" she leaned up and kissed Ryan's cheek.

Marty, from the hammock, called out, "I thought you didn't swing that way, Mrs. Georgia."

"If you were the only other option, I would." Marva noted that Ryan was holding something behind her back. "What do you have there, Ryan?"

"Nothing." The survivalist blushed.

Marva decided she really liked this match-making thing. Maybe when she got back to the States, she could start her own daytime television show for lonely hearts. She could certainly do better than that nasty XXX show on MTV. "Show me."

"It's nothing."

"Look at the beautiful flowers!" Arturo shrieked, bouncing over.

Ryan wondered if killing Arturo would piss Shannon off even more. She decided not to risk it. Right now, he was the closest hairstylist, and she didn't want to risk further alienating the luscious, now shorthaired, blonde.

Taking a whiff of the orchids, Arturo pranced around Ryan. "Who are those for? Hmm? Or shall I guess?"

"Go away."

"Oh, Channon! Channon! Come look at what Rambo Ryan –" a quick glance at Ryan confirmed this nickname was not appreciated "– did I say that out loud?—has brought for you!"

"Hair growth formula?" Shannon inquired crossly.

Ryan winced. Maybe flowers weren't going to be enough. And it had taken her a long time to find some that hadn't been tampered with. Gamely, she pulled the flowers from behind her back and presented them to the object of her desire. "For you."

Shannon melted a bit inside. Ryan hadn't really meant to cut off all her hair, after all. And she did look very adorable standing there with an armful of orchids. She stepped forward and bent down to smell the blossoms.

And immediately pulled back, screaming, as a bee stung her. "Ow! Ow! Ow! Ow!"

Marva closed her eyes and groaned. So much for food. H—E—double hockey sticks! She knew she should have saved a couple of the fish from this morning.

Marty began laughing from his position as he watched Shannon clutch her nose and run around in circles. Lesbians had no clue how to get a woman. He never had a problem. Visa was accepted everywhere he wanted to be.

*   *   *

Ryan didn't reappear in camp until that evening. The hungry castaways sat around the campfire wishing their hunter/gatherer and Shannon would kiss and make up. Marty, especially, hoped they would be naked at the time.

Joe and Dawn had returned to camp early in the evening, after being conspicuously absent all day. Pete, the cameraman, had come back with them, smoking a cigarette like it was his last, best friend.

Shannon stared at Dawn. Something was different with Farm Girl. Something had changed. Something significant.

Someone had gotten some today. And it wasn't her!

Dammit.

If only she weren't mad at Ryan, she would tackle the object of her affection and give Rita and Bender a coronary. It would also be instructional for Rita. She just knew Rita had never heard what a real orgasm sounded like.

Ryan approached Shannon cautiously, much like small children do Michael Jackson. "Hi," she said softly.

"Hi," Shannon managed.

"You feeling better?"

Shannon rubbed the tip of her nose. The stinging had stopped earlier in the day when Arturo had made a paste of ground eucalyptus leaves and spread it over her face. Fortunately, she had washed it off before their non-dinner. "I am. Thanks."

This wasn't going so badly, after all. Ryan was relieved. She reached into her pocket and pulled out the gift that she and Tiffany had crafted for Shannon. "This is for you."

Oh, yeah, Ryan is definitely getting laid tonight, Shannon thought happily. She accepted the gift and removed its leafy wrapping. Nestled inside the greenery was a beautiful, carved, shell hair comb. "A comb? A comb!" she shrieked. "You chop off my hair, and you give me a comb!"

No, Ryan is definitely not getting laid tonight.

"I thought it'd look pretty in your hair. You can use it as a hairpin…as your hair grows out again!" Ryan was backpedaling on the sand. Shannon had a murderous look in her eyes. Ryan had seen it once before, while studying the tapes of one of Clinton's speeches. It was the look he gave the aide who snatched away his Big Mac as he was going on stage. They never found his body. Though they had replaced him with a fairly lifelike clone. The aide, not the president. Ryan scratched her head. Actually, the other would explain quite a few things.

She didn't have time to continue contemplating this new conspiracy, as Shannon was continuing to advance on her.

"Shannon, sweetie, honey, darling," Ryan began throwing out all the endearments she had reserved for Tiffany all these years, "I'm really sorry about your hair. It was an accident, I swear. I was only trying to save you."

Shannon stopped her advance. Maybe she was being a bit irrational about this. Could this all be the product of PMS? She was feeling a little bloated.

Ryan sighed in relief. It worked. Tiffany would be her role model for all future dealings with Shannon. "It looks really, really sexy, actually."

That's what she needed to hear! Shannon's hand went to her hair and fluffed it a bit. "You think?"

"Oh yeah," Ryan groaned. "Although, I'd like you bald."

The moment was shattered.

Shannon's eyes narrowed. "You're such a man!" she spat.

"I am not!" Ryan protested. "That's just an ugly rumor the ATF started that time I outsmarted them. Like Janet Reno has any room to talk!"

"Argh!" Shannon stomped off.

*   *   *

Marva found Ryan sulking in the jungle. She watched as the survivalist spoke softly to her knife. At least, it looked like she was talking to her knife. Marva hoped she was mistaken. "Ryan…"

"Go away." Ryan settled further back against the tree. She knew she never should have come out of the Kentucky woods. She should have stayed where she was safe. Instead, she had been enticed out of the tranquility she knew, all for the love of a few dead presidents. And they weren't even her favorites. Benjamin Franklin was a far better inventor than a commander-in-chief.

"It's going to be all right."

"She hates me, Marva." On the ground, Ryan scratched out her name and Shannon's, intertwined.

"No, she doesn't hate you." No one could look that turned on 24/7 and hate the object of her desire. "She just needs you to go that final step." At Ryan's confused look, she continued, "You need to serenade her."

"You mean sing?"

Marva nodded.

"Out loud?"

"She needs to hear you," Marva pointed out reasonably.

"What should I sing?"

Maybe this wasn't such a good idea after all. "A love song. You do know a love song, don't you?"

Ryan rested her hand on her chin, mentally going through the vocal selections on the jukebox at Archie's Grub and Tackle, one of the better eating establishments in Kentucky. "To All The Girls I've Loved Before?"

"No."

"Never Make A Pretty Woman Your Wife?"

"No."

"If You Can't Be With The One You Love, Love The One You're With?"

"Okay, maybe singing isn't the way to go." Apparently a romantic survivalist was as much an oxymoron as military intelligence, educational standards and compassionate conservatism.

Ryan kept thinking. She had to win Shannon back. And, if it took singing to do it…she was going to come up with just the perfect song.

And then, like the runs after a trip to Mexico, it came to her in a blinding, ferocious flash.

"Come on, Marva. I've got some wooing to do."

*   *   *

As everyone settled down to go to sleep, a clear alto was heard drifting on the night breeze. The sound was a country ode to a green-eyed girl, obviously meant for the novelist.

Shannon listened intently to the lyrics, once she got over her surprise at the pleasant quality of Ryan's voice. She especially liked the reference to her lips tasting like mountain honey and her body being as warm as homemade wine. Oh, yeah. She'd let Ryan have a long drink if she were here now.

Shannon sighed. Maybe she could get used to short hair. It was easier to care for. Didn't get sticky on her neck in the jungle heat. Had more body.

No matter what, she could definitely get used to a certain loopy survivalist.

<Fade out>

Castaway Farewells (Jason, Russell and Tanesha)

Jason sat and faced the camera, his expression sober. "Hi. I'm Jason Wilcox. I want to apologize to all the viewers of Castaway for my insensitive and inappropriate comments, which were aired in this episode.

"I believe that all Americans are endowed with innate intelligence and inner beauty. As a future senator from the great state of Massachusetts, I look forward to representing all of our proud citizens.

"All of us have moments of weakness. I ask for you to forgive mine." He paused and smiled, a tear glistening in the corner of his eye.

Pete pretended to turn off the camera and lowered the lens so that Jason could not see the red light. "Got it, man."

"Great. Thanks!" Jason replied. "Did I sound sincere enough there? I mean, those special interests groups are so damn sensitive. You make one little comment, just one, and suddenly…I mean, they should get a life, ya know?"

"What do you plan on doing now that you've been kicked off the island?"

"You kidding? I'm getting laid. Gonna find me some nice island girl—brown sugar is so sweet, ya know?—and bang the hell out of her."

Pete snickered, proud of himself. "Have a good time, Jason." He wondered how much Jason's future father-in-law, Senator Penent, would pay him not to air that part of the tape.

<Fade out>

*   *   *

The producers of Castaway regret to inform the viewing audience that Russell has been disqualified from competition. Apparently, he had been trading sexual favors for Kraft Macaroni and Cheese (Original).

<Fade out>

                *   *   *

Camera in hand, Pete pointed to a short wooden stool. Tanesha walked over to the stool, and kicked it out of her way. Back erect and shoulders straight, she crossed her arms over her chest.

"You'd better start your filming, you blubbery-assed cracker. 'Cause I got something I wanna tell America! Bring on the camera!"

Pete scrambled into position. On the fear scale, Tanesha fell somewhere just below Ryan, but above everything else on the island, including 200 varieties of snakes. Even the poisonous ones. The red light began to flash. Tanesha began ranting in her best Jesse Jackson voice.

Pete stifled a giggle, his chuckles shaking the camera. He could never think of Jesse Jackson without hearing that 'Green Eggs and Ham' skit from 'Saturday Night Live.' God, he missed television! Well, not all television. Not the crap he was filming.

"Are you paying attention?" Tanesha suddenly shouted at the cameraman.

Pete nodded frantically, bobbing the camera yet again.

"I was a victim! A victim of the white man's wrath! A victim of racism! A victim of sexism! Held down and repressed by 'the Man!'" she sneered. "Brothers and sisters, are we going to stand by while they rob of our dignity? Our opportunity? Our potential? Isn't it enough that they put sterilization drugs in our fast-food fried chicken?"

Ahh....Pete nodded with new understanding. Now he knew why, amazingly, Tanesha and Ryan seemed to get along so well together. They were both insane.

"In conclusion, I'd like to add, 'Can't we all just get along?'"

"Cut," Joan called from the background. She approached Tanesha with a relieved smile on her face. "I'm so glad you to added that bit about 'getting along.' For a minute I thought you were advocating..."

Joan's words were cut off when her face and Tanesha's fist collided. A round of cheers broke out. Pete and the rest of the crew dropped to their knees and bowed respectfully as Tanesha left the hut.

\<Fade out\>

Panelist's Article: Strangers in a Strange Land by Itasca M.H. Onager, B.A., M.A., Ab.D.

Many pundits have remarked upon the similarity of "Castaways" to the "bread and circuses" of ancient Rome, opining that those contestants who are not competing solely for the "bread" are desperately seeking (like those tuning in, they suggest) to fill not just empty pockets, but empty lives.

Whatever. The fact is that this pseudo-sport is a vapid program pandering to the worst in human proclivities.

On the other hand, it does have the potential to demonstrate my theory about social change. Based on weeks of arduous research among the Ainu of Japan, gorillas of Rwanda, and "valley girls," I have concluded that ALL societal progress derives from exposure to superior ideas from the outside, usually ideas from a charismatic "stranger" who galvanizes the group's journey to greatness through inspiration or intimidation. When a society comes into contact with more than one "stranger" at a time, by the way, the outsider who is MOST strange will carry the day.

Admittedly, the circumstances of this serendipitous field study COULD be better: the contestants are not only strangers in a strange land, but they are also, like, really, really, strange. And they aren't really a "society"—they don't know each other and don't want to. (Well, except for those two bodacious babes!) And the contest requires them to pretend to act as a group while actually plotting against one another. And they are operating under the 24/7 surveillance of a camera crew instructed to do whatever it takes to produce sensational footage or join the ranks of the unemployed.

Other than THAT, however, the conditions seem IDEAL. I have no doubt that by the time the series comes to its shattering climax, it will have conclusively demonstrated the validity of my revolutionary hypotheses.

Humph! Maybe THEN those geeks at the University of the Great Lakes—Ypsilanti will pull their pointy heads out of their UGL-Y heinies and finally grant me that Ph.D!—IMHO.

Episode Seven

Ryan's Hope

Joan sat behind one of the crew huts, desperately trying to figure out a way to electrify a boom mic. The damned castaways were so lackadaisical about the competitions. If the network wouldn't give her a cattle prod, she'd make one of her own! She figured it wouldn't kill any of them...unless it started raining. Of course, it rained nearly every day, but Joan didn't want to focus on inconvenient details.

She also couldn't figure out how Pete was going to be able to hold it, but the network had insurance for such potentially ugly little incidents. Besides, Pete was nearly dead as it was. Twenty-four days on the island had reduced the cameraman to lumps of fat and rolls of skin. He looked like a deflated Pillsbury Doughboy.

And to think she had slept with him.

Joan shivered, a chill racing down her spine. She should get extra compensation for that act of personal degradation. Little did she realize that next year she would be paying Pete to keep him from showing the videotape of their little encounter at the company Christmas party. Damn, sneaky cameraman! Joan learned from the experience, however, and did the same thing to Bender a year later.

"Joan!" one of the production crew called, rounding the corner.

"What?" she snarled, jumping as the battery pack she was hot-wiring delivered an unexpected shock.

"Uh, they're ready for the challenge. I finally found them all."

Joan's eyes narrowed. That was another problem. Her production crew was so inept; the little squirrelly castaways were able to sneak away for 'private time' almost anytime they wanted. This meant that Joe and Dawn were constantly gone—though the crew was getting better at finding them. Pete chain-smoked whenever he watched them. Stupid putz! At least he could watch through a camera lens.

Ryan and Shannon were much harder to locate. That whacko survivalist kept laying false trails to lead Joan's crew into the quicksand. An evil chuckle escaped Joan's lips. At least she knew Shannon wasn't getting any. The whole island would know when that particular event occurred again. Greenpeace had already filed an official complaint against the network for the unexpected migration of native birds from the island. Joan knew what had spooked them.

Hopefully, this challenge would put some life back into the show. It was pretty simple, actually. All the castaways had to do was rappel down the side of the cliff on the north beach. Of course, there wasn't any ground below the cliff. The contestants would go straight into the water, and from there, swim against the current, about fifty yards through the inlet to the beachhead.

God, she loved her job.

The beauty of it all was the luxury item the winner would receive.

*   *   *

Marty held the hollowed-out half coconut in one hand and stared at its contents. He looked up at Joan, his vision slightly blurry due to the head wound he had received when the waves had smashed him against the rocks. If he hadn't used Arturo as a buffer, he might have been more badly injured. "What the fuck is this?"

Joan smiled, resembling a psychotic June Cleaver. What was in the coconut would have been used for the challenge…before she had decided to make it a bit more interesting. What were the writers thinking? A card game as a challenge? God, that was almost as boring as an Al Gore campaign speech. Almost. Fortunately, she had saved the episode with her quick thinking. "Your reward."

"My reward?" he repeated, spitting out another mouthful of seawater. "I get bashed against the side of a cliff, then nearly drown, and all I get is a fucking deck of playing cards?!"

"It's entertainment."

"I'll show you entertainment, you scrawny-assed bitch!" Marty began advancing on the host.

"Hola, chico!" Arturo called out as he pulled himself up onto the beach. "Come help your little mattress!"

Marty whirled around, very aware that this was being videotaped for broadcast. If he let that comment go unchallenged, he would never be able to bend over to pick up a nail at a construction site again. "You are not my mattress!"

"Well, it did not seem that way while we were out on the ocean of love, eh, big boy? You were pressed tight against my back…"

"A little help over here!" Marva cried, dragging Dawn onto the sand. Dawn's arm was bent at an unnatural angle and her neck was wrapped in seaweed. Marva looked like an oil-slicked seal. At the last minute, Joan had ordered the dumping of a barrel of oil into the beach inlet. It had made their pathetic rescue attempts all the more dramatic. Joan had seriously considered setting fire to it, but was worried the smoke might obscure filming.

Screw you, Regis! Without Kathie Lee you're nothing but a monochromatic windbag! Joan couldn't wait to see the numbers for this episode.

Next to wash ashore was Joe. He looked like a swordfish-fisherman who had been skewered by his prey. Spitting out a clam—he didn't even want to think about how it got into his mouth in the first place– he rubbed his face carefully, lest any sea urchins were still attached.

"Joe!" Dawn moaned, bringing him back to the present.

He raced over to his…significant other? Nah, they were just sleeping together. Right? Nothing too significant, right? Though she was really pretty and sweet, and he loved being with her. And his kid would love her.

His kid.

Jesus! What if Dawn was pregnant?? They had tried using a sea sponge as a contraceptive device, but it seemed to be more trouble than it was worth. "Are you okay?" *Don't be pregnant, please don't be pregnant.*

Marva rolled her eyes. Men! "Yeah, she's fine, Joe. Everyone's arm is supposed to bend backwards at the elbow."

Relieved that Marva didn't confirm a pregnancy, Joe now blanched at the sight of Dawn's arm. That couldn't be good. "You'll be just fine," he lied. *My God, they might have to amputate!* He faked a smile.

Next out of the water was Ryan, carrying Shannon over her shoulder. Shannon was spewing most of the ocean down Ryan's back. Ryan kept lightly smacking Shannon's butt as they made their way over to the rest of the castaways.

"Ryan?" Shannon choked out. Receiving an affirmative grunt, Shannon continued, "If you're trying to clear my lungs, you really don't need to hit my ass."

"Oh." The survivalist opted for just resting one of her hands there instead. Even better.

"See you all at the tribal council tonight!" Joan chirped. She bent over Dawn to see if it was worth flying in a doctor for the minor injury.

"Stay away from her, you bitch!" Joe growled, pushing the host back. Seeing the host's indecision about helping Dawn enraged the good-natured bartender. Maybe he was in love. He had previously thought the manicurist from Queens had ripped his heart out and eaten it while they were married. *Nice to know it's still in there.* "We aren't sticking around for some stupid tribal council. Dawn and I are getting out of here! This little hellhole isn't worth it. No matter how much we might win. Now, order us a helicopter." Joan kept a false smile plastered on her face throughout Joe's tirade. "Oh, and we will be suing your ass, too. I'm a bartender. I know every God damned lawyer in Hackensack!"

Now, that was a real threat. Joan's eyes narrowed. She'd have to make sure they edited out that little comment. She didn't want anyone to get any ideas.

Turning to the camera, she said, "The tribe has spoken. And survival of the fittest continues." Damn! She had planned something a little special for tonight's tribal council. *Next time.*

*　　　　　　*　　　　　　*

The camp was subdued that night. They were now down to the final five contestants, since Joe and Dawn had volunteered to be the next two voted off. Shannon was amazed to still be on the island. Well, not all *that* amazed. The eleven who had been voted off, or disqualified, had been pretty pathetic. Except for the noble Joe, leaving with his girl. If she were into men, which she wasn't, she would find that hugely attractive. She wondered if Ryan would do that for her.

I bet she would for Tiffany. Shannon tried to imagine what tragedy would have to befall Tiffany for Ryan to leave. An emergency sharpening probably wasn't enough of a reason, but, God forbid her tip should get broken, or the handle nicked.

Was it really wrong to pray for the safety of a knife?

Ryan and Shannon were snuggling in one of the swaying hammocks. Arturo was moisturizing. Marva was leaning against a tree and humming her son's favorite lullaby. And Marty sat by the fire, shuffling cards.

"I'm bored," Marty announced.

Arturo immediately perked up. "Oooh! Let's play a game!"

"Not celebrity charades again," Marva groaned. "You always do Diana Ross."

An indignant look crossed the hairdresser's features. "But of course. She is DIANA! She is SUPREME!" He swished his hips and struck a pose.

"You are so queer," Marty said needlessly. He looked at the three beautiful women with whom he shared the island. Arturo was certainly no competition. He had the perfect game. "No, let's play a man's game: Poker."

"We don't have money," Shannon murmured from her spot in the hammock.

"We don't need money, girlie. We have everything we need to bet with." He pinched at the collar of his Hawaiian shirt. "Our clothes."

Suddenly, Ryan perked up. "Strip poker?"

"Yup."

"Great! Let's play!" Ryan jumped out of the hammock so quickly that it spun around and dumped Shannon on the sand. "Oops, sorry, baby," she apologized, giving the writer a hand up. Ryan reached around and helped Shannon wipe the sand off her butt, getting momentarily distracted.

"I don't know," Marva hesitated. She was a Baptist, a wife, and mother of two. *Hmpf*. Marva scowled. Those two little monsters were the reason she now had sagging breasts. *Screw it*. She would play. "Oh, what the heck, I'm in," Marva drawled.

Arturo bounded over to where Marty was sitting, settling himself beside the burly construction worker. "I am a lousy card player, but a great sport!"

Ryan marveled at Marty's genius. She should have thought of this earlier. What better way to conduct a strip search without a person knowing it? Marty was from Seattle...home of Microsoft...he was probably web enabled. Marva was from Stone Mountain, home of the great confederate monument...she probably harbored dreams of revolution. And Arturo was living in San Francisco...home of all counterculture and all freaks generally...And, well, hell, she just wanted to see Shannon's breasts. They were so pert and firm and succulent and...

She should have done this a long time ago! Of course, it would be a shame to have to kill everyone else who saw Shannon naked. As a child, her report card always said 'does not play well with others'.

They sat in a circle, and Marty dealt the first hand. "Five card stud, nothing wild."

"Ooo, stud," Arturo trilled. "I like this game!"

Marty pointed to a space between Marva and Ryan. "You. Sit. There."

"No need to be mean." Marva gave Arturo a reassuring smile. "You stay there, Arturo."

"Fine, fine, fine," Marty grumbled.

The first hand went pretty quickly as the players sized each other up. In more ways than one. Marva lost, and everyone waited expectantly for her article of clothing. She smirked and put in one of her sandals.

Play progressed rapidly. Within a few hands, the already scantily dressed castaways were less dressed. Except for Ryan. She hadn't lost a hand.

Arturo was down to his swim trunks, having divested himself of his earring, bandana, shirt and shoes. Marty was doing pretty well, having only lost his socks. He was eagerly studying Marva's breasts, which had been bare for a few minutes. *Nice. But saggy.* And he was comparing them to Shannon's, which had just been exposed as the blonde tossed her bikini top onto the pile. *Now, there's a nice set of melons.* He wondered whether Ryan would kill him if he reached over and checked their ripeness.

A quick glance at the survivalist confirmed that she would, probably before his hand even reached its destination.

Ryan was drooling. She kept imagining where her lips could be. Where they were meant to be. She wiped her mouth with the back of her hand.

Shannon's breasts were glowing with the admiration they were receiving. Her nipples were taut, practically begging for Ryan to give them some attention. The kind of attention only Ryan could give them. Well, that wasn't really true. A lot of people had given them attention in the past. But she was willing to reserve them for Ryan in the immediate future.

"Ryan," Marty repeated, punching her lightly on the arm.

"C'mon." Ryan grasped Shannon's hand and began dragging her down the beach. This was simply too much! How much could one woman be expected to endure? It had taken every last ounce of Ryan's will power not to jump across the table and take Shannon right there, in the middle of that damn poker game. But she was *still* going to gouge out every single ogling eyeball that had gotten a good look at the luscious writer's boobs.

Well, maybe she'd leave the women, Marva and Arturo, one eye. Shannon was a babe. It was understandable that they would look.

"Ryan…Should…Shouldn't I put my top on?" Shannon tried not to stumble as the taller woman increased her pace.

"NO!" Ryan barked. "Do you want me to have to cut it off your body?"

Pale brows drew together. Was that a trick question? "Umm…No?"

"Good." Shannon wasn't moving fast enough, so Ryan scooped the smaller woman into her arms and began jogging. Shannon would need all her energy later. Oh yes. She would have Shannon this night. And more importantly, Shannon would have her. That fact was as inevitable as the swell of the tide. Or as Tiffany rendering Marty a soprano. It *would* happen.

Shannon sighed and gazed fondly at Ryan. This was just like the romantic ending to 'An Officer and a Gentlemen'! Only without that beady-eyed Richard Gere. And frumpy Debra Winger. And that hideous, overplayed, croaking duet. Shannon scowled. Damn! Now that she thought about it, the movie really sucked!

"How far are we going?" Shannon asked impatiently. She wanted Ryan *now*! Who knew that exhibitionism was such a turn on? Okay, she did, and so did the patrons of that 'Dykes on Bikes' leather bar just outside of Denver. Damn Jose Cuervo! But Ryan didn't need to know everything about her, did she?

Shannon let out a shaky breath. Ryan's stare during the poker game had got her so hot and bothered that she had to forcibly stop herself from leaping over the table in the middle of the game! It was embarrassing. But Shannon was past caring. She shifted in Ryan's arms, thrusting her starlit breasts in the survivalist's face.

Ryan stopped so quickly that sand flew in all directions. "This is far enough," she moaned, already devouring what Shannon had so eagerly offered. Without detaching her mouth from its prize, Ryan laid Shannon on the beach.

At the feeling of the cool, damp sand against her naked back, Shannon's eyes—which had been screwed tightly shut in ecstasy—flew open. Damn, how could she have forgotten about the sand? "Ryan...Mmm...Let's go someplace...ooooh, yeah, harder is good..." Shannon's words were whisked away by the sensuous feeling of soft lips against her impossibly hot skin. *Please bite down! Yes!*

"You smell so good," Ryan moaned, her lips lingering at Shannon's neck. Suddenly, Ryan pulled back and stared at Shannon with fiery eyes gone pale in the moonlight.

Shannon gasped. Ryan looked like a goddess. An **unbearably horny** goddess to whom the young writer was prepared to pay homage until she passed out. Or until her sand wedgy became intolerable. Whichever happened first.

"I know I should be more romantic," Ryan continued, bringing her hands up to Shannon's cheeks (the ones near the writer's teeth), "and you deserve that. You really do, Shannon." Ryan took a deep breath.

"But does it have to be right now?!" she blurted out desperately. It had taken hours to make Shannon's comb and to think of that snappy fish message. She couldn't wait that long tonight!

Was Ryan crazy? Scratch that. "Romance later, hot monkey sex now!"

"Thank you, God!" Ryan moaned, attacking Shannon's chest with renewed vigor.

Shannon threaded her fingers tightly into Ryan's thick hair...*Hair. That damned Tiffany!* She felt a surge of irrational jealousy. How could she, a flesh and blood woman, compete against six inches of 'precision-honed perfection'? God, this was maddening! She sighed wistfully...she couldn't compete. She could only hope that Ryan's heart was big enough for both of them.

As if reading her thoughts, Ryan paused, then began kissing her way up Shannon's throat. "You look so fabulous with short hair. Nothing makes me feel the way you do. I want you every second of the day. If I couldn't have you right now, I think I'd die," she whispered hotly, dragging the tip of her tongue around Shannon's ear.

Shannon swooned. Jesus, Ryan was really getting good at this! She'd have this relationship stuff licked in no time. But first she had more important things to lick. *No,* Shannon told herself. They were always being interrupted, and she couldn't risk another day passing without Ryan finding peace of mind. The darker woman was clearly beside herself, and that was something Shannon wanted to fix. Oh, baby, she wanted to! She **needed** to do this. If she didn't, she wasn't sure how many of the castaways would still be alive to take the next challenge.

"OFF!" Shannon suddenly shouted, pushing Ryan away. "Every stitch of clothing. I want you completely naked and under me!"

Ryan nodded frantically. She didn't have to be asked, well, told, twice. Scrambling off Shannon, she stripped down to her birthday suit in a matter of seconds.

Unable to resist getting a closer look at Ryan standing nude in the moonlight, Shannon jumped to her feet as Ryan's tank top hit the beach. "God, you are so unbelievably gorgeous, Ryan," Shannon hummed appreciatively, as she circled the naked woman, dragging her nails lightly across sensitive skin. As much as Shannon wanted to blaze forward, a big part of herself was begging her to slow down, to savor the moment.

Ryan moaned, then shivered under the light touch. Was Shannon going to tease her? Nonononononono. She said hot monkey sex now! Not teasing! Doubts assailed Ryan's mind. Maybe Shannon really *was* a spy meant to slowly drive her insane by making her fall in love with her and then denying sexual completion? Oh God! When did the Feds become geniuses?! Their plan was totally working!

Shannon reached around Ryan from behind and wrapped her in a warm hug, a throaty groan escaping at the feeling of her nipples pressed against Ryan's beautiful back. Shannon leaned closer and placed a gentle kiss between Ryan's shoulder blades, tasting her salty skin. Sweeping aside the taller woman's hair and standing on tiptoe, Shannon whispered against Ryan's nape hairs, "Don't worry, sexy. I'm not even thinking of teasing you."

OH MY GOD! There really was an implant! And Shannon was using it to read her mind!

"What's wrong?" the shorter woman asked worriedly, unconsciously tightening her hold on Ryan as she sensed the survivalist's obvious anxiety.

Ryan went rigid and held her breath. Closing her eyes she tried desperately NOT to think of the exact location of her hidden community (56.6 miles west of Louisville on Highway 60, and 6.4 miles south of county road 61, turn right at the dead dog)—nor the location of the money buried in Mason jars in her backyard (beneath the birdbath)—nor her top secret, super-classified computer access information (logon: conspiracy, password: trustnoone). NOOOOO!!!! She had thought it all!! The implant must have artificial intelligence capabilities!

"Ryan? Did I do something you didn't like? Or..."

Ryan whirled around in Shannon's arms, grasping the surprised woman by the waist. "How did you know I didn't want to be teased?" she asked warily. *Pink Elephants. Pink elephants. Pink elephants.*

Shannon burst out laughing. "You mean besides the fact that you're the poster child for…"

"Sexual frustration!" Ryan interrupted with a growl. Of course! Shannon didn't need to read her mind at all. She had read her tightly-wound, quivering body, which fairly begged for attention. Attention from a certain luscious, young writer, who was to die for.

"So, everything is okay?"

In answer, Ryan swooped down and passionately kissed Shannon, swallowing the smaller woman's whimpers as their tongues fought for space in each other's mouths.

Shannon's arousal flared again, and after several intense moments, she tore her lips from Ryan's. "On the ground. Now!"

Ryan immediately dropped to the beach, taking Shannon down with her, spreading her legs to accommodate the shorter woman's body nestled tightly atop hers. Ryan reached into Shannon's shorts and groaned at the feeling of slick, bare skin. "No undies?" Ryan murmured around sweet, deep kisses, vaguely disappointed. Those high-cut, black, silk panties Shannon wore were so hot! Ryan's mouth began to water, just remembering the cool, delicate fabric under her fingertips.

"Mmm…that reminds me," Shannon whispered softly, nipping at Ryan's lower lip. "I have something for you." The writer reached into her pocket and pulled out a piece of black silk cloth. "This is…well, um…" Shannon suddenly felt like an idiot. It had seemed like a good idea at the time. Of course, she had been drinking some concoction that Joe and Marty claimed to have 'specially aged' for several days.

"Your panties?" Ryan reverently took the silky fabric from Shannon's fingers. "Thanks, sweetheart." She sniffed and swallowed hard. "A girl can never have too much underwear," Ryan repeated a bit quizzically, recalling that truism as her dearly departed mother's last words to her. Well, that and 'it's only fun until somebody loses an eye'. *God, I miss you, Mom!*

"Silly." Shannon slapped Ryan's arm, then bent down and gently kissed where she had just hit. "They're um…not to wear. It's a polishing cloth for…" Shannon blinked. Was she really going to do this? Then she gazed down into Ryan's soulful, affectionate, *still* incredibly horny eyes. Yes. She would take the first step towards peace. "It's for Tiffany. See?"

Shannon held the material up in the moonlight. It had been cut into a neat square, and the letter 'T' had been lovingly stitched in the corner, using strands of long blonde hair as thread. Shannon's eyes narrowed as she considered just how much extra 'thread' the castaways now had. *No. I'm going to make nice to the 'other woman' for Ryan's sake. Besides, I have to admit that I like the short hair. And the fact that there are absolutely no mirrors on the island, and that it will take years and years to grow back, has nothing to do with it!*

Ryan gasped. Shannon was reaching out to Tiffany! Even after what she had done. The survivalist gulped back tears. Only someone who *really* cared about her would be capable of such a profound, heartfelt gesture. Did Shannon love her the way she loved the writer? She could only hope. "Thank you," Ryan finally said. She could hardly wait to show Tiffany. She had told the magnificent blade that there was nothing to be jealous about!

Shannon grinned broadly, tossing the cloth onto the pile of Ryan's crumpled clothing. "You—are—very—" Shannon punctuated each word with a tender kiss on the lips, "welcome, Ryan." Then she began kissing her way down Ryan's neck and chest.

"Shannon?"

"Hmm?" Shannon muttered, as she wrapped her lips around the very tip of a taut nipple. The blonde let out a contented purr as she began to suckle in earnest, her own center pulsing in time with the movements of her mouth.

Ryan writhed beneath Shannon, nearly dislodging her. "Mmm…Damn!" the brunette cried hoarsely, as Shannon began a gentle tugging motion with her lips. "But…but Shannon?"

"What is it, sweetheart?" Couldn't Ryan see she was workin' here?

"I've got sand…EVERYWHERE!" came the frustrated reply, even as Ryan's hands moved to Shannon's hips. Grinding their bodies together, Ryan moaned at the flawless contact.

"Oh God." Shannon's head dropped forward, and her nostrils flared. How could she be expected to maintain a conversation when Ryan did stuff like that? It was impossible! Then she remembered what the taller woman had said. "Sorry." She smiled apologetically. "But it's my turn on top!" Shannon slid her hand between their bodies and began softly stroking Ryan's inner thighs, allowing her fingertips to graze Ryan's flooded center.

Ryan gasped. Okay, maybe she could live with the sand for now.

The younger woman moaned against Ryan's breast, surprised she hadn't come from listening to the fabulous sounds that Ryan was making. They were driving her wild! "Oh, baby, you are soaked."

The prophetic words were still hanging in the air when a huge, unexpected wave crashed down onto the women's intertwined bodies, drenching them with salty sea water and depositing a hefty amount of seaweed, leaves, and other ocean muck right on top of them.

"Ack! Gross!"

Ryan spit out a mouthful of seawater. *Well, at least that washed the sand out of my ass,* she thought wryly, pulling a large palm frond from her face. The taller woman reached up and knocked away a small, flapping fish, which had managed to tangle itself in what was left of Shannon's hair, and a pile of seaweed.

Shannon stood up and began picking the huge clumps of limp vegetation off her body. *Those fuckers who made from 'From Here to*

Eternity' never showed anything like this happening! I miss my boring, queen-sized bed!

Ryan smiled, her sexual appetite only increasing as she watched Shannon pick a dangling piece of seaweed off her pink, erect nipple. There was no stopping Ryan's libido now. Nothing, not even that cruel, prankster bitch, Mother Nature, could dampen the flame Shannon had lit.

Ryan's smile shifted into a leer. Her writer looked like a topless, X-rated version of the 'Creature From the Black Lagoon'. *Damn, she's beautiful!* "C'mon. Let's get cleaned up." Ryan stood and nuzzled Shannon's throat. "Phfptt!" She spat away a large, black, water bug.

"Ryan, we can't go back to the showers at camp and have sex right there in front of everyone!" A pause. "Can we?"

A dark eyebrow arched. Shannon was turning out to be delightfully naughty! "We have an entire ocean right here." Ryan gave Shannon a 'come hither' smile and began backing into the lightly churning surf.

Shannon growled. She'd always wanted to do it in the ocean.

Without getting arrested.

But at least she had gotten to take off her beeper in the jug. The one damn time Rita couldn't find her.

When the older woman held out her hand invitingly, Shannon quickly stripped off her sodden shorts and followed Ryan into deeper waters. A few feet from her survivalist, Shannon froze, her gaze shifting to the water. "Ryan, don't the sharks come out to feed at night?"

"Whatever." Ryan surged forward, pulling Shannon into a breathless, soul-searing kiss.

The possibility of being eaten flew right out of Shannon's mind. Well, by anything other than Ryan, that is. Shannon wrapped her legs around Ryan's waist and determinedly snaked her hand between their bodies once again.

Ryan let out a languid moan as the blonde's gentle touch turned into a purposeful stroking. The taller woman's belly clenched tightly, her breath coming in short pants, her attention riveted on the throbbing between her legs and the tender lips dancing across her skin.

"That's it, sexy," Shannon cooed softly into Ryan's ear. "Feel how much I want you, how badly I've wanted to do this for you."

Ryan groaned, her toes digging into the sandy ocean floor, and her desire increasing with every beat of her pounding heart. "Oh God," she whispered harshly. "That's so…" She forgot what she was going to say when her hips jerked forward, taking in the length of Shannon's fingers.

"I love touching you like this, Ryan," Shannon mumbled, her eyes drawn to Ryan's soft lips. The motion of her fingers never wavered as she maintained the steady rhythm dictated by Ryan's hips. Leaning closer, Shannon tilted her head, and Ryan ducked down for a kiss. But the blonde pulled back, repeating the action several times until Ryan remained still, allowing the writer to lean in and sensuously trace Ryan's full lower lip with the tip of her tongue, before pulling the lip into her mouth and sucking gently.

Ryan's thighs quivered as Shannon released the taller woman's lip and moved to the hollow of her throat, licking softly and dragging her free hand down Ryan's back to her buttocks.

Closing her eyes tightly, Ryan threw her head back and hissed as though she'd been burned.

"Yes," Shannon urged, feeling Ryan begin to pulse around her fingers, her own arousal mounting. One more deep thrust of sure fingers and Ryan let loose a thunderous roar that tore through Shannon, sweeping the younger woman away, right along with her lover.

Ryan's arms tightened convulsively around Shannon, as she buried her face in soft, pale hair, her body trembling with aftershocks.

Shannon let out an enormous breath and unlocked her legs from around Ryan's waist, sinking deeper into the water, which now seemed cool against her overheated skin. Smiling, Shannon looked up into suddenly sheepish, blue eyes and wriggled her pale brows.

"Yeah, yeah. I know. I might not be able to fish here for a few days," Ryan muttered as her face colored. She was sure she'd scared away every bit of aquatic life for miles.

Shannon burst out laughing. If she was Queen of the Jungle, then her beautiful lover was most definitely King of the Sea.

<Fade out>

Castaway Farewells (Joe and Dawn)

Joe and Dawn sat side by side on a small padded bench in one of the production tents, while Pete changed his camera's battery pack. No amount of persuading by Joan could convince the couple to do separate 'farewells'. After a blunt reminder about the contract they had signed, however, Dawn and Joe agreed to make a quick, joint statement.

Joe wrapped his arm around Dawn's shoulder, mindful of the sling and crudely fashioned splint that the island's substandard medical staff had provided.

The young farm girl smiled broadly as the room began to blur and the heat from Joe's arm grew more and more intense, spreading a delicious warmth throughout her system. God, whatever Joan had given her was awesome! She felt great! And Joe smelled really good.

"Ready when you are, Pete," the bartender said impatiently.

Pete nodded, and after one more adjustment, the camera's red light began flashing.

"We're leaving the island, together," Joe announced firmly, his gaze softening when he thought of the young woman by his side. "We're going to combine our winnings and open our own bar in Indiana."

Dawn frowned and shook her head 'no'.

"Kansas?"

Another negative response.

Shit! He knew it was one of those useless farm states. "Ohio?"

Dawn shrugged. Close enough. They all grew corn. Leaning forward, she placed a soft kiss on his bearded cheek, giggling as the short, bristly hairs tickled her lips.

Joe flushed and leaned away from the suddenly amorous farm girl.

"C'mon, Joe," Dawn moaned huskily, pulling the man back against her.

Pete began looking around for his cigarettes.

Doing his best to ignore the lips that were now sucking his throat with an almost superhuman strength, Joe looked directly into the camera. He opened his mouth to speak, but Dawn surged forward, plunging her tongue into his mouth as she pulled him into a desperately passionate kiss.

Joe whimpered.

Pete whimpered.

Joan, who was hiding in a dark corner, watching the taping, whimpered.

Bravely, Joe pulled away again. "Dawn, sweetheart," he admonished gently. He gazed into black pupils the size of nickels. "You're stoned!"

"Umm...Hmm..." Dawn giggled again. Then suddenly, she became aware of the camera. "Hi, Mama!" She waved her good hand. "You'll never believe what Joe taught me to do with my -" The bartender clamped his hand over Dawn's mouth and grinned weakly, the sounds of Dawn's father loading his 12 gauge shotgun in his head.

Dawn slapped away Joe's hand and began unbuttoning her cotton tank top. She was hot.

"What did you give her?" Joe demanded angrily. Okay, not too angrily. He really just wished that they were alone. And that Dawn wasn't injured.

Pete finally took pity on Joe when the young woman straddled Joe's thighs and began grinding her hips against his stomach. Besides, it wasn't like he didn't already have this on film. Three times. "Just say 'goodbye', man!" the pudgy blonde whispered loudly.

Joe nodded but it was Dawn's cheerful voice that filled the hut. "Goodbye, man!"

<Fade out>

Panelist's Article: A Novelist Writes by Maggie Goodheart

It's strange the way the mind wanders when you're sitting in a bookstore window, your hand beginning to cramp from signing too many autographs. Yesterday, for example, I was thinking about Castaway.

One of the many writing techniques I utilize in my novels (the latest of which, 'Blue Touchpaper', is available from all good bookstores) is Ruskin's 'Pathetic Fallacy'. Crediting Nature with human emotions is a device that has been masterfully used by many novelists, and can substantially raise the tension and heighten the atmosphere of a story.

I think I detect its subtle presence in Castaway…in the moments when a typhoon maliciously targets Paradise Island, or when sadistic monkeys and crabs try to stop two horny women from making love.

That's not all though. Whether by design or happy accident, Castaway not only makes use of the Pathetic Fallacy, it also features Pathetic Phalluses.

Most of the male team members (and many of the female ones too, but that's another story) are, for want of a better word, limp. In fact, the phallus that stands most erect and tall is not a *real* one at all (though it could prick you) and even has a female name. I'm talking about Ryan's knife Tiffany, of course.

All of which goes to show: sometimes fact *is* stranger than fiction…or more pathetic, anyway…and the mind of the novelist works in mysterious ways.

Must rush. Got another book signing to go to. Wonder what I'll think about today!

EPISODE EIGHT

Something Wicked This Way Comes

Exhausted after an impossibly long day of shooting, Pete finally stalked off into the jungle, tripping over an exposed root on his way out of camp. The cameraman's overstressed, naturally flabby body rejected as foreign the new muscles that this job was forcing him to develop. Pete cursed and kicked the root, then yelped over his now injured foot.

Two cameramen followed Pete into the jungle, chuckling evilly. The crew had a pool going over the pudgy blond's life expectancy. They sincerely hoped he wouldn't figure out that they'd weighted his camera bag down with rocks. Pete was a friend and all. But hell, the pool *was* up to fifty dollars!

As the last cameraman disappeared, the castaways breathed a collective sigh of relief. They settled into their makeshift beds and hammocks, each dreading whatever demented challenge Joan had cooked up for the next day. They shut their eyes, waiting for the nightmares to begin.

For the first few weeks, except for the tribal council meetings, the contestants had pretty much been left alone during the evenings. But now, all that had changed. Pete had explained that a copycat show called 'Peeping Tom', set in a house in New York City, was eating away at their ratings. Shannon snorted to herself. Those stupid fuckers at network programming (a.k.a. Rita and her dogs). How many filthy voyeurs did the BTBC actually think were out there? It wasn't like *all* of Rita's ex-husbands had Neilsen ratings boxes!

In a desperate bid to boost their ratings, the challenges were becoming more and more extreme. Joan, the psychotic network hussy, whose cackle haunted every islander's dreams, was getting increasingly desperate. Shannon truly expected the next challenge to include hand-to-hand combat, more boa constrictors, or full frontal nudity. The blonde bit her lip, suspecting that Joan would somehow find a way to combine all three if it were possible.

But no matter *what* the challenge was, Shannon couldn't wait to kick Marty's chauvinist pig ass! Annoyance with the construction foreman had recently given way to outright repulsion. The relentless camera coverage, combined with the miserable humidity and the stress of competing for a million dollars, had rendered all the islanders weary and irritable. Green eyes narrowed dangerously. Of the remaining castaways, Marty was by *far* the worst.

More than once, Shannon had physically restrained Ryan to keep the survivalist from castrating the man. Of course, she now promised herself that, if Marty opened his yack one more time, she'd simply let nature take its course. Shannon resolved to visit the tall brunette in prison regularly, wondering idly if they had heard of conjugal visits in this part of the world.

The first time Shannon had calmly informed Ryan that she couldn't just kill him outright and feed him to the crabs (Shannon unconsciously clutched her left breast), Ryan had insisted that Shannon break the news to Tiffany herself. Shannon sighed, remembering her heart-to-heart talk to the 'other woman'.

"Here!" Ryan thrust the razor sharp blade in Shannon's face. "*You* have to explain to her why we can't make the gene pool a happier place."

"You're kidding, right?"

"Do I look like I'm kidding?"

"Um…Yes?"

Ryan simply arched an impatient eyebrow.

Cringing, and half-expecting some fool to jump out and shout, 'Smile! You're on Candid Camera!' Shannon tentatively reached out and grabbed the blade between two outstretched fingers.

"She doesn't like to be held like that."

Shannon stared at Ryan for several seconds before speaking. "What in the hell are you talking about?"

Ryan reached out and stroked the shiny handle. "It's like you're afraid of her or something."

"Imagine that."

Ryan rolled her eyes. "Grasp the handle and let her warm your palm. Don't hold her between your fingers." *Feel the love, sweetheart!*

Shannon wrapped her fingers around the handle. Noting Ryan's satisfied nod, she swallowed nervously and focused on the knife, still not quite believing what she was about to do. "Umm…you see, it's not appropriate…"

"Tiffany," Ryan immediately interrupted.

Shannon's gaze darted upward. "What?"

"You didn't say her name. It objectifies her not to personalize your conversation. Call her Tiffany."

Green eyes narrowed suspiciously. *Objectifies?* Shannon scanned the bushes for hidden cameras.

"Shannon?"

"Okay. Okay." The writer took a deep breath as she gripped Tiffany. *Ryan is just eccentric. Eccentric is doable. I could love eccentric.* She felt a warm, comforting palm come to rest between her shoulder blades, then begin a

gentle tracing motion across her back. Shannon's eyes fluttered closed at the touch. *Oh, yeah. I could love eccentric.*

"Shannon?"

"Right." An exhale. "Tiffany, you can't go around cut-
ting off men's testicles…unless of course you ever meet
Trent Bender." Shannon grinned evilly. The sound of
Ryan clearing her throat refocused her attention.
"Anyway, it's illegal and just plain wrong." *There.* She
paused, hoping that was enough.

A long, painfully silent moment passed before Shannon
decided that it wasn't, and added, "I'm *truly* sorry."

"That was great, baby!" Ryan said happily, kissing the
top of Shannon's head and taking back the blade.

"Well?"

"Well, what?"

"Is she happy now?" Shannon's hands moved to her
hips. "Does she understand?!"

Dark brows drew together in confusion. "How would
I know? Damn, Shannon, it's not like she talks back,"
Ryan snorted. "She's a knife, for Christ's sake!"

And with that, Ryan headed off toward the beach, leaving a slack-
jawed Shannon staring at her retreating form.

An uneasy feeling pulled Shannon from her thoughts. Her stomach
churned, and her face twisted into an uncharacteristic scowl. Something
was coming. Something bad. She could sense it deep in her bones, and felt
the irrational need to escape camp and find Ryan. Ryan had fled the constant attention of the cameras several hours earlier, under the guise of
hunting for some real food, much to Joan's annoyance.

Shannon lifted the blanket she'd inherited from a departed castaway,
and padded down the beach until the camp's softly-glowing fire was
barely visible out of the corner of her eye. Smoothing the blanket out

across the soft grass at the beach's edge, she lay down and gazed up into a sky lit with a million stars. The breeze was stronger here and Shannon closed her eyes, allowing the wind to roll over her as she tried to ignore her roiling stomach.

"WHY AREN'T YOU ANSWERING YOUR PAGER?! I'VE BEEN CALLING YOU ALL NIGHT!" a voice boomed from behind Shannon.

Shannon flew to her feet. "I'm sorry! The batteries must be…" Shannon whirled around, then froze. "Oh my God," she whispered.

"Hi, Shannon. How's tricks?" A wicked smile gleamed through the darkness.

"It can't be!" *I knew I shouldn't have eaten those mushrooms after Ryan told me not to! But this is too horrible to be a nightmare! Oh, Jesus. It's my real life!* "Hello, Rita."

Smirking, Rita looked her employee up and down. "You look like shit, honey."

"Don't call me that!"

Rita began to chuckle. "What happened to your…" She gestured to Shannon's new coif.

Shannon immediately tucked a blowing strand of short, shaggy hair behind her ear. "I like it this way!" Green eyes scanned the beach for Ryan. The survivalist was nowhere in sight. "What are you doing here?" Shannon hissed to Rita.

"Why, I'm here to see who shoved a stick up the golden goose's ass." Rita made a tsking noise. " Ratings are way down."

"That's not our fault. I…"

Rita held up a hand. "Save it, honey. Have you done what I asked?"

"I'm here, aren't I?"

"Shannon," Rita warned, drawing out the younger woman's name.

Shannon stamped her foot in the sand, for the first time missing the high heels she normally wore to work. "I am not sleeping with one of the men!"

"Oh yes, you are." Rita began circling the shorter woman, her eyes roaming proprietarily over her employee. "Were you always this tan and skinny?" she commented enviously.

"No, and I'm not going to sleep with one of the men! Do you even watch this sucky show? This isn't skinny. I was starving until last week! I'm surprised you can't see through me!" A faint odor suddenly grew stronger as the wind shifted. Perfume. Soap. Shampoo. Shannon sniffed. Tide with Bleach? "You smell." How come she hadn't ever noticed these things before? Well, except for that nasty perfume that was attracting every mosquito on the island to Rita. She'd always noticed that.

"*I* smell?" Rita laughed, squashing a bug against her cheek. "Why do you think I keep moving? I'm heading upwind."

"Go away," the writer ground out, as she discreetly sniffed her armpit. Ryan had never complained.

"I don't think you realize what's at stake here." Rita's face turned to stone. "You *will* do this." She began clicking her perfectly painted nails together nervously. Shannon should have been agreeing with her by now. What the hell had gotten into her assistant? Other than Ryan, of course. "This wasn't just my decision. Bender said we needed to up the heterosexual content of the show."

"He said that?"

"Well, actually, he fired four other executives, and said, 'Those bitches are ruining my show! I wanna see some good old-fashioned, *normal* fuckin'!'"

"But…"

"Dawn and that hunk of a man, Joe, are gone. And Marva's married. So she's out. Besides, we all know married women don't screw. Just ask my four, no, five ex-husbands."

Shannon shot Rita a skeptical look.

"Besides, we got a good look at Marva's saggy tits during that strip poker game, and Bender gave them, I mean her, the thumbs down."

"You filmed that?!"

"You'd be surprised what we've filmed."

"Pigs!"

"Of course. This is television, sweetheart."

"Don't call me that either!"

The platinum haired woman shook her head in confusion. Why was Shannon making such a big fuss about this? "As I was saying, Marva is out. And I don't see Miss Camouflage jumping back across the fence anytime soon. So that leaves you."

"I won't."

"You will…assuming you want to keep your job and that severance pay we prom…er…discussed." Rita hadn't screwed all those lawyers for nothing.

"Discussed? What do you mean 'discussed'? We had a deal!"

Rita smiled, and Shannon's heart sank.

The young writer was torn. She felt like a puppet with Rita pulling the strings. But she couldn't be unemployed, could she? She'd have to work two or three jobs to earn as much as she made with the BTBC. When would she work on her novel? No. She had bills to pay. Responsibilities. How could she allow her Guatemalan foster child to starve just because she was too selfish to have sex with one of the men? Okay, so she didn't have a Guatemalan foster child, but her credit card bills were really, really big!

Rita's smile grew larger. Shannon was caving in like she always did.

"Rita, I can't. You don't understand. I…I mean, I think I'm in love."

"Don't be a fool, Shannon."

Shannon let out a deep breath. She was finished being Rita's puppet. She could survive unemployment. She could survive damn near anything! 'Castaway' and Ryan had taught her that. There was no way she was going to betray Ryan's tentative trust. Not for anything or anyone. "No," she said simply, rendering Rita speechless.

"I see," Rita finally commented. She pretended to think for a moment. "Well, if we can't up the hetero content, we'll have to boost the ratings another way." *Time to pull out the big guns.* "I suppose a scandal involving one of the castaways would serve the same purpose," she drawled. "I could always hire a few of my favorite private detectives to do a little digging into Ryan's past." Rita eyed Shannon intently, wanting to be sure she was crystal clear. "I'm sure we could find *something* the viewing public and FBI would find interesting."

"You wouldn't!" Shit! Ryan was right. Just because she was paranoid didn't mean people really weren't after her. And when Rita began digging for dirt, she *always* found something. Whether it actually existed or not.

Rita remained silent as Shannon chewed her lip. *No matter what it takes, I can't let her hurt Ryan. I won't.* "I refuse to actually have sex with either of them."

"Just foreplay then," Rita agreed eagerly. Something was better than nothing. She'd already investigated Ryan and she was disgustingly clean. Who'd have guessed? Unlike other wacko survivalists, Ryan just preferred to stay the hell away from people. Rita had to give brunette credit for being that smart.

Shannon made a face. "I'm willing to…." She blanched at that mental image. "No, I won't do that. Maybe I could…" That one was even more disgusting. "Eww…Nope, that's not gonna happen either." Furiously rubbing her temples, Shannon bit the bullet. "You'll get…"

"Something good?"

The younger woman swallowed hard, but nodded reluctantly.

"With Marty."

Green eyes widened. "Arturo is a man, too!" Damn! Kissing Arturo would be like kissing another girl. Arturo was so far past being a gay man he could almost be considered a lesbian

"Ah…ah…ah…" Rita waggled her finger. "I told you before that he didn't count. As far as you're concerned, Arturo's penis is purely cosmetic."

Shannon grimaced.

"Do we have a deal?"

Shannon squeezed her eyes shut, trying to push aside the wave of queasiness that swept over her, as she considered any sort of physical contact with Marty and his hairy back. *God, if this isn't love, I don't know what is. Only for Ryan.* "Deal."

"I knew you'd see things my way!" Rita exclaimed happily, swatting away another mosquito. Tomorrow she would be on the first plane back to dog-eat-dog, sterile, crime-ridden Los Angeles, where pollutants killed all the mosquitoes.

Just as God intended.

Hearing a faint rustling sound, the women turned toward the bushes, but quickly dismissed the noise as a bird. It had been a few days since Ryan had had Shannon, and several of the braver feathered creatures had moved back to their natural habitat.

Marty held his breath, praying they wouldn't investigate his hiding place. He had finally found them, after stumbling through the jungle for far too long in the darkness. Shannon didn't know how to lay false trails as well as Ryan. He *knew* he'd get to see some good girl-on-girl action eventually. Damn, those network people were geniuses. What could be a bigger ratings-grabber than two red-hot lesbians going after each other, week after week? Nothing he could think of.

But who was that blonde with Shannon? Ooo—maybe they were going to meet Ryan here for a threesome! That had always been his deepest wish for 'Charlie's Angels'. It had kept him watching for years. Wishing he had some beer and peanuts to go with the show, Marty wiped a drop of anticipatory drool from his chin, and settled into his hiding spot.

"So tell me a little bit about Ryan," Rita asked. "Is she as wild as she looks?"

Marty cocked his head, listening closer. He was wondering the same damn thing.

"Don't even say her name!" Shannon snarled.

Rita looked at Shannon innocently. "What? No girl talk?"

"Bitch." Shannon took a menacing step forward.

"Wait!" Rita quickly stepped away. "My lips are sealed." That didn't seem to appease the angry blonde. So she upped the ante, to avoid physical pain. "No one has to know you're a BTBC employee. Your paycheck will be deposited as soon as I get back to LA," she lied. *Not bad, under pressure,* she thought happily.

"Goodbye, Rita." Shannon began stomping away. "I'm going to go and throw up now."

"I know you'll make me proud!" Rita called after her, moving into the jungle. *Now which way did that nice cameraman say to go?* Pete had pulled Rita out of a warm pool of quicksand, after Joan had explained, in detail, the exact route to the castaway's camp. *Somebody's gonna get lucky tonight,* she sang to herself, slapping another bug.

When the coast was clear, Marty stood up from his hiding place. Shannon worked for the network? He scratched his stubbly chin as he strode back to camp. Knowledge was power. And right now, Marty was feeling *mighty* powerful.

*   *   *

Breakfast in the Alpha camp was strained. Strained fish guts, to be exact. Ryan hadn't been able to catch as many fish as she had hoped and they had to do something to spread them around.

Ryan couldn't figure out what was going on. Ever since Pete arrived and started filming, Shannon had been sitting across the fire from her. Next to Marty. And she kept leaning across him to ladle out more soup. Was Shannon deliberately trying to get her turned on? Ryan scratched her head. This relationship stuff was really confusing.

Marva was happily slurping down her soup. She was relieved their stay on the island was almost over. As one of the last five contestants on the island, she was guaranteed winning at least one hundred thousand dollars. That should be more than enough to pay off the mortgage, buy a new truck and fix poor Edwina's teeth.

The foreman glanced down as he felt Shannon's breast brush against his forearm…again. It felt good. Really good. And he'd like to feel more of it. But—his testicles twitched—it would have to be over Ryan's dead body. Literally. Otherwise, he wasn't risking the family jewels for a quick grope. This didn't stop him from leaning into Shannon, however.

Shannon's skin crawled as Marty pressed into the tender flesh of her breast. She was still thinking of how it felt to have Ryan's mouth attached to that particular appendage. She didn't want to have to cut it off simply because it came in contact with Martin's nasty skin. *You're doing this for Ryan, Shannon. Just remember that.*

Arturo was blissfully unaware of any discomfort around the fire.

"All right, it's that time," Pete announced, shifting his camera pack to his other shoulder. Poor bastards.

"God, I hate that time."

"¿A que hora?" Arturo asked.

Ryan cocked her head. Something didn't seem quite right with Arturo. But she couldn't quite put her finger on it. Kinda like she couldn't put her finger on Shannon. Blue eyes narrowed dangerously. Marty was going to lose his fingers altogether, if they got any closer to Shannon's bra snap.

What in the hell was Shannon doing?

Had she dreamed everything between her and Shannon? She lifted her coconut shell soup bowl and sniffed. She couldn't detect any drugs. But, if they were going to use mild, mind-altering drugs, the government would be sure they were colorless and odorless.

Was it all a dream?

Was she in 'Dallas'?

Was she even on an island? Was this like the moon landing? Perhaps they were on a sound stage in Southern California and all of this was fake.

Maybe her Kentucky hideaway wasn't real either. Were her parents really gone? Her brothers? Was she even Ryan? What if she was a pod person?

Those taken are always the last to know!

"Ryan?" Marva called, breaking into her thoughts. "Ryan?"

The survivalist looked up with wary blue eyes. "Maybe."

Marva leaned down and felt the brunette's forehead. It was cool, but Ryan's face was flushed. Maybe she was coming down with something. "Are you ready for the competition?"

Ryan shook her head, clearing her thoughts. Maybe they were being beamed into her head by the microwave manufacturers. That would explain things. So many possible conspiracies to unravel. "Yeah, I guess." She looked around the campsite. "Where's Shannon?"

The homemaker made a vague gesture. "She went ahead with…Marty." Seeing Ryan's fallen expression, she laid a comforting hand on her shoulder. "I'm sorry."

"Are you real?"

Marva leaned down and kissed Ryan's forehead. Southerners understood and accepted eccentric people. Hell, they invented the word. "I am. Come on, let's go kick some ass."

*   *   *

The contestants stared at the obstacle course that had been laid out before them.

"Is the ring of fire really necessary?" Marva asked nervously. It looked like a hula hoop that had been set aflame. She had seen tigers jump through something like that in the circus once.

Joan smiled. *Oh yes, it was necessary.* With any luck, someone's hair would catch on fire. The burning plastic was emitting toxic fumes that had already sent several of the crew into coughing fits. *Wimps.*

"So, first we have to walk the plank over the quicksand, then swim across the lagoon with the sea snakes, then jump through the ring of fire, and finally run back along the beach?"

"Barefoot," Joan amended, but didn't mention the broken shells she had strewn along the beach earlier that morning.

"Why barefoot?" Ryan challenged.

Joan shrugged, smiling malevolently. The paranoid always ask inconvenient questions. "Everyone ready?" She watched as they all took off their sandals.

"I am!" Shannon giggled like a schoolgirl, and batted her eyelashes at Marty. The writer prayed that her stomach would behave and she wouldn't puke on his feet right here and now. The confused look Ryan was giving her wasn't helping much either.

"You are one chica loca," Arturo stage-whispered to the blonde. He would never do anything to make Ryan upset. She scared him.

Ryan's eyes narrowed. "Chica loca?" she repeated. "Crazy girl?"

Arturo held up his hands and backed away. "I didn't mean anything by it."

Spanish? Ryan scratched her head. Something wasn't right.

"On your mark, get set, go!" Joan thundered.

The five took off running, glad to have only one more challenge after this one.

They raced the short distance to the five thin logs laid over a pit of quicksand. It took but a moment to realize that the logs had been slicked with leftover oil from the last challenge.

Shannon frowned. *I bet that was Rita's idea. The bitch.* Carefully, she made her way over the pit. At one point, she nearly fell into the murky mess, but a strong hand caught her. She turned to thank Ryan, but blanched when she realized it was Marty. *Oh God, don't let him think I owe him anything.*

I saved her ass, now it's mine. Marty leered at the anatomical part in question.

Marva crossed herself. She wasn't Catholic but it seemed appropriate. She was sure Marty was about to die.

Strangely, Ryan seemed not to notice. She was focused on Arturo. "Where in Brazil are you from?" she asked, slowing down until she was even with the prancing man.

"Rio." They made it to the water's edge. Arturo put his toe in the water and cringed. "Floaties, please. A little help."

*   *   *

Marty crossed the finish line, the trail of blood from his cut and bleeding feet staining the sand behind him. "I won, I won!" he crowed, jumping up to celebrate. He immediately regretted that decision. He wondered if Joan would let him have a couple of Band Aids.

Still preoccupied, Ryan carefully made her way down the beach. *Spanish. Arturo from Brazil speaks Spanish.*

He was a plant!

"See you five at tribal council tonight."

Marva pulled a piece of shell out of her heel. "Do we really have to hike the two miles to the council? Surely we could vote in our camp."

Joan shook her head emphatically. They had to walk to the set. She had paid good money to import several hundred bats. She was planning on releasing them during the castaways' hike, and taping the resulting hysteria. "Be there."

*   *   *

"I'm going to turn into a vampire!" Arturo shrieked. "I'm going to be a blood sucker!"

"Well, some kind of sucker," Marty muttered, earning himself a swat from Marva.

Ryan looked at the bat impaled on the end of Tiffany. It had finally stopped twitching, and its tiny fangs had retracted. *Wonder how these things taste barbecued?*

"This is getting ridiculous!" Shannon roared. The writer marched over to Joan and stood toe to toe with the host. "Bats are *not* indigenous to this island! *You* had them brought here!" Shannon had done some research on the island for Rita when the show was still in its pre-production stage.

Seeing an opportunity, Marty queried, "How do you know that?"

Shannon's expression transformed into that of a deer caught in the headlights. Or at least like Clinton in the hallway by the oval office. "Uh…" She looked across the set and saw Rita, who was out of camera range, shake her finger. "I…I…"

"Yes?" Marty was feeling very powerful. *One million dollars here I come!*

"I was a geography major in college."

"No, you weren't." Ryan reached into her backpack and pulled out a tattered 'Meet Your Fellow Castaways' brochure. "Communications."

"English Literature!" Shannon corrected. *Wait, that didn't help.* "I had a double major," she finished lamely.

"Isn't geography about land formations? Zoology is about animals," Ryan persisted.

Green eyes glared at Ryan, willing the survivalist to be quiet. *Now is not a good time to be paranoid, honey.*

Marva decided to help out. She didn't know what was going on between Shannon and Ryan, or Shannon and Marty, or Shannon and the island, but she really wanted to get this over with. "Have you seen any on the island before, Marty? I think it's pretty obvious they were imported for the ratings."

Joan's mouth dropped open. She hadn't expected the little housewife to be quite so outspoken. *Bitch. Bet you're going home tonight, though.* The crew had another pool going for who the final survivors would be after the tribal council tonight. Of course, if the vote didn't go the way she had bet, she'd just change the votes before reading them on-camera. "Let's start the council."

"Wait!" Ryan interjected. It had been bothering her all day, kinda like an itch in the crack of your ass that you can't quite reach, and now she had it. "Someone here is not who they say they are!"

Shit, shit, shit! Shannon closed her eyes and waited for her world to collapse.

"Arturo is not from Brazil."

Shit, shit…huh? Shannon peeked open an eye and looked over at the hairdresser.

"Si, I am."

"That's the whole point," Ryan countered. "You speak Spanish."

"Si."

"They speak Portuguese in Brazil."

Arturo winced. "They do?" Damn that sexy, no-good, lying Raul!

"Who are you? Where are you from?" Ryan demanded, advancing on him.

Shannon interposed herself between the two. "Put Tiffany away, Ryan."

"Tiffany?" Marty scratched his crotch. Damn, he wished he had popcorn. Was there a third woman involved? That would be really hot.

Betrayed blue eyes met Shannon's. So Shannon had finally torn herself away from Marty long enough to notice her, huh? She had never told anyone else Tiffany's name. And now it had been broadcast to the entire viewing audience. Unfortunately, she didn't know that audience amounted to about three people, who had no lives.

"Arturo," Shannon looked away from Ryan, unable to meet her hurt, confused gaze. She tried to take charge of the situation. Someone had to. "Can you tell us what's going on?"

"I…I…I'm not from Brazil."

Ryan felt a flood of relief course through her. *I knew it. I am not paranoid. I am just sensitive!*

Shannon couldn't believe her ears. *Is there anyone on the island who doesn't have a secret past? Jesus! Is this a fucking soap opera or stupid reality show?* "Where are you from?"

He began weeping. "I'm from Tijuana! I came over when I was six. But, no one wants a hairdresser from Mexico. Brazil is another story! They love exotic Brazil! So, I tell them I am from Rio. And I do the flamenco."

"I thought the flamenco was from Spain."

Arturo wept louder. He should have known he couldn't trust a man who could refuse a hot oil treatment! Well, at least the kind they gave at the salon.

"Flamingo?" Pete asked. "He does a pink bird? That's sick."

Marva rolled her eyes. And people thought Southerners were dumb.

"Can we vote?" Marty asked. If they could get the voting over, maybe the girls would get naked.

Joan was thrilled. This was going to be a good episode after all! "Sure. Let's assemble the tribal council and…"

"Whatever…" Marty marched over to the voting hut. He wrote his vote on the paper provided there. "Arturo. Time to go home. Wherever that is."

Next in the hut was Ryan. "I like Arturo, but I don't trust him now."

Marva voted for Arturo as well. "I have many reasons for this. First, Marty won immunity. Second, I refuse to vote off another woman. Well, at least one born a woman anatomically. And third, going alphabetically, Arturo is first."

Shannon walked in, wrote 'Arturo' on the paper, and left. She refused to say a word. When she got back to L.A., she was going to personally replace Rita's hair bleach with battery acid.

After Arturo voted, Joan went and gathered the ballot box. She brought it to the center of the tribal council set. " Remember, the decision is final. Those voted off must leave immediately." She paused dramatically, savoring her time on-camera.

"Can we hurry this up a bit?" Marty complained. "It looks like it's gonna storm."

Joan barely resisted giving him the finger. "The first vote: Arturo."

Arturo gasped and covered his mouth. "Me?"

"Arturo," Joan read again.

"Two?" Arturo asked. "Are we sure they are not votes to stay?"

"Arturo," Joan said again.

"Tres?"

"Arturo," Joan read for the fourth time.

The hairstylist looked at all the other castaways. "You all voted for me? Even you, Channon? Even after the makeover?"

Shannon hung her head in shame.

"And the final vote...Marty."

Marty held up his immunity token. "They can't vote for me! I have immunity!"

Joan frowned. *Why did there always have to be some fuck-up? Could it be because the contestants don't have two brain cells to rub together between them?*

"So who's the second person to get tossed?" Marva asked cautiously.

Joan shrugged. "No one. Only Arturo. The other vote was invalid." There. That was easier.

"I want to change my vote!" Arturo screeched, even as a couple of the production crew were leading him away.

Shannon smirked. "I don't suppose we could vote you off the island, Joan?"

<Fade out>

146

Castaway Farewell (Arturo)

Pete rolled his guys. "Ya gotta stop bawling or we've never going to get this, Arturo!" Damn. It was already past dinnertime. And the crew was having tacos and refried beans in honor of the fallen Mexican hairdresser.

Arturo wiped his eyes with a tissue supplied by the cameraman and opened his mouth to speak.

Pete hurried into position but no sound came from Arturo other than a loud hiccup that was followed by more heart-wrenching sobs. "For the love of God, at least pretend you've got a pair!" Pete groaned. Arturo had been bawling and bitching ever since his 'secret' came to light.

Arturo held the sodden tissue against his cheeks. "I...I..." the Mexican took a calming breath, "I don't expect you to understand, you lover of demon, lying women!" he spat.

Pete could only agree. "Damn, you're a bitch," the cameraman muttered. Arturo reminded him of all the two-faced, soul devouring beasts (aka women) he had dated who always wanted to leave baseball games during the seventh inning stretch and never appreciated the true greatness of beer.

Suddenly, Arturo stood up and thrust one hip to the side, resting a palm on his slender rear end. "Joo women are all alike!" His limp wrist swung a shaky finger toward the camera. "Joo cannot be trusted! My mammy was right!" He bared his fangs like a cat in heat.

Jew women? Pete scratched his head, not even bothering to focus or move the camera anymore. He had always heard Hispanics were anti-Semites, but being a happy, Midwestern, Lutheran, white boy, he didn't give a rat's ass.

"I fix jour hair, I wax jour upper lips. I draw attention away from jour ugly noses, poorly shaped eyebrows and beady eyes. And in the end, jour kind betrays me. Benedict Arnold! Tokyo Rose! Mata Hari! I'm talking to joo, Raul! Joo know who joo are! Don't joo change that channel, cabron! When I get home, joo had better have your skinny ass out of my beautiful apartment and my waterbed fumigated." Arturo stopped ranting but then added as an after thought, "And don't even think of touching my Yentl CD!"

Pete's eyes widened when Arturo suddenly ended his tirade and squared his shoulders. "It doesn't matter that Channon and Ryan and Marva betrayed me." He really couldn't blame Marty. The construction foreman's attraction for him could only be kept hidden for so long. He had only voted Arturo off the island because of his fear of coming out. "I am so over it now," Arturo announced wiping his tears with the back of his hand. "In fact, I feel pretty. Oh, so prettyyy...." His words lengthen out until he was belting out the happy tune, his body gyrating to his own beat. "I feel pretty.........and witty.......and GAAAAAAAAAAAAAAAAAAAAYYYYYYYYYY."

"And I pity...any girl that isn't you todaaaaaaaay." Pete couldn't help but join in.

With a nod to the cameraman, Arturo gathered his used tissues and pranced out the hut. He'd heard rumors that the resort where the departing castaways were housed had a disco and a weekly talent show.

He could do all their hair and makeup. Who needed a million dollars?

<Fade out>

Panelist's Article: Sick, Sick, Sick! by Dr. Maura

I again would like to extend my thanks to BTBC for allowing me this input into the series. Frankly, I don't understand why you didn't use the suggestions I sent in. I believe the Homo agenda has, again, infiltrated the upper echelon of management. Why else would the offer of the complete library of my radio tapes for the Castaways and their staff to listen to on the island be turned down?

My heterosexual husband came home last week with some videos. He had been away for a few weeks, shopping for a loaf of bread. Funny, he was unable to find any bread in a three state area. Anyway, he brought home some videos he found lying near a dumpster, no doubt thrown there by someone who decided to change her vile lesbian ways. These videos revealed some of the very sexual positions we have seen in this series.

Again, I must shout my mantra: this is sick, sick, sick! We viewed the videos numerous times, going as far as using the slow motion feature on our American-made VCR to make sure what we saw was really what we saw.

I simply don't understand why anyone would want to dress up and perform such acts. It isn't Christian. And, if anyone does happen to come across an old video from 1986 titled "The Stockings in Maura's Closet", it is just a coincidence the actress looks so much like me.

I am sickened by this series. Trying to equate the love between two women with the love between a man and a woman is unreasonable. Why, next thing you know, people will be saying that love is love regardless of gender. Pshaw, stick that in your water-filled pipe and smoke it.

EPISODE NINE

Breakfast at Tiffany's

The next morning, Ryan awoke early. Shannon hadn't slept beside her, further confirming her belief that what she thought was a 'relationship' was really nothing more than an implanted memory, meant to distract her from winning the prize money. The government was smart. Very smart.

She would have to be smarter. Ryan vowed to focus on being better, stronger, and faster. To do that, she would need food. Remembering where a bunch of squirrels was nesting, she headed off into the jungle for some breakfast.

Shannon heard the survivalist leave the camp, and snuck out behind her. She hadn't slept well at all. The island got chilly at night, and without Ryan to snuggle with, it had been colder than Hillary Clinton's right tit. Which was downright frigid. Or so an ex-girlfriend who had spent the night in the Lincoln bedroom had assured Shannon.

They walked inland for about half an hour, Shannon being very careful to follow Ryan's trail. Fortunately, the brunette wasn't trying to hide her tracks, so it wasn't difficult. Tiffany was cutting a wide swath through the jungle. Finally, Ryan stopped and began examining the trunk of a large tree.

As Ryan looked for the telltale squirrel inlet, Tiffany kept trying to etch the bark. "What, girl? What do you want to write?"

In response, Tiffany carved a heart in the bark. In the left half, she added an 'R' and in the right, an 'S'.

Ryan sighed. "No, Tiffany, that was all a dream. We imagined it. I knew it was too good to be true."

"It wasn't," Shannon answered, stepping out into the open.

How did she sneak up on me like that? "What are you doing here?" Ryan moved to stand in front of the carving.

"I followed you."

"Why?"

Shannon kept approaching, moving slowly as she swallowed her own nervousness. "To apologize."

It wasn't a dream or implanted memory! Shannon and I really were together. And...she really was fawning all over Marty yesterday. After what we shared. "Okay," came the very hesitant response.

"Remember when I told you that I used to work for the network?"

Ryan nodded warily.

"That was half true. I am kinda freelancing for them right now."

"You are a plant?" Ryan had to remind herself that big, bad survivalists did not cry.

An emphatic shake of the head was Shannon's reply, her heart clenching at the sight of watery blue eyes. "No. But they try to make me do things. And yesterday, they told me I had to flirt with Marty. Or..." Small, blonde writers didn't have any rules against crying, so she did.

Being careful to sheath Tiffany first, Ryan stepped over and gathered Shannon up in her arms. "Shh, it's okay."

"No, it's not!" Shannon pushed away from Ryan. "I'm sorry, Ryan. I should have told that wicked Rita to go back to hell. But Ryan, she says she has something on you. And if I don't do what she says, she'll expose you."

Ryan laughed. "Has something on me?" She began laughing even harder, until her body was shaking like Monica Lewinsky's thighs. "There isn't anything on me, Shannon. My mother gave birth at home. I don't have a birth certificate or a driver's license or a social security card. To most of the world, I don't exist." Ryan shrugged. "And for those who take the time to really go looking, well, there's nothing to find. I'm totally clean."

"That bitch!" Shannon roared. "That lying, sneaking, no-good, conniving, plastic-inflated, peroxide-coated bitch!" She reached over and carefully extracted Tiffany from Ryan's belt. "Would you like to help me out, Tiffany? I have someone I would very much like you to meet. I think we should invite Rita for breakfast at Tiffany's." She chuckled evilly, thinking of the hapless bat that Tiffany had impaled the night before.

Ryan's hand carefully closed over her baby. "Tiffany is a gentle knife."

"She wanted to cut off Marty's balls," Shannon countered.

"Good point. But can we kiss and make up first?"

Shannon smiled. "Oh, yeah."

As their lips met and the kiss deepened, both women lost themselves in the urgency of the moment. Ryan crushed the petite woman against her, glad to know she hadn't been brainwashed, as she had feared. Shannon clung to the sturdy frame of the survivalist as though her life depended on it.

God, this must be true love. I hear gunfire, Ryan thought.

God, this must be true love. I hear fireworks, Shannon thought.

As the kiss continued, so did the explosions.

Finally, the two broke away from each other and cocked their heads to listen more carefully. "Uh, Ryan…is that what I think it is?"

Ryan nodded grimly. "I'd say we've been invaded."

*   *   *

"What do you mean 'invaded'?" Shannon huffed as Ryan pushed her to the ground, and they began low crawling back toward the beach.

Ryan snorted. It didn't take a genius to identify M-16 fire. She sniffed the air. A left-handed shooter using hollow point bullets and no flash suppressor had probably shot off the rounds. Ryan looked fondly at Shannon's innocent, uncomprehending eyes. God, the American school systems were negligent!

When the camp came into view, Shannon opened her mouth to speak, only to find Ryan's palm clamped firmly over her lips. Ryan silently pointed to the corner of the camp as she slowly removed her hand.

Pete, the cameraman, was lying in a heap on the sand. Marty and Marva were tied together in a nearly obscene face-to-face position that the survivalist could only assume was some exotic form of torture. For Marva.

Several militant-looking, highly unattractive, shorthaired, overweight, exceptionally hairy women, wearing thick glasses and combinations of corduroy and flannel, despite the heat, guarded the prisoners. *The COWS!* Ryan's mind screamed. She knew that bitch YunKungFooey would find a way to cause more trouble!

"Stay down and keep quiet," Ryan whispered to Shannon. "I don't want to be rescuing you, too."

Green eyes narrowed. "I resent that! What makes you think I'd be so easy to kidnap?" she whispered back indignantly.

A slender eyebrow arched. "Call it a hunch."

Shannon stuck her tongue out at Ryan. Then she noticed something out of the corner of her eye. Something she never thought she'd see again. "Bu...is...is that who I think it is?"

"Uh huh. One and the same."

"I should have drowned her when I had the chance."

Ryan could only nod. "Okay, here's the plan. I rush in and save them. You stay here."

"That's a plan?"

"Yup."

"But she's got a gun." Shannon motioned toward Yun-kyung, who was the only COW with a firearm. The rest held only big sticks.

"So?"

"So, she'll shoot you!"

Ryan frowned. Her girl really needed to have a little faith in her.

"I've got a better plan," Shannon said confidently. "One that, hopefully, won't get you shot." The writer leaned over and placed a soft kiss on Ryan's cheek. "I've become rather attached to you, sexy." She gently brushed the spot that she had just kissed with her thumb. "And I don't want you with any holes that you didn't have at birth."

Ryan grinned broadly, then cocked her head to the side. She had planned on a surprise attack, wherein she would rush the Asian COW. She figured she could take two or three bullets before they would really slow her down. But it couldn't hurt to humor Shannon. After all, they'd just made up. "Okay, what's your plan?"

*   *   *

"Shut up, blubber belly!" Yun-kyung shouted at Pete, who was moaning pitifully from his prostrate position on the sand. "You've only been our prisoner for 15 minutes. The Geneva Convention does *not* require that we give you a snack!"

"But I missed breakfast!" he complained bitterly.

"Tough! That's what you get for working for that environmental demon, Joan!" the vet sneered. "I saw on television, how she poisoned that pristine lagoon with the most horrific, insidious pollutant the world has ever known."

"Nuclear waste?" Marty asked.

Pete shook his head. "She was saving that for this week." Pete choked, as the butt of Yun-kyung's gun pressed deeper into his throat. "But I had nothing to do with that. I love the environment!"

"Don't think we haven't traced the mountain of Snickers wrappers and Mountain Dew cans to you, sloth!"

A chorus of affirmative grunts, cheers, and 'Amen, bio-friendly sister', met Yun-kyung's words.

"Oh, man," Marty grunted. "We are so screwed! Start thinking of your last wish, Mrs. Georgia, 'cause those COWS are on their way to martyrdom, and we're doomed." The construction foreman pressed his hips even more tightly against Marva's. If this was his last chance to get lucky, he wasn't going waste it.

Marva made a disgusted face. "Ewww. What in the hell is that?" She brought her knee up sharply, exactly the way she had learned in her church self-defense class. Marty's eyes rolled back in his head, and he began squealing like a pig.

"You're right, Marty." Marva gave the man a satisfied smirk. "I do feel better now that my last wish has come true."

Marva turned toward the COWS. "I demand to be the first one killed!" she shouted.

Yun-kyung focused on Marva. She hadn't really gotten a chance to talk to the Southerner when she was a castaway. Her thoughts turned bitter. Of course, if she hadn't been *sabotaged* and *unfairly* voted off the island, she would still *be* a castaway. But at least, Shannon and Ryan had been voted off. She had been almost sad not to see them when she and her sisters stormed the beach. They were the main reason she was out the million dollars.

Yun-kyung had intended to use the prize money to start a campaign against companies that made fly swatters. Sure, there were trillions of flies *now*. But who knew what the future would bring?! Who would land on and eat the world's many shit piles? "Don't you understand how important our work is?" she said to Marva, her voice impassioned.

The housewife refused to answer, but Marty snorted derisively, hoping that somehow Joan had been able to call in the South China Sea equivalent of a SWAT team before she was captured. He'd seen another part of the 'herd' heading toward the production area, intent on capturing the show's host.

Before Yun-kyung could shoot Marty, a hideous wail rang out.

Dark eyes widened. *What the…?*

Then she heard it again. Only this time the sound was even more piteous. "It must be a wounded animal!" the vet cried. "GO! Find it and bring it to me! I will heal it. For free."

The COWS lumbered into the jungle in search of the hideously crying, injured beast, leaving their leader to guard the castaways.

*   *   *

"Louder!" Ryan hissed.

"God, Ryan, I'm wailing as loud as I can!"

The taller woman smirked down at Shannon from her position in a tree. "Heh. We all know that's not true."

Shannon had the good grace to blush. "That was…um…under *extraordinary* circumstances."

Ryan's eyes glazed over with lust. Oh yeah. Extraordinary was one way to describe it. Shannon was made for her. And there was no way in hell she was going to let the luscious blonde slip out of her life when 'Castaway' was over. Not without a fight.

"Someone's coming," the writer whispered. Worry suddenly clouded Shannon's expression. "You'll be careful?"

Blue eyes rolled, but Ryan decided Shannon didn't need to know that she had done this before. Several times. Hell, she'd *taught* this at Jeeter's Self-Protection for Individualists Camp last summer. "Of course I will, sweetheart." Ryan lifted her eyebrows and tilted her head toward the nearby bushes, where Shannon had promised to hide, and the writer disappeared into the underbrush.

Three COWS approached the area cautiously, scanning the ground for the sorry beast. Shannon moaned again, drawing the Berkeley and Wellesley grads directly under Ryan's position.

Shannon watched, enthralled, as Ryan silently dropped out of the tree. She picked off one woman at a time, rendering each unconscious, while the other COWS searched nearby, oblivious to the survivalist's actions. They never even knew what hit them. Shannon flushed. God, Ryan was sexy! She knew the dark-haired woman was a physical person by nature, that much was obvious, but to actually see with her own eyes, what she'd only imagined Ryan capable of…that was another story.

Ryan used a length of vine and finished hog-tying the last COW with flourish. "Okay, Shannon," she stood up and brushed off her hands, "you can start…"

Ryan's words were cut off as Shannon hurled herself at the survivalist. "Uff!" The taller woman's back slammed against the jungle floor, and Shannon immediately straddled her waist.

"Damn, that was so hot, Ryan." The writer's lips attached themselves to Ryan's throat.

"Oh…sh…baby, we're on a mission here," Ryan ground out, as Shannon's hands found their way under her tank top.

The blonde moaned. "You're right, honey. I'm on a mission."

"What about the COWS?" *Willpower. I must be strong!*

"Let them get their own woman!"

A rustling in the bushes indicated that more COWS were on their way. "Hurry up and take care of them, Ryan," she commanded softly. "I want to finish this discussion." Shannon kissed the older woman deeply.

"I will, sweetheart," Ryan promised as she moved into position again. "I dedicate the next skull fracture to you." She sniffed self-consciously. Nobody ever made her feel like a woman, the way Shannon did!

*   *   *

"Where are they?" Yun-kyung asked. She'd sent the last of her team of COWS to find the wounded animal at least 15 minutes ago. How many women did it take to successfully carry out one order?!

"Maybe the animal ate them," Pete snickered.

Yun-kyung rammed the tip of the rifle up Pete's nose, expanding one of his nostrils. "Quiet, Satanic Minion!"

Yun-kyung closed her eyes in frustration. There was that pathetic wail again. She couldn't take it anymore! "I'll be back," she called over her shoulder, convinced that the castaways wouldn't be able to escape their bindings before she returned.

Just as the vet slipped into the jungle, Shannon popped out from behind a bush and moved over to her fellow contestants and Pete.

"Oh, Shannon! I'm so glad to see you," Marva groaned pathetically. Being this close to Marty all morning made her want to wash with lye soap and bleach. But at least, Pete hadn't filmed it. Bo, her husband, God love him, would certainly string Marty up for pressing against her like she was some wanton hussy. Of course, no jury in De Kalb County would convict Bo of anything. He had been quarterback at Jefferson High School, and his senior year they'd won the State Championship. Marva sighed happily. God, she loved Southern jurisprudence.

"I'm sorry we couldn't get here sooner. The last two COWS were enormous. We ran out of vine to tie them up with."

"You've captured them?" Pete asked.

"Uh huh." Shannon beamed. "Well, I lured them into the jungle, while Ryan captured them."

"You're the hideous beast?" they all exclaimed.

Shannon nodded. "I hope Ryan is careful with Yun-kyung."

Marva squeezed Shannon's shoulder. "She'll be fine, Shannon. She's probably caught her already."

"Shouldn't we go see what happened to Joan and Rita?" Pete asked. Not that he really wanted to. But there was food in the production area and he'd now missed lunch as well as breakfast.

Shannon considered the request for a moment. "All in favor of rescuing the bleached-blonde, turbo bitches from hell, raise your hands."

No one moved.

"There's your answer, Pete."

"But if something happens to them, they might cancel the show, and then no one would win the million dollars," Pete reasoned. For the love of God, today was hot dog day!

Marty, Shannon and Marva all frowned.

Shannon sighed. "Let's go."

      *   *   *

In the production hut, Rita and Joan were tied back-to-back. The second team of COWS previously sent by Yun-kyung to find the 'Castaway' host was in the process of going through the food stores and giving all animal-based products a proper burial.

"I can't believe you allowed this to take place!" Rita hissed, straining at the ropes that bound her to the host.

"Me? Me? Who was too cheap to pay for any security here on the island? Despite the fact that drug traffickers regularly use it to store cocaine to evade international police!" She had been so happy when she found that stash, behind the third palm tree to the left of the big rock, outside the cave. It had almost made staying on the island bearable.

"Those aren't drug traffickers, you idiot! Those are studio employees! And it's part of our executive compensation package!"

Joan groaned, thinking of all the money she had wasted over the years. "Dammit! I want a promotion when this is over!"

Right then, three COWS trooped into the hut. "All right, which one of you is in charge here?"

"I am!" both bleached blondes cried out.

"Okay, then you're both the first to die for the cause of all animals processed into handy meat patties, to be cooked your way at substandard restaurants."

"She is!" came their next reply.

The COW with the firearm scratched her butt. This was harder than expected. "Come on, tell me. Don't make me have to shoot you both." It would be better if they had one later for leverage.

"Have you been watching the show at all?" Rita queried. Were there any animal components in televisions? Or were the COWS all too busy playing in their softball leagues?

All three shrugged. "Nah…it looked kinda lame."

Rita made a mental note to begin including some COWS in her next focus group. "Well, she's the host of the show! The one who poured the oil in the lagoon! The one who imported the bats! The one who dumped your leader in elephant crap! It was her, all her!"

"Me? Me? Who was it that came up with the stupid idea for this show to begin with?"

Rita snorted. "That was some person in Dutch TV." *We don't have one original idea at the BTBC. Why else are our other programs 'Police Cops', 'Who Wants To Bury A Multi-millionaire?' and 'Gerri Wringer'?*

"And who has been sending me cables encouraging me to do all those heinous acts? Who said to 'pump up the danger level', to 'make it sexy' and to 'fillet the COWS'?"

Horrified gasps all around.

Joan smiled maliciously, going for the kill. Literally. "Aren't you the one who told me to put animal protein in the rice that Yungster was eating?"

"That's it." The COW had heard enough. "You're dead, blondie." Seeing the confused looks on the women, as both of them were blonde, the COW amended, "Old blondie."

Rita shrieked. How dare they call her old!?

*   *   *

Ryan had been watching the crew area for several minutes. Yun-kyung had, instead of coming to find her alone, headed in this direction for backup. Ryan was just about to make her move when she heard loud thrashing in the jungle to her left. Coming along the path were Shannon, Marva, Marty and Pete.

So much for sneaking up on the camp. Ryan stealthily moved through the underbrush and intercepted the foursome. "Shh, come with me," she directed and turned to lead them back to a safe place.

Shannon immediately grabbed her hand. She was so glad to see her lover unharmed. And she was still more than a little worked up from before. As they moved through the jungle, she let her hand glide over Ryan's ass.

Ryan, for her part, gave a little yelp when she felt the smaller hand cop a feel. She glanced over her shoulder and smiled at the playful expression she found on Shannon's face. "Later."

Once they were at a safe distance, Ryan knelt down and used Tiffany to draw a diagram of the camp. "All right, here's what we're up against. There are five huts in the production area. The COWS and Joan and some other anorexic person are in the center one. But we have some mad COWS still roaming around here...and here." She made sketches in the dirt to illustrate her point. "What we need to do is take out the big COWS –"

Marty snorted. "You can tell the difference?"

Ryan allowed a brief smile to cross her lips. It was true. They were rather interchangeable. "The outdoor ones," she conceded. "So, we'll take them down, and then we can deal with the head COWS."

"And then have lunch?" Pete asked hopefully. Just to piss off the COWS he wanted to have a weenie roast. He figured their phallic shape would add insult to injury.

Everyone shrugged. Lunch sounded fine. No one mentioned saving Rita or Joan.

*　　　　　*　　　　　*

Yun-kyung strode into the main tent the moment Joan was being untied for execution. She had thought better of wandering into the jungle alone. If the animal was that badly injured, she should take someone else with her to help. Especially with so many of her minions missing. "What's going on here?" she demanded, dark eyes taking in the scene.

The COWS snapped to attention. "We were going to execute this one—" she gestured to the weeping Joan "– so that people would know we're serious."

Why must all brilliant revolutionaries be saddled with idiot followers? Yun-kyung sighed. "We're not killers."

"Thank God!" Joan sobbed.

"We're here to protest the abuses committed to the animal life on the island. Remember?"

Rita shook her head. "You're pathetic! What kind of terrorist are you? Jesus! I've dealt with actresses who were more mercenary than you are! Kathy Lee Gifford would eat you COWS alive," she sneered disgustedly. Her wrists were getting chaffed for this?

The COWS were forced to nod their agreement. Nobody did 'bitch' like Kathy Lee.

Joan glared at the studio executive. "Are you trying to get us killed?"

"Like she has the balls to do it!" Rita snorted.

Yun-kyung stamped her foot. "Enough! Two of you need to go back to the castaway camp and get the four hostages I left tied up. Then we'll make that fat cameraman broadcast our demands to the world!"

The armed COW squinted. "We have demands?"

Yun-kyung wished for a wall to beat her head against. "Of course we do!" Jesus, Mary and Joseph! "Go! Now!"

✳   ✳   ✳

The sound of an animal in obvious distress was heard in the crew area. Yun-kyung scowled. *What did the BTBC do to the island to cause such pain to the animal population?* In a rage, she turned to Joan and Rita. "What did you do? Set up traps around the perimeter?"

"Huh?" the blondes answered in tandem.

"Listen to that noise! The pain! The suffering! The anguish!" The veterinarian could hardly stand it a moment longer.

Joan began laughing. "That's not an animal. That's Shannon getting laid." *Lucky little bitch.*

"What?" *That's impossible! Unless…unless Ryan is still on the island!* Yun-kyung slapped her forehead. It all made sense now. The insane survivalist had taken down her fallen COWS. Pointing the rifle at the network women, she warned, "Stay right here." Then she stalked out of the camp.

In the jungle, Shannon continued on with her pathetic wailing. While Marva, Marty and Pete hid in the underbrush, Ryan dropped out of the trees and took out the wandering cattle one by one.

When Shannon felt the barrel of a rifle pressing into her neck, she went mute.

"I should have known." Yun-kyung couldn't believe she had fallen for this ruse.

"Little help, please?" Shannon called, finding her voice again.

Ryan had just finished hog-tying the last COW, when she heard Shannon's cry. Rushing back to where she had left the luscious blonde, she stopped dead in her tracks when she saw Shannon held hostage.

The brunette scratched her head. Somehow the scene didn't seem right. She had a brief flash of a memory of Shannon being held with a knife to her throat. But that didn't make sense. Tiffany and her kin would never hurt Shannon. She shook her head, clearing the image. She needed to focus on the here and now. "Easy does it."

"Easy does it? Easy does it? What? Do I look like an egg?" the Asian ranted.

"Huh?" Ryan replied. Damn, the vet really was loony. What did eggs have to do with this?

The environmental terrorist blew out a deep breath. "You kept saying 'easy does it'. Like fixing an egg over easy."

"What does breakfast food have to do with anything?"

"I'm not talking about breakfast!"

Broad shoulders shrugged. "I didn't bring it up. You did." Ryan gave Shannon a reassuring smile, which the younger woman immediately mirrored.

"I did not! I don't eat eggs!"

"Why not?"

How many times did she have to explain this? "Because I don't eat other living things."

"Eggs aren't living," Ryan countered reasonably.

"They were!"

"I don't think so."

Yun-kyung shoved Shannon out of her way and stalked over to the survivalist. "My God, are you really that stupid?"

"No, but you are, bitch," Shannon said behind her, picking up a large branch and smacking the smaller woman with it. Yun-kyung crumpled to the jungle floor, and Shannon rushed into her lover's arms.

"God, I love you," Ryan whispered reverently, hoping she could talk Shannon into substitute teaching at Jeeter's next spring. The luscious blonde was a natural!

*   *   *

Several hours later, Ryan had repaired the radio, allowing Joan to send out a call for help. The local authorities came and corralled the COWS, herding them away from the island. In an unusual act of compassion, Joan decided to forego the immunity competition and go straight for the tribal council.

Pete managed to somehow shoulder the camera, despite having one hot dog sticking out of his mouth and another grasped in his free hand. Since his near brush with death, all thirty minutes of it, he had been eating non-stop. If he was gonna go, he was gonna go his way. And that was fat, dumb and happy.

"This is the next to last vote. The two who emerge from this tribal council will be competing for the one million dollar prize," Joan informed the viewing audience. She had planned on drawing it out, but she was so over this show. She couldn't wait to get back to her life in Los Angeles. The first thing she was going to do when she got there was burn her passport. "Who will it be?"

The four remaining castaways waited for their moment in the voting hut. Marva was sent in first. "This vote is for my husband, who would do significant bodily injury to Marty if he were here. Honey bear, I'm sending Marty home. Do what you will." *No witnesses, baby!*

Next in was Shannon. She quickly wrote down Marty's name. Ryan was next, and she too voted to evict the construction foreman.

Finally, Marty came into the hut. "Marva, sweetheart, you have a cute ass…but saggy breasts. Time for you to go."

Joan went into the hut and retrieved the votes. Bringing them back to the tribal council, she began reading them off. "Marty."

"Bitch," Marty muttered.

"Marty."

"Pardon me, *bitches*," he amended.

"Marty."

"Bite me."

"Please, there's not enough Listerine in the world for that." Marva shuddered at the mere thought of it.

Joan paused dramatically. The next vote would decide who, besides Marty, was voted off. She was sure the ass hadn't voted for himself. "And..."

The three women all leaned forward.

"Marva."

"Fiddlesticks," the housewife sighed. She turned to Ryan and Shannon. "Congratulations, you two." To Joan she said, "I don't care what you say, but I won't go back to the mainland in the same boat as him."

"You're not going back to the mainland. You and Marty are spending the night here in the crew quarters. Tomorrow, we bring back the last five voted off, and then the seven of you will choose who is the final castaway."

Marty spat. "What? You mean I don't even get a fucking hot shower and a decent meal?"

Joan smiled thinly. "No, but I think we have a few more hot dogs." *Prick.*

The construction foreman pointed a thick finger at Shannon and Ryan. "I wouldn't start counting your winnings just yet, girly-girls."

<Fade out>

Castaway Farewells (Marty and Marva)

Marva sat demurely in the good-bye hut, her hair damp from the hot shower she had just indulged in. Well, it was far from an indulgence. She was intent on getting any remnant of Marty off of her skin. She wondered if anyone would miss him after Bo had him 'disappear'.

Doubtful.

"Hi, Bo. Hi, Edwina. Hi, Hubert! I am so looking forward to seeing all of you again. And hi to Mr. Biggles, our pet pig. He's a big fan of the BTBC." Mr. Biggles always squealed during the 'Police Cops' series, happy to see pigs on TV.

"Well, I'm excited that I got this far in the contest. I bet no one would have bet on me making it to the final four." Pete nodded. He was sure she would have drowned that first day. "But never count a Southern lady out of anything. We have a way of living to see a better day."

Marva took a sip of the orange juice in front of her. "I'd like to thank Ryan, who is really one of the sweetest people I've ever met, for her help while on the island. Ryan, you and Shannon are welcome to come visit us up in Stone Mountain anytime. After I buy my children ear plugs, that is."

And a pair for Bo too.

"See y'all at the big tribal council tomorrow!"

\<Fade out\>

       *   *   *

Despite his loud protests, Marty was shoved into the good-bye hut. He walked into the center, and faced Pete's camera.

"Is that thing on?" he demanded.

"Sure thing," Pete answered, nearly wetting himself with the look Marty was leveling at him.

"I have only one thing to say: This is far from over!"
And Marty stormed out.

<Fade out>

Panelist's Article: Castaways and Amazons by Poopsie Gebilhiney, Ph.D.

"Once again, I find myself in the enviable position of serving as a commentator for 'Castaway'. I am honored to have been offered this opportunity again, especially after the fiasco surrounding my last effort. I have obtained the services of a new assistant who will faithfully edit my comments as she transcribes them before they are forwarded to the 'Castaway' staff. Claire, doll, just make sure you make me sound really, really smart when you send this. That bitch I had before left in comments that made me look ridiculous. She's probably humping whatever poor slob she conned into hiring her after she got back to the states.

"The Amazonian studies that I have been pursuing have provided an uncanny contrast to the study of human nature that the 'Castaway' contestants have afforded. The Amazons are community oriented. The needs of one must never become more important than the survival of the whole. This is in direct opposition to the contestants of 'Castaway'. They willingly sacrifice each other for the survival of the one.

"The most recent tapes that I have viewed depict the savagery and brutality that one would expect of a tribe located here on the Amazon River. However, these peaceful inhabitants of the jungle that I've been studying work together to feed, clothe and house everyone. Their only quirk is that they sometimes get a little cranky and perform unspeakable acts upon the captives of neighboring tribes that they war against. The addition of processed sugar, preservatives, and artificial coloring due to the addition of Fruit Loops into their diet seems to have heightened their aggressiveness, and the entire tribe now seems to be suffering from sugar induced mood swings and hyperactivity. This is not a surprising development. It is probable that most, if not all, of the contestants on 'Castaway' were raised on such a diet as the Amazons are now experiencing, and their sudden deprivation of these unhealthy foods is now inducing certain withdrawal symptoms and possibly accounts for at least some of the bizarre behavior.

"The one exception seems to be Ryan, who I am convinced, most likely never ate anything prepackaged in her life due to her paranoia. And Arturo…who.. well, I just give up trying to explain him!

"In the tapes that I viewed, I heard the name 'Tiffany' mentioned. I didn't recall any such contestant. Then my new assistant pointed to Ryan's knife and assured me that 'Tiffany' was the knife's name. The Amazons have a similar cultural view of their tools and frequently name their blow guns and darts. Before a monkey is darted in the hunt, a small chant is said over the blow gun and dart that in effect means: "Okay, Bessie, do your stuff. We're gonna have tree kill tonight!" but in terms more in line with Amazonian culture and expressions.

"This has been an interesting experiment. The producers of 'Castaway' are to be credited with the concept of putting people who could be anyone's next door neighbors into a very challenging and foreign environment and then studying their reactions. The contestants are to be credited for the lack of homicides committed under these extreme conditions.

"This has been Professor Poopsie Gerbilhiney, PHD, from the Amazon Jungle.

"Now, Claire…where's that sexy nightie I bought for you on our last trip to the trading post? What do you mean, a cold day in hell when I get to see you wear it? C'mon, Claire, even a cultural anthropologist's gotta get some! Claire? Claire!"

Guest Panelists' Parting Comments

A Compilation

We have asked our panelists to contribute their final thoughts as we reach the conclusion of 'Castaway' next week.

✶   ✶   ✶

Poopsie Gerbilhiney, Ph.D. says:
"This is Professor Poopsie Gerbilhiney, PHD. If you get this message...SEND HELP!!!!!! Claire, the ungrateful bitch, set me up! Apparently, I violated some sacred tribal law and am now engaged to the oldest man in the tribe who expects to father a multitude of sons with me, if his rude gestures mean anything. They're coming for me now...and they have sharp, pointy things. 'Castaway' was fun...it was interesting...an anthropological wonder! Now get me the hell outta here!!!! Oh, and could you get me Ryan's number?"

✶   ✶   ✶

Maggie Goodheart says:

Endings. Don't you just love 'em? And don't us novelists just hate 'em? A poor ending can ruin a fine story; a good one can provide the finishing touch.

"What's the problem?" you ask. "Simply go on until the end, then stop." Excuse me but: Phooey! "OK then," you say. "Isn't there a saying: 'It ain't over 'til the fat lady sings'?" Yes. But what if your story doesn't feature a plump opera singer?

Pick up any 'How To' book on plotting a story and you will find the chapter about endings includes: circular, linear, trick, happy, and sad. So many choices; what's a girl to do? The answer is of course, to choose an ending suitable for your particular story, one which your protagonists have worked hard throughout to achieve, one which, above all, SATIS-FIES, yet perversely leaves the reader wanting more.

Which means, in the case of 'Castaway', going out with a BANG. (Btw, Can I make one final plug for my latest novel: 'Blue Touchpaper', available at all good bookstores?)

In other words, I'll go home happy if the series ends with some hot monkey sex between Ryan and Shannon.

See! I knew there was something we could agree on in the end.

                    *   *   *

Dr. Maura says:

Over the course of this show, we have be exposed to various types of deviant behavior. As you know, this is just sick, sick, sick. I have searched for my soul, I mean, I have searched my soul to come up with the solution to save people from dysfunctional life choices.

I believe that I, alone, can cure some of these problems —bring their actions into comportment with the rest of the normal people who listen to my show. I feel the only right way to do this will be for me to fly to Paradise Island and do some one-on-one therapies which have been successful in helping a reasonable number of people become heterosexual.

I must start with Ryan. Her psyche is the one most askew. With her strong belief in minimalistic survival, she has shown that she is already rebelling against normalcy. The abnormal attachment to her knife, Tiffany, is in a way bordering on pedophilia as it can't be more than a few years old. The bit of bestiality with the hermit crab...well again, sick, sick, sick. Yes, Ryan, I'm coming for you, loudly...I mean quickly. The depths of your cerulean blues will not be the same after I get my hands on you.

*　　　　　*　　　　　*

Itasca Onager says:
We tried to reach sociologist Itasca Mead Hagetaka Onager to solicit her final thoughts on Castaway. IMHO was not available. We did, however, find this message on her answering machine. It will have to suffice.

You have reached the office of Assistant Professor Itasca Onager: I will be away from the university through January 1. I am en route to the Amazon, where I plan to join eminent anthropologist Poopsie Gerbilhiney in her study of the effect of food preservatives on the native cultures there.

[HONK!] Damn, there's the taxi!. "I'll be there in a minute!"

Where was I? Oh yeah. You know how sometimes you just KNOW something? Without hours and hours of tedious research? Anyway, I logged on to the Castaway site the day Poopsie's first commentary was posted and—well, maybe it was the throbbing beat of the drums in the show's mesmerizing theme song, but the moment I saw her face, I KNEW that she was the mentor and partner I'd been lusting for since childhood. And her commentary! I had to stop reading after the first paragraph or two. It was just too powerful, too...Let's just say it reached down and touched something inside me that...

[HONK HONK!] "Keep your pants on! I'm coming!"

Anyhow, long story short I'm heading for South America today to offer to fill any aching voids Poopsie may have. If you've got business with me, leave a message on the machine at the "Beep." Unless you're one of the members of my dissertation committee. In which case, you can stick it up your...

[B-E-E-E-E-E-P!]

EPISODE TEN

One for the Money, Two for the Show

It seemed only fitting to Shannon that it had rained all night. *God is pissing on me,* she thought gloomily. She had a bad feeling about the tribal council later that day. *After today, after tonight, Ryan won't be here any more. She'll be on her way back to Kentucky, and I'll be heading toward Los Angeles. Maybe I should be like every other lesbian on the planet and buy a cat. Great, Shannon, the only way you can have pussy is to buy it? How pathetic! I've got to do something. I'm not giving Ryan up without a fight.*

Ryan walked into the camp, holding up two lobsters. "Good morning! I thought we could celebrate."

Shaken out of her miserable thoughts, Shannon smiled. "Lobster for breakfast! How decadent!" She rubbed her stomach. "I'm starving."

"And tonight we get to sleep in a real bed." Ryan was used to roughing it, but she did miss her deluxe, extra-firm, innerspring mattress. Even survivalists have bad backs.

"And a hot shower!" Shannon nearly swooned at the thought of soap and shampoo. She felt like that chick in the Herbal Essence commercial—it would be an 'organic' experience.

Ryan dropped the lobsters in the pail over the fire. "Our last meal here." She looked across the fire at the blonde she had come to love. "What are your plans for after this is done?"

"Umm…well…after I kill Rita, I don't exactly have any." *As long as I don't get caught, I won't be doing time.*

"Tiffany won't help you."

"Why not?" Shannon demanded, more than a bit annoyed. *This 'Tiffany is a gentle knife' is only so much bullshit!*

"I was kinda hoping…"*Damn! This is hard!* It reminded Ryan of the first time she learned to assemble an M16 blindfolded and one-handed. But with perseverance, she had become the best in her survivalist unit. Ryan took a deep breath. "See, I was thinking…well…"

Shannon could tell something important was about to happen. "Maybe if you told Tiffany," she suggested. That idea seemed to appeal to the brunette. She took out her knife and stared at it lovingly, sending a twinge of jealousy through Shannon. *Will she ever look at me that way?*

Ryan sighed. She had already practiced a hundred times with Tiffany. But at least this time, Shannon would hear the words. "I have a nice place. It's big, and far away from prying government eyes—I get it scanned every week to be sure—and it's beautiful." Ryan swallowed hard and put the knife down, as she stared intently into Shannon's eyes. "I was hoping you'd like to join me there. We'd have a cabin, and my two brothers, and you could write all day."

Shannon's heart soared, relieved beyond words that Ryan wanted to make a life with her, since she wanted so much to be with the survivalist. But something else caught the blonde's attention. "Two brothers?"

"Younger brothers. The baby is Patrick, the older is Sean."

"You sure you're not IRA?"

Ryan scratched her head. "What's this got to do with retirement?" She paused a moment and then laughed. "Gotcha."

Shannon wiped her mental brow, grateful for the teasing, glad Ryan could joke about her own idiosyncrasies. If Ryan hadn't asked her, she was going to invite Ryan to come out to LA. She was glad she didn't have to. "I'd love to, Ryan."

"Really?"

"Really."

"You're sure?"

Shannon nodded. "I'm sure."

"You won't miss California?"

"California is full of freaks and network executives."

Ryan wasn't sure there was a difference, but couldn't argue with that assessment. "Well, good, glad we got that settled."

"Shouldn't we shake on it, at least?" the writer teased, coming around to Ryan's side.

"Okay," Ryan held out her large hand.

Shannon bypassed it and immediately took Ryan's mouth in a deep kiss. It was their best kiss ever, in Shannon's opinion: hot, wet, deep, longing and without hermit crab intervention. She didn't want anything with the name 'crab' included in her love life.

"That was a handshake?" Ryan asked after they broke apart.

"Well, a modified one." Shannon kissed her nose, causing the survivalist to wrinkle her brow.

"Don't go sealing deals like that in Kentucky."

"I promise."

"Good. Let's shake again."

*　　　　*　　　　*

Ryan and Shannon made their way, one final time, through the jungle. "You would think," Shannon grunted, nearly tripping over a fallen tree, "that for once, we could hold the council at our campsite."

Ryan grabbed a snake by its tail and flung it into the jungle. Last week those would have been good eating. Today they were just annoying.

That was the fourth snake Ryan had tossed. *Fuck! I bet Joan put a bunch of them along the trail this afternoon, just for us!* "Joan! Rita!" Shannon bellowed. "I'm going to put one of these in your beds tonight! Then we'll see how funny you think it is!"

In front of her, Ryan chuckled. The guys at Jeeter's were so gonna love Shannon.

Finally, they made it into the council clearing. Already seated were the last seven castaways to be voted off the island: Marty, Marva, Jason, Arturo, Joe, Dawn and Tanesha. Together they would form the final voting jury, deciding who would win the million dollars.

Shannon smiled over at them. Only Arturo and Marva smiled back. *Well, that can't be a good sign.*

"This is the final tribal council meeting," Joan intoned from her place on the set. She couldn't believe that she went to Brown for this. Of course, Brown was nothing more than a school for rich kids who couldn't get into Harvard, but it was still better than state schools. "This afternoon, the tribe will decide who will be the winner. And who will just go home."

Ryan shrugged. The 'loser' would still win half a million dollars. Government surplus was cheap. No matter what, she and her community were set.

"So, we've been here awhile together," Joan continued. "Alliances have been formed. Trust has been betrayed. Danger has been escaped. Today, it all ends." She turned to the jury. "What does it feel like to be losers?"

Marty bristled. "Oh yeah? Who's the loser here? I hear you're only getting a hundred thousand for this show. I get more than that for making it to the final four. Seems like the only loser here is you."

"Yeah, well, I get book publishing rights, and you don't, asshole!" Joan countered easily. She was cutting out all of Marty's comments anyway. Of course, who would buy a book about this whole ridiculous thing? They'd need another marketing tie-in. Maybe that ridiculous knife Ryan was always talking to? *That would appeal to all the nutcases who would find this shit interesting. I wonder how much I could bilk them for?*

"Can we get on with this?" Shannon demanded.

"Please, I am wilting over here," Arturo moaned, fanning himself. Truth be told, he looked fresh and dewy. Shannon vowed to get his secret later.

Joan frowned. She would so *not* miss the blonde annoyance. "So, we're down to Ryan and Shannon. Tell us, Jason, do you think it's more than a coincidence that they're sleeping together?"

Jason looked at the camera with bleary eyes. He had obviously been on a bender since getting kicked off. It was then that Ryan and Shannon noticed the young island woman, who couldn't be more than sixteen years old, seated behind him, her arms around his waist possessively. "I don't know and I don't care. Let me repeat that I am extremely tolerant of all diverse lifestyles, whether they be gay or black."

"Black is not a lifestyle!" Tanesha exploded. "You ignorant cracker! I didn't choose to be black!"

"Hey, I didn't choose to be gay," Shannon countered.

"Oh, please, this genetic stuff is bullshit! It's a choice. You just couldn't find yourself a good man."

"Damn right!" said Marty, adjusting his family jewels, finally agreeing with something Tanesha had to say.

Joan nearly beat her head with a coconut. The last two Midwestern viewers had just turned off their television sets with that outburst.

"I'd like to find a good man," Arturo cooed, winking at Marty.

"Do that again and you'll..." Marty stopped. He couldn't think of any threat that would worry Arturo. Other than a lack of skin care products. And he couldn't have his coworkers hearing him threaten to take away someone's facial lotion.

Dawn moaned. Her arm was still throbbing, and the meds didn't seem to be touching the pain anymore. The only thing that helped was

Joe. And she needed help now. She moaned again, differently this time, and placed a hand on Joe's thigh.

Joe moaned too. They really needed to get new meds for Dawn. He wasn't twenty-one anymore. And he hadn't bothered to get Russell's stash of Viagra before he left for home.

Before she lost control of the council entirely, Joan called out, "Okay, let's finish this up." She gestured to Marty, "Start the voting. Remember, you're voting for who should be the winner, *not* who you want off the island."

Ryan leaned over and kissed Shannon's cheek. "Good luck, sweetheart."

She received a kiss in return. "Same back."

Rita, on the sideline, cursed. *Sure, the dykes kissing would titillate, but where is the drama, folks? The cutthroat competition? The backstabbing?* God, she missed Hollywood.

Marty stalked over to the voting hut and wrote down Ryan's name on the paper. "I'd never vote for that two-faced Shannon."

Next in was Arturo. He wrote one name. Scratched it out. Wrote another. Scratched it out. Wrote both. Sighed dramatically and wiped his brow. "I must vote for my Channon. And I also must say that her makeover is looking very good. If you, too, are in need of a new look, visit my salon in San Francisco."

The third voter was Marva. She quickly wrote down Ryan's name. "Ryan, thank you for everything."

Joe and Dawn entered the voting hut together. "Oooh, alone at last," Dawn murmured, kissing Joe.

Pete pulled out another cigarette. He was really gonna miss these two.

"No, no, no, dear," Joe protested, pushing her away.

"Yes."

"No."

"Yes."

Joe shrugged mentally and tried a new tactic. It worked in Bugs Bunny cartoons. "Yes."

"No." Dawn frowned. That didn't work. "Where are we?"

"In the voting hut." He led her over to the paper. "You need to vote between Shannon and Ryan."

"Okay." She wondered who those two people were.

"Dawn, honey," Joe prodded.

"What?"

"You need to vote."

"Okay." Dawn's eyes fluttered closed.

Joe decided to take things into his own hands. So to speak. With Dawn around, he'd never need to, in that way, again. He walked over and wrote down Shannon's name twice. "You're a great kid, and Dawn and I wish you all the best."

That woke his lover up. "Kid? You want kids?"

"Let's talk about that later." Grabbing her by the arm, he helped her back to her seat at the council meeting.

Tanesha strode in and quickly wrote down her vote. "Ryan. She kicks ass and takes names. For a honky."

The last to vote was Jason. "Shannon. If I have any hope of a political future left, I certainly can't vote for Ryan."

Pete was shocked. Four votes for Shannon, three for Ryan. Joan was going to have a stroke. He couldn't wait to get that on film.

*   *   *

"NOOOOOO!!" Marty roared. This whole damn thing was fixed! Shannon wasn't a real contestant. She worked for the network. She couldn't win! Pushing Pete aside, the furious man stalked away from the other castaways and a stunned Shannon. "I don't believe this bullshit!"

"You," Marty pointed an angry finger, "blonde network bitch!"

Both Rita and Joan turned around.

"Not you." Marty shook his head at Joan, and then gestured at Rita. "I want the one who looks like she's been around the block a few times."

Rita gasped. Why did people keep saying that?

"That would be you," Joan snickered. Leaning over, she pressed her lips against Rita's ear and whispered, "Mommy dearest."

Rita gasped again, her face twisting into a scowl. Joan was going to ask for her hush money payments to be increased after that whole kidnapping thing. She just knew it! The greedy, conniving, evil, blackmailing, bitch of a daughter!

Rita's heart nearly burst with motherly pride.

"That's right. You—me—jungle—right—now!" Marty grabbed Rita by the hand and began dragging her into the trees.

Rita took a deep breath to scream but paused, realizing that, as unlikely a prospect as it was, someone might actually rescue her if she did. Her mouth clicked closed. "Ooooo…" she squealed, a combination of fear, anger, and arousal as Marty yanked her along a bit faster.

"Shut up." When they were out of earshot of the other castaways, Marty pushed the programming VP up against a tree, pinning her there by her wrists. He frowned and looked down. With a grunt, he shifted his thighs. 'Little Marty' wasn't supposed to be enjoying this. This was business!

"You're not going to get away with this!"

"I'm not?" Rita asked interestedly, quite certain she would get away with whatever it was he was talking about. A woman didn't get to her level within the network without confidence and ability. And fucking the right people. That never hurt either.

"I know about Shannon." Marty tightened his grip on Rita's wrists. He leaned in and, almost against his will, took a deep breath. *Ummm…* She smelled clean, and he was pretty sure she'd have shaved armpits.

"What about her?"

He jerked his head back. This was no time to get preoccupied with feminine hygiene. *Ewww…* The words caused Marty's arousal to plummet. "Don't play dumb with me! I know all about your fucked up, evil plan."

Rita rolled her eyes. "Which one?"

"The one involving the castaways!"

"I repeat. Which one?" Men were so slow.

"ARRRRGGGHHHH!!" This wasn't going the way he thought it would! "I know Shannon works for you. She can't win the million. It's against your own rules."

Rita didn't even blink. "What do you want?"

"You, for starters." Little Marty was already back in the saddle, having put those nasty thoughts of female issues out of his tiny mind. Big Marty leered and thrust his hips against Rita. Then he tensed, expecting a nut-crushing blow like the one he'd received from Marva the day before. But it never came.

"So you expect me to have sex with you in this hot, sweaty jungle, merely because you know something you shouldn't?"

Marty nodded.

"Okay." Rita shrugged.

That was way too easy. Marty's eyes narrowed. It must be a trick. "I have more demands."

"But I still have to have wild, nasty, untamed, jungle sex with you, right?"

"Well, yes."

"Okay. Just checking."

"If you don't meet all my demands, I'll go to the press and tell the world that this entire contest was rigged."

"But we're still having sex?"

"You don't get it, do you, you stupid broad?" Marty ground his teeth together. "What I'm going to make you do will crush another contestant, probably ruining her piss poor life."

Rita shrugged again. "Whatever. Shit happens. But you're still going to force me to have sex with you, right?"

Marty frowned. "Well, I wouldn't say 'force'. I mean…"

"What kind of wussy blackmailer are you?" Jesus! First the COWS, now Marty. Extortion was simply a dying art. "Amateur!" she taunted. "You should take me right this very second! We can talk about the money later."

"Really?" Marty asked interestedly. Rita did appear to be a master manipulator. She would know about these things.

"Of course!"

Rita yanked her wrists free and grabbed hold of Marty. In a lightning quick move, she had the man pinned against the tree in the mirror image of how she, herself, had been held only seconds before.

"Very funny, babe." He smiled condescendingly and gave Rita a wink. Then he yanked his hands. When they didn't move an inch, he yanked again. His eyes widened with the realization that he was held firm. By a woman! As disconcerted as this made him feel, he had to admit, Little Marty was lovin' it!

Rita leaned in close, her warm breath against his cheek causing his lips to twitch. Wreaking havoc on his senses, she purred, "Watch and learn, jungle boy."

*   *   *

"DIE. DIE. DIE. DIE!!!"

Shannon was straddling Rita, choking the life out of her, pounding her head against the sand to punctuate every word.

"DIE. DIE. DIE. DIE!!!"

"Channon, girlfriend!" Arturo, with the other castaways hot on his heels, rushed over to the catfighting women. Well, it wasn't really much of a catfight anymore. The crew was trying to hunt down some masking tape. They thought it would be neat to outline Rita's body in the sand, for the local authorities. "You've got to stop this instant. You can't kill her."

"Oh yes, I can!" Shannon hissed between clenched teeth. "I'm doing my God damned best!" A drop of perspiration rolled off the tip of her nose and plopped onto Rita's cheek.

Rita tried to speak, but couldn't. Her lips were beginning to turn a lovely shade of purple.

"Channon! Are you crazy? Oooo...look at that color her eyelids are turning," Arturo pointed out conversationally. "That reminds me of Tijuana's big Dia de los Muertos Ball I used to go to every year. Oh, chica, in '92, I met the most beautiful man dressed like a zombie, named Jose..."

"Shannon," Marva interrupted. She could see Arturo was lost in some bizarre, gay, Mexican fantasy and was no longer helping. "What are you doing?"

"What does it look like? I'm strangling this no good bitch." A diabolical, near-orgasmic look crossed Shannon's face.

"No. No. No." Arturo shook his head violently, ending his trip down memory lane. "You're doing something far worse than that. You're mussing her hair!" He bent down and plucked a strand from Rita's crown. "Clairol 32. Nice choice for mature women."

Mature?! Rita willed Shannon to squeeze a little harder and end her misery.

"He's right, baby. You need to let her go," Ryan commanded softly, suddenly appearing at Shannon's side. She estimated that Rita had a good twenty seconds of life left in her, but seeing the mood Shannon was in, she decided not to wait until the very last second.

"Bu...bu..." Shannon looked up at Ryan, who shook her head sadly. "FUCK!" Shannon exhaled explosively as adrenaline coursed wildly through her. "Okay. Okay." She closed her eyes in a silent bid for control, allowing several tense seconds to pass before muttering, "Umm...

Ryan, could you…?" She motioned to her hands, and Ryan began prying her fingers from Rita's throat.

The writer rose to her feet and planted her hands firmly on her hips,
turning still raging eyes on the gasping, choking woman. "If I had one
wish—It would be that your ship home would sink! Or your plane
would crash! Or your broomstick would catch fire!" she shouted. "If it
weren't for Ryan, you'd be dead, dead, dead!"

"Here we go again," several voices moaned as the crew resumed their
hunt for tape.

"DEAD! DEAD! DEAD!!!"

"Shannon," Ryan placed herself between Shannon and Rita.
"C'mon." Without waiting for an answer, she began steering the
younger woman down the beach.

"Oh, Shannon?" Rita choked, rising to her knees and clutching her
bruised neck. "Remember that little 'discussion' we had?"

Shannon froze, knowing instantly that Rita was talking about her
promised severance pay. "Yes?"

"Forget about it, honey."

"Ahhhhhh!!!!!!!!!!!!!!!" Shannon turned on her heel and launched herself at Rita, only to be intercepted in mid-air by Ryan.

"Hold still." The survivalist began carrying a ranting, cursing
Shannon down the beach over her shoulder, having to tighten her grip
when Rita's taunting laughter set Shannon off again.

Joan stared down at her womb donor. "You are pure evil," she said
seriously, deliberately not offering her a hand up. The younger blonde
shook her head in simple awe. *I have so much to learn!*

"I am," Rita agreed unrepentantly, as she stumbled to her feet. "Now,
radio the boat so I can make this hellhole a memory." Rita smiled sweetly, sending a chill down Joan's spine. "Oh, and before I forget. I've got
something to tell you about your newest job for the network."

Joan was afraid to ask; there was something wicked about Rita's
expression. "What is it?"

"You'll be hosting our next reality show: Gulag."

Oh my God.

Rita continued merrily. "We'll send you and sixteen contestants to a jail in Siberia. You'll be given a nail file and some matchsticks and six months to get yourselves free. This time you'll get to live with the contestants so you can help move the show along."

Joan gulped. "When does it start?"

"That's the best part: filming begins next month."

*   *   *

"Put me down!"

"No."

A smack to the ass drew a yelp from Shannon. "Ryan!" The blood rushing to Shannon's head as she hung upside down over Ryan's back was making her dizzy. "Please, honey." Not that a good spanking from Ryan wouldn't be a lot of fun. In fact, she made a mental note to add it to her 'to do' list for when they got back home. But now just wasn't the time.

Ryan began softly caressing the stinging butt cheeks she had smacked.

Shannon lifted her head and sighed, "Ooooooh, that's nice."

The taller woman laughed. It was nice. **Very nice.** Ryan was still a little, okay, *a lot,* giddy that Shannon had agreed to come home to Kentucky with her. Her thoughts were awhirl with the visions of the new cabin she would build for her love. After a long discussion with Tiffany, Ryan decided she would tell Shannon that they'd have to live in a tent for a few months, until their new cabin was finished...later.

Much, much, later.

"Ryan, sweetheart, I'm going to pass out."

Ryan immediately stopped and lowered her now limp bundle to the ground. "Sorry." She smiled fondly at the beet-red face. "Are you over your urge to kill that woman yet?"

"Nope." Shannon shook her head and flopped down on her back, throwing her arm over her eyes. "There's still the boat ride to Bora Bora. I hope the sharks are hungry." For a fleeting second, Shannon felt sorry for the aquatic predators. In a fight to the death, she would never bet against Rita. And even if they did manage to kill her, she was sure the demonic crone's fake tits and multiple collagen injections had rendered her indigestible. Like corn. Only tougher. "I'd better do it myself," she finally admitted.

Ryan sat down next to Shannon and brushed a stray lock of pale hair from her face. "What's wrong? This should be the happiest day of your life." *It is for me. I've got my girl and enough money to start my own survivalist school. What more could a woman want?*

"It is the best day of my life, Ryan!"

Ryan's face creased into a grin. In her heart, she knew that Shannon wasn't talking about the million dollars.

A faint hum caused the women to turn their heads and gaze down the long stretch of beach that separated them from the rest of the castaways. The boat, which had been anchored off the beach while the contestants voted for a winner, was slowly chugging to shore.

"It's almost time to go."

Shannon nodded.

"I know it's kind of a goofy question," Ryan scanned the beach and then the jungle, "but are you going to miss this place?"

The blonde closed her eyes again, considering the scratchy sand, the days of living on only dry, white rice, the typhoon, the crustacean that had seemed nearly as attached to her nipples as Ryan. She thought of the biting insects, oppressive heat, and the challenges that had nearly killed her on several occasions. Then she blinked, allowing green eyes to focus firmly on Ryan. A wistful smile replaced her rueful one. "Maybe just a little," she admitted, glad that the absolute best thing about 'Paradise Island' was going home with her.

Ryan bent down and gently kissed her on the lips. "Me too. Hey, are you going to tell me why you nearly killed that lady?"

"Lady?! Ha!" Shannon snorted derisively. "That was no lady. That was Rita. My former boss and Satan's role model."

Blue eyes narrowed dangerously. That was the woman who ordered Shannon to flirt with Marty. "Damn! I should have let you kill her!" Tiffany had wanted to help get Rita. Oh God! Now *both* women in her life would be upset, and Ryan didn't know if she could take that.

"I know."

"But why now? You're rich. You don't need to go back to work for her." A sinking sensation filled Ryan's chest. Had Rita somehow talked Shannon into going back to California instead of coming with her to Kentucky?

"It's nothing like that, sweetheart," Shannon promised, instantly recognizing the look of worry on Ryan's face.

Ryan let out a relieved breath. "Then what?"

"She's giving the million dollars to Marty, not me," Shannon said flatly.

"WHAT?!" Ryan sprang to her feet and unsheathed her baby. It was time to play. "She can't do that!"

"He knows about me, Ryan. Marty knows that I used to work for the BTBC. He's threatening to go to the press with the information and claim this whole show was nothing but a network scam."

"So? You were fired! You don't work for them anymore. They *have* to give you the money!"

"It doesn't matter what's really true. The scandal alone would cause the BTBC to lose advertisers. And Rita told me that if the negative publicity hurt the BTBC badly enough, they'd file bankruptcy, and then nobody would get their prize money."

"Fuck the money! It's the principle!" Ryan took a step back toward the waiting castaways and crew, hell-bent on finishing what Shannon had started.

"No!" Shannon grabbed Ryan's hand, tugging on it until the raging woman relented and dropped next to her on the sand. "Honey, I know you don't care about the money." Shannon stroked Ryan's palm with her thumb, feeling her angry, pounding pulse through the lightly callused skin. "But I can't cost everyone their winnings. I won't. The BTBC *has* been hurting financially for years. Rita's right. If they lost their advertisers because of bad publicity, Bender would file bankruptcy, and no one would get a dime." *Including you,* she added silently.

"But…"

"I don't have a choice! I won't cost Joe and Dawn their bar, or Arturo his own salon, or…"

"But…"

"And God knows, little Edwina needs those fangs fixed."

Both women shivered. As much as she wanted to argue, Ryan knew Shannon was right. Especially about Edwina. They'd seen the photograph Marva kept tucked safely away in her bra. Of course, Marva's moment of maternal pride was slightly marred, when Marty exclaimed that Marva's saggy tits left more than enough room for a small photo *album* in the top of her bra, not just one picture. But to her credit, Marva didn't actually slug him until he said that he wished he had someone like her daughter, Edwina, on the construction site, because that girl looked like she could gnaw through solid steel!

"So the world thinks that you won the million, but Rita is going to give it to Marty just to keep him quiet?"

Shannon nodded miserably.

"I'm going to kill that prick Marty and then go after Rita." Ryan moved to get up, and, again, Shannon stopped her.

"It took me my whole life to find you, Ryan." Green eyes softened, and Shannon scooted a bit closer to the survivalist, reveling in the primal attraction and love she felt for the darker woman. Money was nice. Really nice. But it couldn't buy what she felt with Ryan. "I'm not waiting twenty-five more years for you to get out of prison. Just let it go, please." And at that very moment, Shannon realized that meant she couldn't take a chance on killing Rita either. God! Life was so unfair sometimes. Knife wounds were so traceable; she wondered briefly about poison.

Ryan hesitantly nodded. She wouldn't kill Marty or Rita. After all, it was at least partially due to Rita that she had met the love of her life. But that didn't mean she wouldn't pay them a little visit when she got stateside. She and Tiffany were relentless. And they both loved Shannon. The thought of a reconnaissance mission with Tiffany caused Ryan's pulse to race with anticipation. But she and Tiffany would bide their time. For now.

Shannon looked at the small boat and then back at Ryan. "They're almost finished loading up."

Ryan stood and put her fingers in her mouth, giving a shrill whistle that the wind carried down the beach. Marva, Marty, and Jason's heads all popped up, and they turned to wave at Ryan.

"You trained the Alpha team? Like horses or dogs?" Shannon asked incredulously.

A smug eyebrow lifted. "I have many skills."

Shannon smirked. *That*, she already knew.

"And I had to use them all. Marty isn't as smart as my horse or dog."

Shannon mentally groaned. Wasn't Tiffany enough competition without throwing Lassie and Black Beauty into the mix? She could see several more heart-to-hearts in her future.

"Let the fuckers come and get us." Ryan sat down behind Shannon so the younger woman could lean against her chest, wrapping her arms around Shannon's slim waist. She'd go hunting for some big game for her love when she got home, and help her gain back all the weight she'd lost on the island.

"Good idea." Rita still needed Shannon and Ryan for the big press conference when they got back to Bora Bora. She wouldn't leave them behind.

Ryan kissed Shannon's neck and whispered in her ear, "Tell me…if 'Castaway' were your ridiculous show, how would you end it?"

"If it were my show, it wouldn't be ridiculous."

"Of course." Ryan chuckled as Shannon thought for a moment.

They both watched as the boat picked up the last castaway and slowly made its way towards them.

"Well, I suppose I would have had one of us win the money. And get to keep it."

"But we've still got my prize money."

"And you'll pay less taxes on only a half a million."

Taxes? Is Shannon insane? Uncle Sam will be seeing a penny of our money only over my and Tiffany's dead bodies! Ryan burst out laughing.

The setting sun painted them in shades of crimson and orange. Shannon smiled, her gaze drifting out over the pristine water and gently rolling waves. "We could sail off into the sunset together. Classic endings are always nice and go over big with the hopeless romantics."

Ryan sighed happily. "Very nice."

A loud clanking noise drew the women's attention back to the boat. Next came a hiss as black smoke began to billow from the boat's stern.

"It's not Navy SEALS," Ryan assured Shannon.

The writer could only stare at her lover with affection and a good dose of fascination. Her life would certainly be a whole lot more interesting from now on. "Gee, Ryan, I feel a lot better. I was really worried about that," she deadpanned.

Ryan patted her knee. "I know, baby. Me too. But they go for the fuel lines, not the engine."

"I don't believe it." Shannon's mouth dropped open when the boat suddenly lurched to one side. "It would be a little unimaginative, but I'd love to end the show with evil Joan, and even more evil Rita, getting their just desserts."

"That would be so trite."

"But satisfying."

"True."

The boat let out a final groan before it began to sink. Rita and Joan were the first to jump ship, each trying to drown the other so that she could claim a dingy life ring that had been tossed overboard. When all their flailing only caused the ring to float out of reach and be picked up by the tide, they each tried to use the other as a floatation device.

"They're really going to kill each other." Ryan cocked her head to the side and watched.

"I know!" The blonde tilted her head skyward. "Thank you, God," she said seriously.

Then it was a free for all, as everyone abandoned the sinking boat. Arturo's girlish screams blended with Marty's vehement curses, as the Mexican began trying to give Marty mouth-to-mouth. Which wouldn't have been unreasonable, except for the fact that Marty was still completely conscious. And they were both still on the boat.

Jason was swimming to shore as fast as he could, hoping to lose his new wife, who, of course, had other ideas. She had learned English by watching reruns of 'Green Acres' and 'Welcome Back Kotter'. There was no way she was giving up her free ride to the land of milk and honey! And washing machines and indoor plumbing. She would tell Jason about her fourteen brothers and sisters, three aunts, parents and both sets of grandparents, who would be coming to live with them, later. After her citizenship went through, and she was pregnant.

Tanesha was still trying not to get her hair wet. Why couldn't 'Castaway' have been set in the ghetto? Shannon would have been trampled, in a stampede for government cheese, the very first week! This show was biased against sisters! There was a reason there were no famous black swimmers.

Pete's body fat allowed him to float along like a beached whale. He had a submarine sandwich and bag of Fritos resting comfortably on his belly, and he allowed the tide to take him where it would. He wasn't missing another damn meal, no matter what!

Dawn and Marva claimed a life raft, while Joe received a kiss from the drugged farm girl. With a supreme effort, he managed to break away and take hold of the rope that would let him tow them to shore. He loved Dawn, but he was honestly surprised that his legs still worked. He felt a sudden surge of pity for Mormon men and vowed to ask Ryan and Shannon about things he could purchase that would make his life easier and keep Dawn happy.

Strangely, as Shannon took in the entire scene, a wistful smile crossed her face. It was different, yet undeniably familiar, and her mind couldn't help but flash back to thirty-nine days ago, when they had all swum ashore, and she had vied for unknown luxury items against a mysterious, beautiful stranger with a big ass knife.

Wide blue eyes met hers. "Rita's boat ride home sank! Your wish came true."

Shannon turned her head and kissed Ryan deeply, letting all the love she felt express itself in one perfect gesture. "*All* my wishes came true," she whispered against soft lips.

"Mine too, Shannon," came the earnest response. "How about ending the show with hot monkey sex?" Ryan's heart felt like it was about to beat out of her chest. Besides, they still hadn't done it in the trees. Her lips wandered to Shannon's shoulder.

The blonde moaned. "Oh yeah. That would be a great way to end the series. Who could resist hot monkey sex?"

"Certainly not me."

Both women stood, and Ryan swept Shannon into her arms. "They can set up camp without us. There's no way another boat can get here until tomorrow. I want to spend my last day on 'Paradise Island' alone with you." Ryan had trained her team well and, like a proud mother eagle, it was time to kick them out of the nest and see if they could fly on their own.

The blonde nodded and flashed her lover a heart-stopping smile. She had a feeling every day with Ryan was going to be paradise.

<Fade out>

EPILOGUE

There's No Place Like Home

"A little to the left."

"Left?"

"Uh huh. There! Don't change a thing!"

"I won't," Shannon vowed, maintaining her white knuckled grip.

"Oh, God, baby, that's perfect. I can't believe how badly I've missed this," Ryan moaned, shifting her position and doing her best to hang on for the wild ride. "I don't think I can stand to live without it *ever, ever* again!" Her hand lifted, and she gently stroked Shannon's head, pushing a lock of hair from the younger woman's eyes.

"I know what you mean." The blonde nodded, her voice dropping to a whisper. "Jesus," was all she could think to say.

"A little more," Ryan coached.

"To the left, honey?"

"Right."

Pale brows drew together, and, while she didn't slow down, she didn't move her hands either. "'Right' as in correct? Or right…right?"

"Hurry up, Shannon," Ryan urged. "Left. Left. Left!"

"All right!"

"No, left! Now!" A sudden movement caused Ryan to jerk to one side. "No, *my* left, *my* left, *my* left! Your *other* left!"

"Oh, shit, Ryan! I can't stop it!" Shannon gasped, her pulse pounding. They were out of control.

"Hit the brakes! The brakes!"

The pickup slid down a small ravine, whose edge it had been dancing along for long moments, coming to an abrupt halt against a tall pine tree. Ryan stared at the shaken driver. "What happened, baby? You were doing so well."

Shannon uncurled her cramping fingers from the steering wheel and turned angry eyes on her lover. "Why don't *you* drive? You know where we're going!"

"Because you need to learn the way yourself."

"It would really help if I didn't have to weave through the trees and boulders and drive over jagged rocks. Not to mention that river we drove through! For Christ's sake, this isn't even a road! It's not a trail or a path. It's nothing!"

"A road?" A slender eyebrow arched. Did Shannon think that she would willingly lead the Feds right to her doorstep? "Perhaps you'd like me to leave out some bread crumbs for the FBI, too? Just to make it a little easier on them?" Ryan snorted. "Next, you'll be asking why I don't have a mailing address!"

"Funny," Shannon said without a hint of humor.

A hiss of steam escaped the hood of the truck, and something fell out of the engine, landing on the uneven ground with a dull thud. *Uh oh.* "I think I killed your new truck, Ryan."

"S'okay." Ryan shrugged, pushing open her door. "I can fix it."

"Why am I not surprised?" Shannon chuckled wryly. *I'm in love with Macgyver...with breasts.* She exited her side of the vehicle, taking a deep breath of cool, pine-scented air. So different from LA, yet oddly reminiscent of the wilderness shop next to the Radio Shack in the mall in Laguna. *God, I'm screwed up! Maybe Ryan is right, and I do need deprogramming.* "How far do we still have to go?" It seemed like they had been driving through the trees for hours.

"Go? We're not going anywhere, Shannon. We're home." With an enormous grin, Ryan opened her arms wide, indicating their surroundings.

"Huh?" Green eyes scanned the forest. Nothing. She had figured Ryan's survivalist community wouldn't have much in the way of modern conveniences, but this was ridiculous. Hadn't Ryan mentioned a cabin? Even the Beta camp had been...well, a camp! *Don't tell me they just throw their blankets or sleeping bags right on the ground. Oooo, me and Ryan in a sleeping bag together. Naked.* Shannon sighed as she warmed to the idea. Really warmed. *And we'd be all sweaty. Hot monkey sex...minus the actual monkeys. I like it.* She turned to the taller woman, and her eyes softened. *She's worth it, Shannon. No matter what you have to give up. Ryan's worth that and more.*

A teasing smile curled Ryan's lips. "Your parking leaves a lot to be desired. But you did get us to the right spot. This is it." Was Shannon blind? The cabin was right in front of her. Sure, it was camouflaged to keep it hidden from prying government eyes. But they were only a few feet away. Ryan shook her head. Shannon had many, many skills, most of which Ryan had no intention of letting another human being find out about. But detecting hidden things was, apparently, not among them.

"Okaaaay," Shannon drew out the word. She knew Ryan would point the way to their bush sooner or later. "Where do you want me to put my stuff?" She gestured toward the cardboard boxes that filled the pickup's bed.

Ryan frowned. Had Shannon been replaced with a robot? That had to be it. The 'real' Shannon would have thrown her to the ground by now, demanding they make love.

It had been—Ryan began counting on her fingers—nearly six hours! This was clearly an imposter. It must have been the robot's *almost* life-like coordination that had prevented it from being able to traverse that last ravine! Shannon was nothing if not dexterous. Ryan bit back a growl of arousal.

And if that wasn't enough proof, as a memento of their trip, the 'real' Shannon had insisted they make love in every state they passed through on their way to Kentucky. They had enjoyed X-rated Kodak moments all over the nation. Ryan grinned happily. It *was* a lot more fun than collecting spoons. Those people were just sick. Anyway, *this* Shannon hadn't even tried to cop a feel since they'd crossed the border.

The survivalist yanked up Shannon's shirt and suppressed a moan at the sight of that deliciously firm stomach. Was it wrong to be turned on by Shannon's doppelganger? She was sure it was and decided she wouldn't tell the 'real' Shannon about her perverse attraction to her mechanical twin. Ryan wondered briefly if the 'real' Shannon would let her keep the remarkably life-like doll. She smiled devilishly. That much fun could kill her.

But what a way to go!

Ryan gasped. The Feds had even remembered that tiny mole on her belly. Damn, they were good. They must have made the switch in that public restroom Shannon had insisted on using in Omaha. *Don't worry, baby! Tiffany and I will find you!*

"Oooo, Ryan," the blonde squealed in delight as curious fingers began poking and prodding her every orifice. She had intended on saving their first Kentucky romp for Ryan's bedroom. But, since Ryan didn't appear to have one, now was good, too.

Abruptly stopping her inspection, Ryan reached inside the truck and grabbed her travel cup—full of root beer. Using Tiffany's exquisite, multifunctional tip, she popped the tight lid. Without a word, she turned and splashed the cup's entire contents in Shannon's face, waiting for her to short-circuit.

Ryan wasn't disappointed.

*   *   *

"I believe you. I believe you! Dear God, I swear by Tiffany's perfect, razor-sharp blade that you're the 'real' Shannon!" Ryan cried out, her voice hoarse from her screaming.

Shannon drew up to her knees, a satisfied smirk crossing her face. "Call me an uncoordinated robot, will you…" her words trailed off.

"You're so right, baby," Ryan admitted readily, gasping for air. "A robot could never do that. I'm sorry I ever doubted you."

With that apology, Shannon finally released Ryan's wrists and rolled off her. Leaning against a rock, she blew damp bangs off her forehead with a mighty puff. After Ryan had thrown her drink in Shannon's face, the younger woman hurled herself at the survivalist. As intent on killing her as she was, wrestling with Ryan had left Shannon breathless and even hornier than normal.

It was *too* possible!

But refusing to give into her baser needs, which were pretty much *all* of her needs around Ryan, Shannon began tickling her lover with a single-minded ferocity that Ryan found truly frightening.

The brunette decided to include Shannon's torture technique as an elective in Jeeter's spring curriculum. She squirmed uncomfortably from her prostrate position in the dirt. God, Shannon was good!

"I made you pee your pants, didn't I?" Shannon asked smugly. She was good and she knew it.

"No!"

"Uh huh."

A low growl sounded from the bushes, pulling both women's attention away from their play. "Grrrr….Grrr…."

"Uh…Ryan, honey?" Shannon jumped to her feet and extended her hand to the taller woman. With wide eyes, she began tugging Ryan toward the truck.

"No worries, baby. That's just…"

"Uff!" Shannon found herself lying flat on her back with 70 pounds of drooling bloodhound on her chest; the hound's long, rough tongue snaking out to lick her face and neck. "Jesus! Gross! Ack! Ack!" Shannon laughed and gagged as she tried to push the droopy face away from hers. Of course, that only caused the hound's sagging jowls to drag through his own saliva, spreading it even further across her cheeks.

"That's Paul Revere. Revere for short. He's our trusty watch dog." Ryan smiled proudly. "Revere's here to warn us of invasion."

"But we've been here for half…yuck! A half an hour already," Shannon sputtered, finally succeeding in pushing the beast off of her chest.

Ryan grimaced and looked at her watch. *Damn!* "Well, it's sort of his nap time." *I thought I broke him of that before I left!*

Revere flipped over onto his back, exposing himself in the process, and begged for a belly scratching from his 'victim'.

Ryan's mouth dropped open in shock.

"Oh yeah. He's totally fearsome," Shannon chuckled as she easily complied with Revere's wishes, paying special attention to a spot on his chest that got his legs and tail thumping wildly. "I'm just glad I wasn't an invader. I would be sooo afraid."

Revere let out a very satisfied growl at the scratching he was receiving, not bothering to give his owner the time of day.

"Benedict Arnold," Ryan muttered to the blissful hound. Blue eyes narrowed. What had happened to her trustee watchdog over the past two months while she had been away? He was lethargic and overweight, looking more like a mutant pig than a dog, and treating Shannon, a total stranger, like his long lost, best friend.

Another few seconds under Shannon's ministrations and Revere was snoring loudly.

The young blonde laughed out loud at the look of surprise, then embarrassment, on Ryan's face. Standing, she kissed the survivalist thoroughly, making sure got Ryan own taste of Revere's drool. "I'm sure we just caught Revere at a bad moment, honey," she lied, trying to wipe the smile from her face. "You finally trained Marty not to pee in the camp. And you only had to rub his nose in it twice."

Ryan ducked her head. Blushing, she dug her toe into the moist soil. "It was really Tiffany that helped him finally break that nasty habit. I was just holding her at the time." *Against his balls,* she added silently.

"Still…" Shannon smiled warmly. "We all appreciated it."

"Well, if it isn't Ryan Daly, my long lost sister!" a voice boomed from behind the women, appearing out of nowhere.

"Patrick!" Ryan laughed, spinning around and hurling herself at the clean-cut young man of middling height and slender build, who was dressed in a neatly pressed polo shirt, faded blue jeans, and leather loafers without socks.

Shannon couldn't believe her eyes. She'd figured on a fuzzy-faced, eye patch-wearing, tobacco-chewing brute of a man. They were in Kentucky, right? She'd seen 'Deliverance'! She was still waiting for the sound of 'Dueling Banjos' to ring out in the forest.

Wait a minute! Ryan Daly? Who the hell is that? "Daly?" Shannon turned and asked her partner. Although Ryan had never actually told Shannon her last name, she was sure the Castaway brochure had said 'Stryker'. Damn. She had pulled up stakes to be with this woman. And she didn't even know her name! *I am not a slut. I am not!*

Ryan recognized the confusion in Shannon's eyes. She honestly couldn't remember which name she'd given the 'Castaway' production people until Shannon had just reminded her. She sighed. So many aliases. So little time. "I'm Ryan Daly." Doubt still lingered in Shannon's expression, so Ryan promised, "Really, sweetheart. I swear. Ryan Stryker is just the name I filled out on my 'Castaway' application for…" a devilish grin creased her cheeks, "tax purposes."

At the word 'tax' both Ryan and Patrick began howling with laughter. *This must be one of those inside joke things,* Shannon finally decided, watching the siblings punch each other's shoulders and stomachs, barely able to remain upright they were laughing so hysterically.

"Is there anything else I should know about you, *Ryan*?" Shannon demanded, hoping, at least, she had that much right. She cringed. What if she had been screaming out the wrong name all these weeks? *I am not a slut. I am not!*

Ryan smiled rakishly. "Well, there may be a few *insignificant* things you don't know about me." She shrugged one shoulder. "But they're nothing to worry about."

Shannon smirked. "Why doesn't that comfort me?"

Ryan grinned again in return. A girl had to have some secrets, after all. There were even a few things so personal, so intensely intimate, that Ryan couldn't share them with Tiffany. Okay, there really weren't. But they had had years to bond! And she didn't want to frighten away the luscious writer. She planned on keeping her.

"You must be Shannon," the young man greeted her, holding out his palm. "I'm Patrick."

"Hello, Patrick. Your sister has told me absolutely nothing about you."

Patrick burst out laughing again. "Figures. Ryan tends to be a little…" Whatever he was going to say was interrupted by a firm slap on the back that knocked the wind from his lungs and caused him to start coughing.

Shannon put her hands on her hips and glared at Ryan.

"Mosquito," the tall woman explained lamely.

A faint rustling of leaves drew Ryan's attention to the ground. This time it wasn't Revere. He was still belly up, sawing logs. "Pat, where is…"

"ARGGGGGHHHHHHHHHH!!!!!!!!!!!!!!!" A beefy young man, wearing fatigues and painted head to toe in camouflage, exploded out of a pit a few feet from Ryan, who immediately threw herself in front of Shannon. Leaves and twigs were plastered all over his body, making him looking like a human bush. His eyes were round and wild as he rushed the survivalist.

Ryan merely sidestepped the charging man, sending him sprawling face first into the dirt. She turned to Shannon and raised an amused eyebrow. "This is my other brother…"

"Patrick?"

Patrick and Shannon laughed, but Ryan didn't get the joke. "No." She
looked confused for a moment. "You already met Patrick. This is Sean.
He just turned eighteen and is a little enthusiastic."

Sean jumped to his feet, yanking two large Rambo-type knives from
sheathes at his waist. He began circling Ryan, expertly spinning the
knives. "Identify yourself!"

Ryan leaned closer to Shannon and whispered conspiratorially, "Sean
is just the teeniest bit," she paused, hating to say the word, "paranoid."

Pale eyebrows shot skyward. Coming from Ryan, that took on a
whole new meaning. Shannon remained behind her companion, glad
for Ryan's strong, protective demeanor. Ryan *was* different...but
Shannon liked to think of her as endearingly quirky. Sean, on the other
hand, looked just plane wacko.

"Put those away, Sean!" Ryan barked. Nobody was allowed to fright-
en her luscious writer.

Sean gripped his knives even tighter, his pale eyes squinting suspiciously. "You look and sound like her...but how do I know you're really Ryan?"

"You could throw a soda in her face," Shannon deadpanned, the tip
of her tongue snaking out and licking a sticky, mostly dried drop of
root beer.

"What's the password?" Sean queried warily. "You've got 10 seconds.
Ten, Nine, two, one!"

Ryan shook her head. Her baby brother could be so—she sighed
internally—'intense'. She wondered briefly where he could have picked
up such an unusual trait. Oh, well, it didn't matter. He had a firm, if
slightly skewed, grip on reality. She could work with that. And at least
he wasn't fat, farting, and snoring like Revere. She'd hate to have to put
down her own brother.

Smiling crookedly, Ryan seriously intoned, "Trust..."

"No one!" Sean finished with a gleeful shout, dropping his blades.
"Ryan! My sister!"

"Sean! My brother!" Ryan yelled with equal gusto, opening her arms to the youngest Daly.

*　　　　　*　　　　　*

"This is amazing," Shannon muttered to herself as Ryan finished giving her the grand tour of the cabin. The structure was completely nestled between several huge, twisting trees. Netting impregnated with leaves, twigs and ivy covered the wood, making the home blend into the landscape almost perfectly. Shannon had been shocked to find she was standing on Ryan's doorstep.

Literally.

"I'm glad you like it." Ryan's head dropped bashfully. "It's not like southern California, but…"

"You're joking, right? This place is fabulous." Shannon opened the door to the last room she hadn't seen and found a large whirlpool bath surrounded by redwood benches and brightly covered clay pots overflowing with beautiful, variegated ferns. For a moment she was speechless, then she began counting. "You have an office, a den, two guest bedrooms, a greenhouse, a gym, a laboratory that I don't want to know anything more about…ever, and a game room in the basement." *I won't be living under a rock!* her mind cheered. *Fuck you, Joan! Fuck you, Bender! But above all, fuck you, Rita!!*

"Not a basement, baby," Ryan corrected, mildly insulted, "a solid concrete survival shelter capable of withstanding chemical, nuclear, and biological attack, complete with its own air and water filtration system, small artillery storage, including light anti-aircraft weaponry, and a year's supply of food."

Shannon's brow creased. She hadn't seen any of those things. "And the big screen TV, pool table, pinball machines and overstuffed, leather Lazy Boy recliners?"

"Umm…" Ryan bit her lip. "Those are necessary items for…for…for…" she thought wildly, "stress relief." Heh. That was pretty good. "Yeah, stress relief."

Shannon laughed. She had other ideas for how Ryan could relieve stress, the word 'naked' figuring prominently in all of them.

"Besides, my 3M stock split last year. I had to buy the boys something for Christmas, didn't I?" Ryan's expression turned slightly petulant; she knew she was busted.

"The boys, huh?" Shannon's tone was playful. "Wasn't that you screaming at Sean to get his lazy, leaf-covered ass out of *your* chair?"

Ryan scowled, but Shannon stepped forward and kissed away the grumpy face. "I'm just teasing, sweetie." She patted Ryan's chest. "I'm happy you've got someplace comfortable that you love."

Ryan wrapped her arms around the shorter woman and looked down, affection and devotion written clearly across her face. "Good. Because your recliner will be ready to be picked up next week."

Patrick and Sean walked by the room, the older man poking his head in the doorway. "She can sit next to me." Patrick grinned engagingly.

Sean suddenly moved in front of Patrick, blocking his view of the women. "Why you? Why not me?"

Shannon's eyes widened. "Can't I just sit next to Ryan?" she offered tentatively. What did it matter where she sat? She didn't even like TV!

"I sit in the middle, baby," Ryan clarified. "They're talking about which one of them gets your other side."

"Couldn't you just move your chair to the end?"

Move her chair? Ryan looked at Shannon like the blonde was from outer space. Didn't she understand that her center position in front of the television was sacred? Like her framed photo of Janet Reno caught picking her nose, the Holy Grail, or Tiffany's sharpening stone. You don't mess with things like that! Suddenly, Ryan's astonished look shifted into a relieved smile. "Yeah, right," she snorted. "Good one, honey. You really had me going there for a minute."

Patrick marched up and stuck his face into Sean's. "Why would she want to sit next to you? She hasn't expressed a preference for sheep lovers!"

"Not smart," Ryan groaned to herself, taking her head in her hands.

Sean flushed brick red. "I told you, I was just checking the wool. That's all!" he ground out between clenched teeth before roughly pushing Patrick a step back. "Besides, she wouldn't be safe sitting next to a little girl like you anyway."

"But I like girls," Shannon promised quickly, hoping things wouldn't escalate further. "A lot."

"Just because I take a bath doesn't make me a girl! 'Course you wouldn't know that, seein' as how we have to shear your girlfriends every fall and dip them for fleas."

"Sissy boy," Sean taunted.

"Let's watch Sean get hot. Baaaa...Baaaaaa!"

Sean threw a solid punch that connected with Patrick's jaw with a loud crunch, instantly dropping the man to his knees.

Patrick retaliated with a vicious strike to his brother's groin, causing Sean to wail pitifully and clutch his privates before his legs buckled beneath him and he fell alongside his brother.

Shannon looked on in horror while Ryan beamed with pride. She'd taught them both of those moves. She sniffed back a tear. They'd been practicing while she was gone. Damn, it was good to be home!

*   *   *

Ryan, Patrick and Sean sat staring at their hands, disbelief marring their handsome, angular features.

Shannon worried the inside of her cheek. After several long moments, when it was apparent that no one was going to say a word, the young writer's patience snapped. "Tell me! I can't stand it! What did you think?"

Still nothing.

"Was it that bad?" Shannon twisted the afghan in her hands, waiting for a response.

"My God, baby!" Ryan finally blurted out. "Was it necessary to be so...so," the tips of her ears turned scarlet, "explicit?" She held up the first four chapters of Shannon's novel. "Don't get me wrong," Ryan smirked. Shannon was wonderfully wicked when she wanted to be. God she loved this woman! "You *did* make your point. It's just that page sixty-nine was..."

Patrick snatched page sixty-nine from his sister's hand and hid it under the stack of pages in his lap, wondering if Shannon's book had melted his laser printer. "Don't read it," Ryan, he pleaded in a whisper. "I do appreciate the irony of its placement, Shannon." He cringed. "But, dear God, I can't hear it again!"

Pale brows lifted. Considering his close relationship with his sister, Shannon was surprised at Patrick's lack of appreciation for alternative lifestyles.

Sean glanced up at Shannon with watery, innocent eyes. "I think it is the single most beautiful thing ever written!" he proclaimed, his emotion-laden voice cracking at the end. "The romance...the passion..."

Shannon's jaw sagged a bit. She suspected that if anyone was going to be bothered by this novel, the chronicle of her stay on the island with Ryan, it would be Sean. This was a pleasant surprise. Tucking a strand of hair behind her ear, she grabbed a tissue from the box on the coffee table and passed it to Sean.

"I haven't been so moved since Aunt Zelda's prune bars!"

A month ago Shannon would have been insulted. Today she took it for the compliment that it was and patted Sean's knee. He wasn't quite as eloquent as his sister, who, despite her initial, dismal attempt at poetry carved into fish, could turn Shannon's legs to jelly when she put her mind to it.

Embarrassed by his outburst, the young man dabbed the corners of his leaking eyes.

"Thank you, Sean. I'm glad you liked it." Shannon smiled warmly. "I didn't know you liked love stories," she teased gently, leaning forward to ruffle the young man's hair. In the month since she'd moved into the cabin, she'd grown quite fond of both of Ryan's brothers.

Sean leafed through his own copy of the novel and pulled out page sixty-nine, mostly to torture Patrick, but also because it was so damn beautiful. He cleared his throat and began reading:

> *Slender hands caressed strong arms, stroking the length of sinewy muscle.*
>
> *"You are so hot. I've waited for this for so long."*
>
> *"I know. No matter how hard I tried, the attraction was too powerful to ignore."*
>
> *Hands threaded their way into dark hair, pulling hard, sweat-slicked, naked bodies together. They weren't sure which was louder: the sound of their pounding hearts or the crashing surf.*
>
> *"Kiss me, Marty. I can't wait another moment! Channon told me you loved me. But I didn't dare believe it was true."*
>
> *"It's true, sweetheart. I can't deny it any longer. I've wanted you from the very start. I've been eyeing men on the construction site for years. Burning with lust for them. Watching their muscular asses every single time they bent over....But none of them made me feel like you do. I love you, Arturo. Take me!"*

"Oh God, stop, stop! Ack. Bleck. Ack!" Patrick grabbed his stomach and began making gagging noises while Sean wiped away another tear.

Ryan laughed and pulled Shannon into her lap. "You did good, baby. This will ruin that prick Marty's life. And it will take years to wipe the grin off Arturo's face."

Shannon smiled wickedly, her eyes taking on a truly evil glint. "I know." *But I'm not finished with Marty yet.* "Why don't you guys go get washed up, and I'll fix us something for lunch?"

Sean and Patrick dutifully scampered off, leaving Ryan behind with her lover. "Having second thoughts?" the tall woman asked, wondering about the sudden look of melancholy that stole over Shannon's face. She began to move out from under Shannon.

"No," Shannon laughed softly. "Just thinking. Go on." She gave her a quick kiss before playfully shoving her toward the door. "See what we have to eat. I'll be there in a second."

Ryan cocked her head to the side, peering at Shannon from the doorway. "You sure you're okay?"

Shannon nodded, tracking the sound of Ryan's footsteps down the hall. She ambled over to her desk and opened a drawer, removing a floppy disk. Deep in thought, she brought the disk up to her mouth and absently gnawed on the end.

Shannon loved Kentucky. She had a wonderful place to live. And a wonderful new family to share it with. Sure, it had been an adjustment. She had known it would be. But, surprisingly, they were all taking the changes in their lives in stride.

The writer loved how she could walk out of her house at night and look at the stars without the slightest concern of being murdered where she stood. Who knew people could feel so free? She felt inspired.

The air was cool and clean, and she wondered how many years she'd added to her life simply by escaping the smog. Traffic was a thing of the past, despite that little road rage incident between Ryan and her brothers when they all tried to park their vehicles in the shed at the same time. But the boys were healing nicely.

She would miss the Laker Girls. But Ryan was worth the sacrifice!

And that's what it came down to. She had Ryan. The love of her life. The biggest part of her newfound inspiration. And that was just her breasts. When Shannon thought of the complete package, inside and out, her heart skipped a beat.

So was this *really* necessary? She tapped her chin for a second or two before an enormous smile split her face, crinkling her eyes and nose. Hell, yes, it was necessary!

Grabbing a pen and envelope, she began writing. It was all she could do to not burst into helpless laughter. Maybe she'd learned a thing or two from Rita after all.

*   *   *

Marva's husband, Bo, cursed as the rental car took another precarious bounce. Marva covered little Edwina's ears and gave Bo a cautionary glare. "Bo, you know how I feel about that!" she chastised.

The big man looked over grumpily. "This is ridiculous. I swear we passed that tree before."

She looked down at the directions Ryan had given her while they were in California. Already the ink was fading from the paper. She was sure Ryan had planned that. "Let's go a little further, and then...oh my God, Bo! Look out!"

Bo slammed on the brakes as he recognized the camouflage-clad figure in front of them. The car skidded forward and came to a halt with a hiss. Ryan bounded around to the passenger side window and leaned in. "Glad you made it!"

"Did we make it?" Marva asked.

"Sure. Just a little further and you'll be at the cabin. Shannon is so excited about your visit." She looked at little Edwina. The child wasn't quite so fearsome with her new dental work completed.

"We're close?" Bo asked, scratching his stomach. He hadn't scratched it in a few minutes and it was important to reestablish his connection to it. He briefly wondered what they'd be eating for dinner. He hadn't seen a Dairy Queen for miles.

"Yeah. We'll leave the car here and walk the last hundred yards. The road gets a bit rough ahead. Even Shannon had trouble with it."

"Road?" Bo questioned.

"In a manner of speaking." Ryan flashed a bright smile. "Come on, let's get going. The longer we're out in the open, the longer they can track us."

Marva silenced Bo's inquiry with another pointed look. She handed their daughter to him and leaned over the backseat to release Hubert from his car seat. "Time to see Aunt Shannon," she announced cheerfully.

*   *   *

Later, Shannon and Marva were in the kitchen, finishing up dinner. "How do you like life here?" Marva asked. She kept looking out the window for Bambi. Actually, more accurately, for the hunter who shot poor, little Bambi's mother.

The writer smiled. "It's nice. Different. But nice."

"And Ryan?"

Shannon paused. How to describe normal life with Ryan? Okay, it was hardly normal, but it wasn't as unusual as being stranded on an island. "Happy." She opted for simplicity in her answer. "The best thing about Ryan is: she's uncomplicated, believe it or not. She has a pretty simple worldview."

"Do you miss civilization?"

Shannon laughed softly. "I don't miss traffic jams, noisy neighbors, or the rat race, that's for sure." She scratched her cheek as she thought.

"Ryan had her brothers add a lot of amenities to this place before I arrived. And I've been surprisingly comfortable and content. Occasionally, I miss the mall, but don't tell Ryan that. She believes they are the epicenter of the FBI's surveillance of the population. She won't enter one."

"At all?"

Shannon shook her head. "Nope. Too many video cameras. She says Janet Reno has enough pictures of her as it is."

The two shared a laugh and began carrying dinner in to the table. At first, Marva had been worried they'd be eating chipmunk (a favorite of her in-laws) or something worse. She had been relieved when Shannon showed her the roast. Well, after she confirmed it was cow.

Bo and Ryan were laughing at the table, reliving their time together in Los Angeles. "I don't think I've ever seen a hairier back!"

Ryan shivered. "It would have been faster if we had used yard clippers."

"I think the duct tape was pretty effective," Bo countered.

The two laughed once more. "We'll have to watch the videotape again after dinner."

"Are you two talking about Marty again?" Shannon asked, setting the meat down on the table.

Bo snickered. "You mean Martina?"

While in LA, Ryan and Bo had sneaked into Marty's hotel room, after having given him a sedative at dinner. While he slept, they shaved his legs, underarms, chest and back, then slipped him into a pink nightie. They were going to shave something else, but neither one would volunteer for that 'sensitive' job, so they dropped the idea. Arturo was only too happy to pose for a series of pictures with the large foreman. He merely asked for copies. Bo and Ryan had videotaped the whole event, as well, so they could enjoy it later. And send copies to Marty at Christmas and other major holidays.

Dinner went well, even with Hubert throwing candied yams over to Revere. The bloodhound ate the tubers happily and wandered over to the table. As a sign of affection, he rested his drool-soaked mug on Shannon's knee. As nonchalantly as possible, Shannon reached under the table and slid her napkin under his jowls. "So, Marva, have you heard anything from our fellow castaways?"

"Oh, sure." She fished into her pocketbook, pulling out a postcard from Las Vegas. "Dawn and Joe eloped."

"Vegas?" Shannon asked. "That's pretty...tacky...and a bit far from Kansas."

"Ohio," Marva corrected.

No, that didn't sound right. "Indiana."

"Iowa." Marva finally remembered. All those Midwest states were the same. Especially the ones with four letters in their names. "She says she and Joe want to be as far away from a beach as possible. It seems they're going to move there. Dawn is going to be a blackjack dealer, and Joe a bartender at the Luxor."

"Great!" Bo boomed. "Someone to stay with when we visit."

"I told you we aren't visiting there."

Shannon glanced at Ryan and immediately discerned they wouldn't be visiting either. "Why won't we be going, dear?"

Ryan rolled her eyes. "The mob."

"The mob doesn't keep records, sweetie. They don't want those surveillance tapes around long either."

"It's not that." Ryan studied her shoes bashfully. "It's...they wanted me to do them a couple of favors."

Shannon was intrigued. This was another thing she didn't know about her lover. "You're kidding. Like what?"

"I know how to disappear people."

Marva dropped her fork.

Bo backed away from the table.

"In the non-murderous sense, right?" Shannon realized she should clarify before the dinner party broke up early.

"Sure. I'm not dead and I've disappeared." Ryan shook her head. People could be so dense sometimes. "Those damn Feds will never find me. And the IRS hasn't seen a nickel from me since 1992. Before then, I just underreported."

Everyone visibly relaxed.

"Sugarplum, you need to tell them about that infomercial we saw last week." Bo decided to change the subject since his wife was looking rather disconcerted. Or maybe it was PMS. Damn, women were complicated!

"Thanks for reminding me." Marva bestowed a fond look on her husband. "We saw Molly and Desiree on this infomercial the other night."

"Selling what?"

"Self-esteem tapes. Molly does the psychobabble, and Desiree the beauty tips."

Ryan was unimpressed. Both she and Bo scratched their guts at the same time. "Did her hair grow back yet?"

"It's still a little short and patchy," Marva admitted.

"We heard from Arturo," Shannon chimed in eagerly. It was fun talking about these people now that she didn't have to see them on a daily basis. Or ever again in most cases. "He and Raul are doing well together. Seems those pictures of him and Marty from Los Angeles were just the thing to make Raul attentive again."

"I bet Marty would love to hear he saved Arturo's love life." Marva leaned over and wiped off Hubert's chin before Revere could beat her to it.

"Nothing could save Jason's love life." Shannon began gathering up the dishes to take them to the kitchen. "We saw him on 'Hard Copy' last week. Apparently his ex-fiancée didn't take too well to his marriage." She laughed recalling the look on his face at the final tribal council. "Her father, the senator, also happens to be on the Senate Subcommittee on Immigration. Looks like Jason might have to move to Bora Bora to be with his wife."

"It couldn't happen to a nicer guy," Ryan muttered, "although he is partially responsible for your makeover."

Marva fought to keep a smile from her face, remembering Shannon's initial reaction to the haircut. Time for another change of subject, she suspected. "Tanesha is doing pretty well. I hear she's giving motivational talks at elite prep schools in New England."

"Prep schools?" Shannon echoed. "New England?"

"What type of talks?" The survivalist knew this had to be interesting.

"Race relations."

"NASCAR?" Bo asked. "God damn, I'd love a job in their public relations department."

"No," Marva patted his arm gently, "race like skin color."

"Where the hell is the fun in that?"

"I want to know what happened to some of those early losers," Ryan admitted. "The ones we kicked off the island early because they were so lame."

"We saw Tony on our visit to Disney World earlier!" Marva gushed, suddenly remembering the sulky teenager who filled up their car. She had been concerned since he kept lighting up cigarettes while pumping gas. Marva had been careful to get the kids and Bo out of the car and into the Gas-n-Sip. It wasn't hard to coax them.

Shannon started laughing, remembering their time driving back from California. "Remember when we saw what David was up to, honey?"

Ryan looked like a deer caught in the reflection of Tiffany's glimmering blade. "We what?"

"When we were driving. Remember?"

The survivalist shook her head. She had been in the passenger seat and had been focused on Shannon's legs. She had really liked the way Shannon's calves looked while she was working the gas and brake pedals. "No."

Shannon laughed amiably, knowing what Ryan was thinking. *Lech* .
"Seems the good preacher has relocated his congregation from a church
in Arizona to…get this…a drive-in theater."

"He's showing them movies?" Bo asked. He couldn't imagine a
preacher showing any of the movies Hollywood was making nowadays.

"No. He's preaching in front of the screen, and people listen to him
on the little boxes they hang in their car windows. He collects money
from them at the ticket booth on their way out."

"My God, what will they think of next?!" Marva exclaimed, laughing.

Revere began barking, and nudging Ryan where she sat. The lanky
woman scratched his furry head, eliciting more drool from the hound.
Revere whimpered and glanced over at the television in the living room.

"Ah, that's right, boy," Ryan praised. She explained to the less astute
at the table. "Revere was reminding me it's time for the debut episode
of 'Gulag.'"

Shannon squealed excitedly, "Wonderful! I hope that Joan freezes her
pointy little breasts off!"

The other two women shivered at the thought, although it got Ryan
to thinking about ice cubes and Shannon and later that evening. She
could do a mean Russian accent, too, from her counter-espionage training. Ryan leered at her little babushka.

Shannon slapped her arm, snapping her thoughts back to the
moment.

The group wandered into the living room and took their places
around the television. The survivalist sat in her overstuffed, Lazy Boy
recliner, pulling the blonde onto her lap. Bo followed her lead and took
the other one, grabbing Marva. Edwina, anxious to not be left out,
plopped on the ground and dragged her little brother down next to her.

Leaning over the side of the recliner, Shannon picked up their safety
caps. Okay, so they wore foil hats to prevent subliminal messages from
seeping into their brains during commercials. To keep herself from feeling completely idiotic, Shannon had dubbed them 'safety caps'. It didn't

change the facts, but it made her feel better. Besides, if it ever came down to it, she would deny ever having seen them before in her life. Out of habit, she plopped one on Ryan's head and then on her own.

Marva and Bo stared at them, slack-jawed.

"You'll find yours beside the chair. I made a couple extra for the kids too," Ryan said, gesturing to them.

"Uh, thanks." Marva, being Southern, knew that this was a sign of hospitality and could not be refused. She helped her family get their hats on and smiled affectionately at Ryan. Funny, the survivalist's behavior didn't seem nearly this odd on the island. Then again, she herself had exposed her breasts while gambling, eaten fish guts (and several things whose origins she didn't want to know about), committed an act of violence against another human being, and played matchmaker for two women. So it wasn't like she could throw stones.

Once assured of everyone's safety, Ryan turned on the television with the remote. They were just in time for the opening music, a mixture of pained wailing and mating pigs.

A light flickered and they could make out several people running in the darkness.

"Why are they running?" Marva wondered aloud.

Gunfire erupted.

Bo leaned forward. "That sounds like live ammo." He looked at Ryan for confirmation.

"Definitely is. I'd say two, maybe three M-16's and a couple of old, bolt-action babies to boot."

Shannon kissed the brunette's hair. "We need to get you another hobby, sweetheart."

Marva asked her follow up question. "Why are they firing weapons?"

Before anyone could reply, Joan's face filled the screen. She was poorly lit, sans makeup and her lips were a vivid blue. "We believe that the Alpha Team has managed to find the supply of arms that was hidden in the Gulag."

More gunfire. Joan dove face first into a snow bank. When she thought it was safe, she pulled out her head and shook it wildly. She looked like a dog drying itself after an unexpected drinking escapade in the toilet. Joan cursed loudly as she tried to remove the snow that was packed up her nostrils.

"Man, she's stupid. Everyone knows the only way to get ice outta your nose is to remove your mittens first," Bo offered sagely.

"What's the bleepin' noise, Mama?" Hubert asked pointing to the television as Joan's face turned blood red and she momentarily lost control. It was the first color she'd had in her frozen cheeks in days.

"Never you mind," Marva shushed.

"I think it's safe to say the Alpha Team has the upper hand right now," Joan whispered into the microphone when the gunfire drew closer.

Shannon crowed gleefully. "Thank you, Jesus! I got the girl, and off that tropical island, and Joan gets to freeze her ass off surrounded by Gulag guards and gunfire. There is a God!"

Marva smirked right along with Shannon and Ryan. "Don't forget that Yun-kyung is in jail, too."

"Yes!" Shannon pumped her arm over what was already one of her most replayed memories. Well, that and the time she and Ryan did it in the drive-through of Taco Bell while driving cross-country. Now every damn time that little damn Chihuahua came on TV, her nipples turned hard as rocks. *Yo quiero…*

"Shannon," Ryan prodded gently. "You were saying?"

"Sorry." She smiled sheepishly. "Anyway, we saw her satellite interview on the 'Jerry Springer Show'. She looked terrible!"

"She's awaiting trial in Borneo. She's hardly going to be looking great."

Shannon shrugged. She was still pissed at the Korean for cutting her fishing line, holding her friends hostage, and threatening to kill them. She was silly that way. "I'll make popcorn!"

*   *   *

Shannon sat on the edge of the bed, nervously clutching an envelope between her fingers.

Naked.

She had a brief flash of doubt. But as she looked at the contents of the envelope, those fleeting feelings of guilt all but evaporated. Ryan wouldn't think less of her. She was positive. Almost.

Ryan rounded the corner into their bedroom. "You called me…." The rest of her words blended into a jumbled mess at the sight of the luscious, young writer perched nude on her bed. Ryan immediately slammed their door shut. She swallowed hard. "You…" Despite her best intentions, darkening blue eyes languorously made their way down Shannon's body. Lingering on the really good parts. "You wanted me?" She frowned when the last word came out a croak.

"I did."

"I'm here."

"I have something to show you."

"I've seen it, baby. But I'll be happy to look again." Ryan practically sprinted across the room, pouncing on Shannon.

"Ryan, I…" Shannon jumped when Ryan's hands began kneading her ass and seeking lips attached themselves to her neck. "Oh God, Ryan. I can't talk when you do that."

"Good."

"But…yes!" Shannon cried out when Ryan's kisses moved down her body to her breast and began sucking a painfully hard nipple. *I do not want a taco now! I don't!* "But, sweetheart…" she moaned, her voice dropping an octave. "I really have to…" *What do I have to do again? Oh yeah.* "You need to see this. It's important."

Ryan frowned. Whenever Patrick or Sean said that it meant they wanted her to pop a really big zit on their backs, where they couldn't reach. She hoped whatever Shannon had to show her was more appealing.

"What I have in this envelope will change our lives." Shannon pulled the crumpled wad from between their bodies.

Ryan breathed a sigh of relief. No zit. Her face was suddenly thrust against Shannon's breast.

"You don't have to stop!" *God, I'm weak!* "I'll just tell you about what's inside."

Ryan nodded. She didn't give a rat's ass what was in that envelope. Her girl was naked, excited, and best of all…under her. Nothing in that envelope could top that.

Shannon shuddered under Ryan's attentions. She was rapidly losing interest in her surprise, so she decided to make it quick. "I sent my…ohhhh! Just like that!"

Ryan nodded vigorously. She was sure Shannon was saying something to her; she'd ask her exactly what it was later. *God, her skin is soft.*

"Um…I sent a copy of my manuscript to Marty."

"That's nice," Ryan mumbled against the pale skin on Shannon's chest.

"Are you listening?"

In response, Ryan's grip on Shannon's bottom tightened, pulling their bodies even closer together.

"Good!" Shannon hissed.

Ryan wasn't sure what she was referring to, but it didn't matter. Awkwardly, she began kicking off her boots. The movement caused the bed to bounce up and down, and Shannon muttered her approval.

"I blackmailed him with my manuscript." Shannon squirmed a little so that Ryan's ammunition belt wasn't digging into her kidney anymore. "In this envelope is a cashier's check for one million dollars."

Ryan's lips hovered over their next target, not moving.

I knew I should have done this after I got out of the whirlpool.

"You did what?"

Oh God. Oh God. She's going to hate me. Marty's not with the government! She'll never understand. Tears filled soft, green eyes, threatening to spill over. "I know it was wrong. But he stole our money! We earned that! I couldn't just let him…"

Ryan stopped Shannon's panicked ranting with a fiery kiss. "You're right, Shannon. You earned every damn penny."

"We."

"Right. We."

Ryan sat up and let her eyes hungrily sweep over her partner once more, finally noticing the towel next to Shannon. A dark eyebrow arched. "Were you on your way somewhere?"

Shannon sighed happily. Ryan understood. "The whirlpool." She raised her own eyebrow and tilted her head toward the adjoining room. "Care to join me next door?"

Ryan nodded, giving Shannon a hand up and a swat on the bottom as they made their way across the room.

"Just a second." The younger woman made a small detour to her desk. Sitting on its polished, oak top were two floppy disks. She picked up one of them and tossed it in the trash bin alongside the desk. "I guess the world will never read "Marty & Arturo: Manly Monkey Love." She burst out laughing and picked up the other disk. "Tomorrow I'm starting the *real* story of how, under the most unusual of circumstances, a very unsatisfied woman found her heart."

Ryan grinned. "Where was it?"

Shannon grinned back. "Funny thing…another woman was holding onto it for safe keeping." Leaning forward, Shannon placed an incredibly soft but persistent kiss on Ryan's lips. She gave a tug on Ryan's shirt. "Meet you in the tub, sexy?"

"You bet." Ryan gave a low whistle as her eyes tracked Shannon's naked body across the room and out the door. Ryan's gaze dropped to her belt, and she removed Tiffany. *What were you saying?* she cooed to her knife. Blue eyes widened. Tiffany was right! Marty had touched the writer. *Their* writer. Or tried to anyway. He'd gotten off far too easily. She waited until she heard Shannon's light splash into the whirlpool before bending over and retrieving the disk from the trash.

Ryan carefully opened the bedroom door. She opened her mouth to call for Sean and Patrick but stopped when Sean ran right into her.

"Sorry, Ryan," he mumbled in a fake Russian accent. He was dressed in all black, with a long, fake beard, hat and dark sunglasses, vaguely reminding Ryan of one of the members of ZZ Top. Or an Hasidic Jew.

"Ah, perfect; you're going to town."

Sean nodded.

"Do you know the address of Shannon's publisher?"

The young man clutched his chest and fake gasped. Ryan knew he memorized the addresses on all outgoing mail. Just in case.

A predatory smile curled Ryan's lips. She had trained him well. "Mail this." She handed over the disk and patted her brother on the back. "And don't tell Shannon. It's a surprise."

"Sure thing, Ryan." He turned. "Are you ready yet, Pat?"

"Ready."

Ryan spied Patrick at the end of the hall dressed as a postal worker. He was shifting uncomfortably from one foot to the other. She shook her head. *Lost the coin toss again.* Just as she reentered her bedroom, she heard Shannon's voice.

"Where are you, Ryan. I miss you!"

The survivalist began peeling off her clothes. "I'm coming."

"Have I told you how much I love you?" the voice called again.

Ryan carefully laid Tiffany on her dresser after laying a gentle kiss on her handle. "I love you too, Shannon." She grinned and addressed her knife. "Ah, Tiffany. There's no place like home!"

<Fade out>

The End.